Lost

As they watched, the ship shimmered and shook and then vanished from sight. Bakker had expected something more. Maybe a flash of light in the best tradition of television special effects. Maybe she expected to hear something, though the ship was so far from the base on Mars that she would never have heard it, even if sound could travel in the vacuum of space. Such was the influence of television, even on a physicist.

Smertz, watching his sensors, watching the scene on the flat screen, looked back and grinned broadly. "I think that's it. I think the ship jumped to light speed."

"You sure?"

"I want to check a few more readings, but yes, I'm sure that we made the jump."

"How fast?"

"What do you mean?"

"Did the ship just jump over the speed of light, or did it go twice the speed, three times the speed?"

"I don't know yet, we're still gathering data."

Bakker nodded but grinned widely. She looked from face to face and finally said, "We've just reached the stars."

It was an hour before they learned the ship had exploded.

**THE EXPLORATION CHRONICLES:
BOOK THREE**

Ace titles by Kevin D. Randle

SIGNALS
STARSHIP
F.T.L.

THE EXPLORATION CHRONICLES

F.T.L.

KEVIN D. RANDLE

ACE BOOKS, NEW YORK

This is a work of fiction. Names, characters, places, and incidents either are the product of the author's imagination or are used fictitiously, and any resemblance to actual persons, living or dead, business establishments, events, or locales is entirely coincidental.

THE EXPLORATION CHRONICLES: F.T.L.

An Ace Book / published by arrangement with
the author

PRINTING HISTORY
Ace mass market edition / September 2004

Copyright © 2004 by Kevin D. Randle.
Cover art by Danilo Ducak.
Cover design by Judith Murello.
Interior text design by Julie Rogers.

ISBN: 0-441-01192-6

ACE®
Ace Books are published by The Berkley Publishing Group,
a division of Penguin Group (USA) Inc.,
375 Hudson Street, New York, New York 10014.
ACE and the "A" design
are trademarks belonging to Penguin Group (USA) Inc.

PRINTED IN THE UNITED STATES OF AMERICA

10 9 8 7 6 5 4 3 2 1

PROLOGUE

THERE WOULD BE NO ONE ON THE SHIP BECAUSE it was simply too dangerous. No one knew for certain what would happen. They understood the theory, but theory translated to paper or computer disk sometimes had the habit of exploding violently and spectacularly. Sometimes those mistakes rendered a large part of the surrounding area, whether on Earth, Mars, in the asteroid belt, or on one of the moons of Jupiter, useless. The radiation might dissipate to safe levels in a hundred years, or a thousand, or a hundred thousand. Such areas often glowed brightly without the assistance of the sun.

Professor William Bruce Smertz looked like the stereotype college professor, a look he cultivated. He had a shock of white hair that he carefully bleached to maintain the color, ratty sweaters that he sometimes cut new holes into, and faded, baggy jeans. He never wore socks, even when the weather was cold, but now here, on the Martian base, the weather was never cold. The weather of the interior of the domes was well regulated.

Smertz sat at a keyboard, which many of those working with him thought of as quaint, watching the drama
play out on a large flat screen. The ship, which had been
orbiting Mars for construction and routine testing, was
now cruising out of the plane of the ecliptic to avoid as
many of the asteroids as possible. It was the focus of the
experiment and the end of months of very hard and theoretical work.

"Are we about ready?" he asked.

One of the anonymous graduate students nodded and
then said, "Just about."

Dr. Sarah Bakker, who was largely responsible for the
experiment about to be conducted because it was she who
had first detected the signal from an alien spacecraft,
stood off to one side, out of the way. Bakker was still a
young woman, though she had lived on Mars for more
than five years and had immigrated after she had completed her education. Actually, as one of the members of
the Galaxy Exploration Team, she had been ordered to
Mars. She had just finished years of research that had led
Dr. Smertz to his discovery, which lead to the experiment.

Bakker was thin, almost skinny, and her once-long,
straight hair was now shorter and curlier than it had been.
Her skin had lost its tan long ago so that she had a pasty
look, but her bright eyes and quick wit convinced everyone that her health was fine.

She asked, "What's the hang-up?"

"Takes a while for the signal to get to the ship," said
the grad student.

Bakker almost snapped at the student and then realized
that the student had no idea who she was. So, she asked,
in a reasonable tone of voice, "That the only hang-up?"

Smertz glanced over his shoulder and said, "I think
we're all set." He pointed at a big red button on the console in front of him and added, "I push this button, and
that should push the ship into light drive. At least that's
what the theory says, and I believe the theory."

Bakker studied the button, which looked as if it had been borrowed from a vaudeville routine, then looked at the banks of computers, flat-screens, television and holo, and then at the long, wide room that held only a few people. The experiment was their first attempt to break through the light barrier. Bakker would have thought that officials, both government and military, would have been present just for the political capital it would give them, but that wasn't the case. Watching it on the closed circuit hookup where they were insulated in case something went wrong, they could claim that they had never supported the project. If it worked, then they could all rush to the closest media center to publicly congratulate Smertz and his team on what they had known all along would work.

Bakker moved forward and then stopped, standing almost directly behind Smertz. On one of the large screens that dominated the far wall, she could see the shimmering shape of the ship. Far beyond and below that was Jupiter, looking like a bright striped ball hanging against a black background.

Smertz looked back at Bakker, and then, somewhat self-consciously, he began to count down, his thumb hovering over the button. At one, he pushed it.

Nothing happened.

Bakker was momentarily taken by surprise and then remembered that the signal, traveling at the speed of light, would take several minutes to reach the ship. She laughed, thinking that television had done that to her. She expected everything to happen instantaneously, because that was how it happened on television. Directors gave no thought to the time lag, because they wanted no break in the action.

The grad student finally said, "I make it another thirty seconds."

But even that meant there would be a further delay, because once the signal reached the ship, its response would travel back only at the speed of light. Distances, even inside the Solar System soon became nearly unmanageable and sometimes suggested that the speed of light was simply not fast enough.

They watched as the ship began to accelerate. It moved slowly at first, and then faster, pointed out of the Solar System. They kept track as it neared half the speed of light, then three quarters, and finally 99 percent, the acceleration more a function of the drive being used than with a conventional rocket, which pushes chemicals out the back of a long tube. It wasn't a push but more a creation of a distortion in space. One that allowed them to watch and one that didn't require the months-long acceleration to the speed of light. The ship was quickly moving faster than anything the human race had ever conceived and built.

"We're getting close," said Smertz. "If this is going to work, it should push on through any moment. We should break the barrier."

As they watched, the ship shimmered and shook and then vanished from sight. Bakker had expected something more. Maybe a flash of light in the best tradition of television special effects. Maybe she expected to hear something, though the ship was so far from the base on Mars that she would have never heard it, even if sound could travel in the vacuum of space, not to mention that the speed of sound was so much slower than that of light. Such was the influence of television, even on a physicist.

Smertz, watching his sensors, watching the scene on the flat screen, looked back and grinned broadly. "I think that's it. I think the ship jumped to light speed."

"You sure?"

"I want to check a few more readings, but yes, I'm sure that we made the jump."

"How fast?"

"What do you mean?"

"Did the ship just jump over the speed of light, or did it go twice the speed, three times the speed?"

"I don't know yet, we're still gathering data."

Bakker nodded but grinned widely. She looked from face to face and finally said, "We've just reached the stars."

It was an hour before they learned the ship had exploded.

CHAPTER 1

[1]

COLONEL THOMAS HACKETT SAT TRYING TO concentrate at an ornate desk that looked as if it had been created for a king in the nineteenth century. Hackett was now pushing forty but looked a decade younger. His hair held no traces of gray, and his dark eyes sparkled with youth. Had he not been a colonel, not been sitting in the office where he was, and not been in charge of the Galaxy Exploration Team, people would have thought of him as a flunky for those who had the real power.

The desk, one of those symbols of power, was not from Earth and had not been built for a king. A craftsman on Mars, who enjoyed working with the local raw materials, created it because he loved to create the ornate. Hackett, who normally rejected symbols of power, proving that he would never make it as a politician, had fallen in love with the desk when he first saw it. For most of one night, he had bought beer for the desk's creator, offering more and more in an attempt to buy the desk. Finally as dawn began to filter through the Martian dome, the man had cracked. To him, anyone who loved his work enough to bargain through the night deserved to be the caretaker of some of it. Upon the condition that the desk would be returned when Hackett was finished with his duties and transferred back to Earth, he could use it. Hackett, of course, agreed.

Now Hackett sat in his office, behind that desk, with his back to the window that would have given him a good view of the Martian city had he turned around to look at it. From that vantage point, he would have seen across several low buildings to the center of the dome, where there was a core of taller office buildings and residential towers. Beyond them was the wall of the dome designed to keep the air in and the Martian cold out. Though Hackett didn't think about it, the dome was just another version of the generation ships that were being built and launched to protect the human race. It was a larger version, with the resources of a planet available, but a version of those ships nonetheless.

There were now more than ten thousand people living inside the dome and another hundred thousand living elsewhere on Mars. That didn't count those in orbit and those who were on their way to help colonize the planet or those who would soon be sent to Mars for a variety of reasons.

He turned his attention to the people sitting in the office with him and smiled. Bakker hadn't said much, but Smertz seemed to want to dominate the conversation.

Finally Hackett held up a hand to stop the flow of words and asked the single question that was important to him. "Why did your ship explode?"

"Well," began Smertz again.

"No," said Bakker, interrupting. She didn't want to listen to Smertz anymore either. "The explosion had nothing to do with the star drive. There was a flaw in the power-plant that should have been detected."

"So you don't know why it blew up?" interjected Hackett quietly.

"Yes, I do know," said Smertz. "Engineering mistake. No, that's not fair. The engineering was flawless. Manufacturing error. We should have caught it but didn't. Manufacturer made the mistake."

"Two billion dollars to build that thing, and it blew up before it even left the Solar System."

Bakker grinned and said, "But everything indicates that it had passed into faster than light travel. We succeeded in breaking through the light barrier."

"I'm not sure that a load of debris circling the sun is going to impress those who hold the purse strings on this, even if it is moving faster than light," said Hackett. "Or rather, that it once moved faster than light."

Bakker looked shocked by Hackett's comment, and her voice rose slightly. "When did you become a bureaucrat?"

"I think about the time the ship exploded and I had half a dozen calls, including those by narrow beam transmission from Earth."

"But the explosion had nothing to do with our experiment," said Smertz. "It was an accident."

"All that was seen on Earth was the flash of light and the failure of communications between the ship and your control center. They assumed cause and effect."

Bakker jumped in again. "But that's what it was. An assumption. The jump to light had nothing to do with the failure of the component."

"Can you know that for certain?" asked Hackett.

Bakker dropped her eyes as if there was something interesting on the floor. When she looked up, she said, "Not a hundred percent certainty. However, I will say this. If there is a causal relation, it is only because of the forces created as we jump to light. It has nothing to do with the concept itself, or the impossibility of faster-than-light. We know that is possible. We probably just did it. The aliens we saw have done it."

Now Hackett held up his hand again, this time to stop the lecture. He said, "I know all this. I just want to make sure that the next ship doesn't explode."

"I can assure you that it won't," said Smertz.

"I don't want to be a pessimist, Doctor," said Hackett, "but I would like something a little more concrete."

"Tom," said Bakker, "this process works. You saw that faster-than-light was possible when we intercepted the alien ship. The science is solid. There was a manufacturing flaw."

"I know. I know. But I'm on the hot seat here. If the next one explodes, then I'm on my way to Earth, and I'll be counting mess kits in Utah."

"Utah is not so bad," said Smertz. "I like Utah."

"Like has nothing to do with it," said Hackett. "But he who counts mess kits in Utah does not see flag rank."

"I don't know what that means," said Smertz.

"It means that Tom will not be promoted to general."

"Oh."

"If we might get off my career potential here," said Hackett, "and return to the main topic. When will you all be ready for the next test?"

"We need to get the modifications complete and then move the ship out to Jupiter," said Bakker.

"How soon?"

"If I was forced to guess," said Bakker, "I'd say about two weeks."

Hackett seemed to visibly relax. "Two weeks."

"About."

"Then I have a career for another two weeks," he said. "I can dream of being a general for two more weeks."

"Unless we get done earlier and the ship blows up," said Bakker grinning.

But, of course, the ship wouldn't blow up because they had found the flaw. At least that was what Hackett kept telling himself. Once in a great while he even believed it.

[2]

ONE OF THE THINGS THAT JOE DOUGLAS ENjoyed about orbit was the feeling of weightlessness. There were people who couldn't handle it and who were sick almost from the moment they entered space. But then there were people who couldn't stand an ocean voyage or air travel without some discomfort and more than a few drugs. Douglas was glad that he didn't have those problems, because he would have missed the joy of free fall.

Douglas was a relatively young man, approaching thirty a little faster than he cared. His attitude had not matured as much as it should have, but then, his attitude was encouraged by a society that viewed him, and people like him, as big kids. They tolerated behavior from Douglas that would have landed others in jail for a night. Douglas hadn't learned to walk that fine line between being eccentric and being immature, but no one had forced him to. He was just too good at what he did for others to allow small annoyances and excesses to inhibit his career.

He was rather small, just under five ten, and weighed, at most, 130. He kept his dark hair cut short so that it looked like a five o'clock shadow that had grown up his face and infected his head. He wasn't strongly muscled, but spaceflight was not conducive to building muscle mass. In fact, he had to fight to keep the muscles he had. He found the gravity on Mars quite unpleasant and wasn't sure how he'd handle the gravity on Earth. He didn't plan to return to Earth any time soon.

At the moment he floated in the rear of the space station orbiting Mars, his hands locked behind his head, looking as if he was relaxing in a hammock. By turning his head he would see the red of the Martian deserts and a little of the northern polar cap. The view would have been exciting if it was the first time he had seen it, but he had been assigned to Mars for more than a year and had seen the scene a hundred times, a thousand times. It was there whenever he wanted to look out at it.

Sally Wilson, the youngest of the crew members, and quite possibly the brightest, floated into the cabin. She was nearly as big as Douglas. She was the same height and about the same weight, maybe a couple of pounds lighter, and like Douglas, she didn't look big. She looked fit.

"Got a message from the ground," she said.

Douglas moved an arm and then a leg slightly, rotating around so that he was looking at her. "They tell you what they wanted?"

"Shuttle on the way up," she said. "Be here in a couple of hours. Looks like you're rotating to the ground. Ordered to the ground."

"Crap," said Douglas. "I don't want to go dirt side. They have gravity there."

"Well, gravity makes the world go 'round."

Douglas looked at her like she had lost her mind and then understood the reference. "They picking up anyone else?"

"Yes. I'm going down as well."

"So it won't be a complete loss."

"Now what in the hell is that supposed to mean?" she asked, staring.

"Nothing," said Douglas. "I just meant that I would have some company. Someone to talk to."

"There's crew on the shuttle."

"Yes," said Douglas, nodding. "But I might not know any of them, and they'll be busy with their piloting duties. They might never come back to see me. I just don't want to be the only cargo."

"Well, I might want to sleep," said Wilson. "Sometimes that's better than talking to you." She smiled as she said it, taking the sting from her words.

Douglas laughed and then spun around again so that he was looking down at Mars. "There are people who actually like it dirt side."

"But you're not one of them."

"Nope. Not by a long shot. I wonder what they want?"

"Well, you'll just have to be patient, because they didn't confide in me. I'm always the last to know anything around here."

"It has to be bad news," said Douglas. "When they go to this much trouble, it's always bad."

[3]

IN THE YEARS THAT STEVEN WEISS HAD BEEN on Mars, working with the Galaxy Exploration Team, he had managed to earn his doctorate with Sarah Bakker's help. It was a distance-learning degree, and while it was not quite as prestigious as having received it on Earth, it was a recognized degree, fully accredited, and it earned him the right to be called doctor. His plan, when he returned to Earth, was to obtain a second degree through a more traditional method and remove any questions about the legitimacy of his distance-learning degrees. But that was for when he returned to Earth.

His office was on the floor below Hackett's, and Weiss liked it that way. With no elevator in the building, it meant that Hackett had to walk downstairs to see him. It never occurred to Weiss that Hackett never visited him, but always used the telephone to order him up. So much for his elevator theory.

Using his own computer, he called up the video of the destruction of the star ship and watched it carefully. He hoped to be able to spot the flaw, whatever it was, and then report that fact to his friends on Earth. It would be the club he used to get himself transferred back to Earth. He was beginning to really, really hate Mars.

Weiss, as a younger man had been thin and looked somewhat athletic. He didn't play sports; he just had the look. Now, on Mars, where the gravity was lighter and the food starchier, he found himself gaining weight, or more precisely, gaining girth. His face was fleshy, and he noticed that his belly extended out so that it seemed to be sitting on his thighs when he sat down. His belt was at its last hole, and it was beginning to look like he would need to buy a new one. There was only so much space to punch new holes, and he had already used it.

The solution, of course, was to eat less and exercise more. Use the facilities where it seemed gravity was heavier. But, to Weiss, that was no real solution because he liked to eat and he hated to exercise. His solution was diet pills, which he had just begun to take.

He was sitting quietly, feet up, studying the flat-screen, when Linda Mitchell tapped on his door. He turned and looked at her carefully, thinking that the slight, dark girl should be interested in him romantically. After all, he did have a doctorate and he was rich, or rather his father was rich, which was about the same thing. She had neither the advanced degrees nor the money.

She said, "I wanted to know what you were going to do for lunch."

"Eat it," he said. "Since you have been here have you ever known me to skip my lunch?"

"No."

He stared at her, surprised by her tone. "Is there something going on that I should know?"

Bright as she was, Mitchell was intimidated by Weiss. She had heard stories about him and about how he had challenged both Bakker's and Hackett's authority. She knew that his challenges had failed, but the point was that he had actually tried it. She also knew that she had no power of her own and if Weiss took a dislike to her, he could make her life miserable. She never thought that either Hackett or Bakker could protect her.

"Not at all. I was just going out to lunch and wondered what your plans are," she said.

Weiss leaned forward and touched a button. The display

on his flat-screen disappeared in a burst of bright color. "Well, I'll accompany you out for a bite, if that's what you're thinking."

Mitchell lowered her eyes, looked at a spot on the carpet and said, "I was just going to grab a sandwich in the cafeteria. Nothing fancy."

"I'll tell you what. Let's get out of the building. If we stay, they can find us and make us work through lunch. I'll even buy."

Mitchell's first inclination was to flee, but she knew that was no real option. Weiss, even though he was not respected, could make trouble for her, so she nodded. After all, she had approached him. Without meeting his eyes, she said, "But I only have an hour."

Standing, Weiss said, "That's all I have."

Without a word, he walked to the door, touched her shoulder to push her into the hallway, and closed his door behind them. Together they walked along the corridor that could have been in a building anywhere. The tile looked like the institutional material used in every office building on Earth, but it was a composite created on Mars that held its shine and wasn't slippery. The walls were currently a light green, but at night they gave off a glow that was bright enough so that a person could walk along without worry of tripping over something. At the far end was a window with the city beyond, but the view was partially obstructed by the side of another, taller building.

They walked down the steps and then out onto a second floor mezzanine that connected to a sidewalk and ramp that eventually lead down to the street. This was a long, wide concrete creation with potted plants, some of which had been brought from Earth and others that had been hybrid on Mars. One whole side of the mezzanine looked like a green wall, or the edge of a forest, except it was only five or six feet deep and there were breaks in the foliage that gave away the secret.

They descended and joined a crowd walking along the

street level, where there were commercial enterprises such
as clothing stores, speciality shops, and more than a few
restaurants. There wasn't much of a nightlife on Mars, and
most forms of entertainment were beamed into individual
homes. A person with the right kind of job, computer access into the net, and a large enough bank account could
get everything delivered. There was no need to get out,
but even so, restaurants and a few nightclubs were always
crowded. Say what you will, the human race is a social an-
imal. Sometimes they just need to see other people.

They found a small sandwich shop that had a corner location. Windows on two sides gave them a good view of
the city around them. Weiss steered Mitchell into it and then
along the wall until they came to a small table near the
back that still had a view through the windows. Weiss,
without thinking, dropped into one chair as Mitchell took
the other.

"They make a mean club here, though I'm fond of the
chicken salad."

"Not real chicken," said Mitchell.

"Nope, but damned if I can taste the difference."

Mitchell looked beyond Weiss. Behind the counter
looking like something from the middle twentieth century,
was a large, rectangular screen. The programming was the
latest from Earth. The newscaster was a young woman
who didn't look as if she had reached her majority and
was dressed from her neck to her feet. Only her face and
hands were showing. In strange contrast, the man, who
was giving the latest football scores, wore almost nothing
and looked as if it was very hot in the studio.

On the pretext of watching the screen, Weiss slid his
chair around so that he was sitting next to Mitchell rather
than across the small table from her. He couldn't have
cared less for the football scores. He was maneuvering
into position for his tactical assault.

Once they had given their order, electronically, by se-
lecting the items on a small touch screen on the table,

Weiss turned his attention to Mitchell. "I was trying to figure out what went wrong on the test when you came in."

"Do you have a theory?"

Weiss shrugged, "I really don't know. I can't see anything obvious. I know Smertz is blaming manufacturing, and that might be the cause, but I don't know."

"It's funny to hear you admit something like that," said Mitchell.

"Well, there is nothing wrong with admitting the truth. If I had a good theory, I'd be the first to broadcast it. Now, well, who knows."

He slipped his chair closer and touched her on the arm. He didn't really look at her, but he let his fingers linger. He focused his attention on the flat screen behind the counter as if distracted.

Mitchell pretended that nothing had happened. "So what is the next step?"

Weiss chose to misunderstand her and said, "We finish our lunch and then maybe look for a more private, more comfortable location."

"I mean what is the next step for Smertz and the others."

Weiss leaned back, stretched his arms high over his head and then seemed to collapse on himself. He leaned forward, both elbows on the table and said, "They're going to have to repeat the experiment once they've isolated the cause of the explosion. When they have that problem corrected, they'll try again."

Mitchell was honestly interested in that. "Will they get the problem corrected?"

"Of course," said Weiss, "eventually. The problem always gets fixed. The Hindenburg exploded but they knew why. Hydrogen and twentieth-century politics. Airship travel never recovered. World War Two and passenger airplanes finally did it in."

"Your point?"

"Like I said. The problem always gets fixed. We might figure out a better way of doing something, but progress continues to move forward. Progress did in the airship, but we fixed the problem."

Mitchell wasn't all that interested in Weiss's take on history and science, but the topic was a safe one. She said, "You sound as if you don't approve."

Now he looked at her, staring into her eyes. He was no longer interested in discussing faster-than-light travel, airship travel, or Earth politics. He had other things on his mind, but he tried to remain cool. "It's not that I disapprove. It's just that sometimes things happen in the name of progress that aren't always the best for the human race or the planet."

She grinned, "Mars or Earth?"

"Now that you brought it up, Mars." He waved a hand around, indicating the tinted windows and the protective dome far beyond them. "Look what we've done already. We've altered the environment."

Mitchell didn't want to get into a discussion of environmental issues with Weiss. It could only lead to trouble, so she sat quietly. She noticed that the food had been set on the counter, but no one had picked it up to deliver it. The lack of robot waiters was one of the charms of the place.

"Looks like our order," she said. "I'll get it."

"Sit," said Weiss. "I'll get it."

He stood up, put a hand on her shoulder, and seemed to push off. He crossed to the counter, grabbed the plastic baskets of food, and returned to the table. He managed to push against her again when he set the food down, and when he sat, he touched her thigh.

She slipped her chair to the right, away from Weiss, giving herself a little extra space. He gave her a questioning look. "Is there anything wrong?"

She smiled weakly. "No. I just like to have my space when I eat. On Mars, we have so little space."

Weiss pulled his basket close and inspected the contents as if he had expected something different. "We all need some space sometimes."

Mitchell kept her eyes on her lunch. She knew that Weiss would keep to himself now, but she didn't know how limited her space was about to become.

[4]

SITTING ON EARTH, ON THE TOP FLOOR OF A hundred and fifty-story skyscraper, with a glass of bourbon in one hand and a fountain pen in the other, Wendelle B. Barnett, called Barney by the few friends he had, was staring at a video screen. Barnett was a fat man, who sweated in the coolest of environments, and who usually yelled when a quiet, pleasant voice would do. He had a full head of hair that was unnaturally black, small, dark eyes, and large lips. He wasn't ugly, but he wasn't all that good looking either. Some women found him attractive, not because of his face or body, but because he had a lot of money and a lot of power. They ignored the physical for the monetary.

Barnett, at the moment, wasn't a happy man, so he was yelling at the screens where some of his staff were displayed on a conference call. He didn't know that his subordinates routinely turned down the volume at their end so that it was sometimes hard to hear him and often impossible to understand anything he said.

Setting the bourbon on his massive, opulent desk, Barnett stood and walked to the window. His view, out over the city was not unlike Hackett's on Mars. Barnett, however, could see a greenbelt that wound through the city along the riverfront, where the land had been carefully sculpted, the trees planted in a regular but pleasing pattern, and brightly colored flowers lined the walkways in crimson and gold waves. He could see a bright blue sky that was only partially obstructed by other, high-rise buildings, and beyond that, the blue water of a lake that disappeared over the horizon.

"I want that damned program canceled!" Barnett screamed at the window. "I want it canceled now, before another ten billion dollars is sucked into it."

Those on the conference call could only see Barnett's back, because he was facing away from the camera as he studied the city beyond his window. They didn't know that his face was now bright red and that sweat was dripping from his nose and chin, making it look as if he had run up the stairs to his office rather than taking one of the high-speed elevators. He looked like he was about to pop a blood vessel.

The staff on the conference call glanced at one another, each insulated in his or her office, some of them in cities thousands of miles away from Barnett. Each was daring the other to say something, but no one wanted to offend Barnett.

He turned, stared into the bank of screens that sat across the office from him in two neat rows, each labeled with a staff member's name and his or her location. He studied them carefully, watching their reactions as each tried to avoid his wrath.

"Do any of you have a comment? Anything? Something banal? Something trite?"

"There is a real threat," said William Bonham. "We know the alien enemy is out there."

Barnett shook his head slowly, then raised his voice again so that he was screaming. "Threat? Enemy? You mean that ship that allegedly passed our system a decade ago? You mean those pathetic pictures that were supposed to frighten us into producing legislation that was exactly what the president wanted?"

"Are you suggesting that it was all a put-on job?" asked Bonham.

With the quickness of a cobra, Barnett threw his glass at the screen. The drink shattered into an explosion of bourbon, ice, and shards, but the screen remained undamaged, being constructed of near-bulletproof glass. It wasn't the first time that Barnett had thrown something at a screen. "You dare to question me?" he roared. "You lowlife, ignorant swine question me?"

"No, sir," said Bonham, beginning to sweat himself. He tried not to squirm as he said, "I merely asked if the government was clever enough to have created this . . . this . . . hoax for the purpose of inducing a national cause and financing a space effort that could bankrupt us."

"Now you're thinking," said Barnett. "Finally a spark of intelligence."

"Yes, sir."

"And even if it is true," said Barnett, calming himself with great effort. "It's now irrelevant. We are launching—have launched—the generation ships that will protect the human race from extinction. We have people on Mars, on Titan, and working in the asteroid belt. There is now no catastrophe that could eliminate the human race."

"So what is the plan?" asked Julie Reasoner. With Barnett calmed and his face now returned to a nearly normal color, she was confident enough to speak.

"Well," he said, "we've dumped enough research and development money into this project. I want to see our losses recovered on a cost-plus basis, but the administration isn't going to listen unless we begin a campaign to let both the general public and our elected officials know how we feel. We shouldn't be required to carry the burden for this ridiculous exploration project for this administration."

"I thought we fought hard to win the contract," said Bonham.

Barnett turned his attention to Bonham and looked as if he was going to erupt again. Instead he said, quietly, "That was before we learned that faster-than-light was impossible and we were wasting our time. The administration is holding firm to the contract, which will cost us dearly if we don't deliver the drive. Fail, we lose the money and another company will take over. It would be a financial disaster for us. It's cost-plus for success."

"But the enemy has faster-than-light drive," said Bonham.

"How do you know that? The administration tells us that. Their pet scientists tell us that, but we don't know that. It is an assumption that might be based solely on faulty reasoning. The observational data might be in error. And now we're draining the company resources to create something that is physically impossible to do."

"There is another test scheduled for two weeks," said Reasoner.

"Which is all the more reason for us to end this relation as soon as possible. Another disaster, another explosion, and we are going to be out the R and D costs, with no way to recoup the losses. I will say it again. It's cost-plus for success not for spacecraft that fail."

"But," said Bonham, "we don't know the next test will fail. The first might have been a fluke."

Barnett stared hard at the screen. "Oh, make no mistake about it. The next test will fail. I know this for an indisputable fact."

CHAPTER 2

[1]

THOMAS HACKETT HAD TOLD SARAH BAKKER
that he would meet her later because he had another
meeting to attend. She had looked at him strangely, as if
she didn't believe the excuse, but since he volunteered
nothing about it, she didn't ask questions. She just
walked out the door, turned to wave, and disappeared
from sight.

Hackett laced his fingers behind his head and turned so
that he could look out on the Martian landscape—or, into
the domed city that happened to sit on Mars but was an artificial construct created by people from Earth. It wasn't
quite the same thing.

Finally, Hackett pushed himself out of his chair and
walked to the door. He waved a hand over the wall plate,
and the lights shut off. It wasn't necessary. If the sensors
had detected no movement in the room after fifteen minutes, the lights would have been automatically shut down.
Any movement would have reactivated them. Now someone would have to actually turn them on.

He walked down the corridor and took the steps down a half dozen levels. When he stepped into the hallway, the lights near him blazed. As he walked along, deeper into the building, more of the lights came on. He turned a corner and then walked to the end of the hall. Hidden there, as far from the entrance as they could get it, was a small office without a sign on the door. For those who didn't know better, it could have been a closet or storeroom.

Hackett tried the old-fashioned doorknob, but it wouldn't turn. Instead he tapped on the door and was tempted to put his ear against it. He doubted that he would be able to hear anything from the inside.

After a moment or two, there was a quiet buzz. Hackett pushed on the door and found himself in an empty office. At least the light was on. Of course the motion of the door could have activated it.

A raspy, male voice announced quietly from the rear, "I'm back here."

Hackett passed through another door and saw a man sitting behind a desk and a woman standing near a computer terminal. She was wearing the standard jumpsuit that had become the unofficial uniform of the civilians assigned to the Galaxy Exploration Team and the official work clothes of nearly everyone on Mars. Hackett didn't recognize her.

The man at the desk, Richard Trask, was dressed in a short-sleeved shirt. He was older than Hackett but had been on Mars for only a year. He was a short man with dark hair and a nearly permanent five o'clock shadow that everyone suggested he have fixed by electrolysis. He liked the somewhat menacing look it gave him.

Hackett glanced again at the woman but said nothing.

Trask said, "She's cleared. If she wasn't, she wouldn't be back here."

"I don't know her," said Hackett.

She grinned. "I can speak and answer questions all by

myself. My name is Monica Stone. I was assigned here just last week."

Hackett raised an eyebrow. "You didn't stop by my office?"

"I did, but you weren't there, and I haven't had a chance to get back up there."

Trask stood up and came out from behind his desk. He sat back on it and said, "That's my fault. She mentioned it, but I told her you were a reasonable man and we'd take care of it when we got the chance."

Hackett looked at her and then at Trask. He smiled thinly and asked, "What ever gave you the impression that I was a reasonable man?"

Trask laughed. "I was told that by Bakker, but I'm not sure we should trust her judgment on this. She seems . . . prejudiced."

Hackett held out a hand. "Welcome to the Galaxy Exploration Team."

"Isn't the title a little . . . enthusiastic?"

"Well, we have some teams out now, moving toward the heart of the galaxy," said Hackett, smiling broadly.

"What does that mean?"

"It means they're out of the Solar System, but barely. It's our first baby step out."

"So the title is enthusiastic?"

"Let's just say it's hopeful."

"If you two are through discussing semantics," said Trask, "maybe we can finish here, so I can get home and get something to eat."

Hackett said, "You called this meeting. What have you got for me?"

Trask reached over, pulled a sheet of paper close, and glanced at it. "You asked us to follow up on these narrow beam transmissions to Earth."

"You got something?"

Trask shrugged. "I don't know what we might have. I can tell you that the real message is embedded inside another, legitimate message, and we had one hell of a time digging it out."

"You got it though?"

Trask glanced over at Stone, who took over. "Yes and no. We have found the messages, and we have decoded some of them, though there is nothing important in them. Others are just gibberish. We can't make any sense out of them."

Hackett shook his head in confusion. "You lost me on that last turn."

Trask took over. "I think, based on our analysis, that some of the messages are gibberish. I've often thought that if I wanted to confuse code breakers, I'd transmit some messages that have absolutely no message. There would never be a way of deciphering them because there is no solution for them. Our competitors, whoever they might be, would spend countless hours, years, and computer time trying to break a code that has no solution. They'd believe that we have an unbreakable code. It could divert attention from the real messages that have a code that could be broken."

"But you didn't transmit this stuff."

"No, but we did intercept it. So now we try to learn what the message is and who sent it."

"And who received it?" asked Hackett.

"No way to figure that out. Even though it is narrow beam, that beam spreads as it moves through space. Anyone on Earth, or the moon for that matter, who has the proper equipment can receive it. We learn who sent it and what it says, and then we might be able to figure out, deductively, who was meant to receive it."

Hackett rubbed his face. "I think we're getting into too much theory here. I think we're way out in the weeds."

"Okay. What we know is that someone is sending narrow-beam messages to Earth. They're using the computer system here so that we can't trace it to a single person. We have decoded only a few of the messages, because they're using a sliding-scale code which means that the code for one message is different for the next. And, I believe they are sending some gibberish, as Monica said, to confuse and irritate us."

Hackett had to laugh. He said, "Then you really have nothing for me now."

"If you count that we know it is happening and we know how it is being done, then we do know something."

"But have you decoded any of those intercepted messages?" asked Hackett.

"Yes, but they're not real impressive," said Stone. She grinned. "One of them had something to do with cats and their litter boxes."

"I didn't know we had cats on Mars," said Hackett without thinking.

"You should get out more," said Trask.

"Weight restrictions," said Hackett. "Why use up your weight on a cat, or even a dog, for that matter."

Trask laughed. "You bring the frozen embryos," he said. "Very little weight, and you can have a viable population in a matter of months. A very diverse population. We even have some lions here."

"I knew that," said Hackett, feeling dumb.

"Anyway," said Stone, "I don't think that was the real purpose. Those receiving it probably have a code sheet where one word means something else. Or the phrase means something else so that there is really no way to figure out the end meaning. The message meant something to them, but not to us."

"And no way to figure it out," said Hackett, nodding, "because it could mean anything, and we can plug any meaning into it that we we I want."

"Exactly."

"So we really don't know much," said Hackett.

Trask shrugged.

"But we do know," said Hackett, "that messages are

being sent, and we know how they are embedded in the other messages beamed to Earth."

"Yes."

"Then let's send our own."

Trask looked at him askance. "What do you mean send one of our own?"

"We transmit a message in one of the codes we've broken, but it will mean nothing to them."

"It tells them we're listening," said Trask.

"But they already know that, otherwise they wouldn't be using codes. Maybe it'll spark some more communication that we can trace to the source."

"Well," said Trask, scratching his chin, "I can certainly work something out."

"It has to be something they can read, otherwise they'll just think it is one of those gibberish transmissions you talked about. Something real, but obscure."

"We'll do something," said Trask.

Hackett was about to leave but stopped. He said, "I don't understand why you can't backtrack this to the source and identify the terminal used for input."

"We can," said Stone, "but after we wind our way through all the various links, we end up somewhere public so that all we know is which terminal was used but not who used it. We're into some Internet café."

"Aren't these things time-stamped?" asked Hackett.

"Of course."

"Then isn't it simply a matter of finding the time stamp and reviewing the video security disks to see who was using the terminal when the message was input?"

Trask looked slightly sick. "Of course. I should have thought of that."

"Get me the times," said Hackett, "and I'll get security to look into it."

When they finally got the answer, it was a surprise to nearly all of them.

[2]

ALTHOUGH BAKKER WASN'T SURE WHAT
Hackett had to do, she had a couple of things that interested her. Nothing to do with the military, or the development of the FTL ship. It was radio astronomy as she had
practiced it on Earth in what now seemed to her to be another lifetime.

She left the headquarters building, which was really a
misnomer, since they only used a couple of floors in what
was otherwise a corporate office, and walked across the
open air plaza, which was another misnomer. The dome
shielded them so that no matter where they were on Mars,
they were actually inside.

She reached another building, this one with a brick fa-
cade constructed of materials native to Mars that had been
mined by some of the first construction crews, and the
doors opened automatically. This was a smaller, shorter
building that was closer to the dome. Input from the telescopes erected outside came inside, through shielded
cable.

She walked through the double door entrance and
moved up the narrow, darkened corridor. There was a reception desk, but the receptionist was gone. Bakker didn't
care because she knew her way.

Finally, she climbed a set of stairs, turned right, down
another narrow corridor. In the distance she could see a
rectangle of light, which marked the conference room and
told her that someone was still in there. She hurried down
the hail and pushed her way in.

"Evening, all," she said.

Ken Peters looked up from a monitor that had been
built into the table. He was about Bakker's age, maybe a
year younger, but without much hair. It had begun disappearing about the time he turned twenty-one and had continued its strategic retreat since then. He'd tried
everything to stop it, but, for some reason, the various

cream and ointment treatments didn't work for him, and he refused any type of implant or surgery. Philosophically, he surrendered completely and had shaved his head. When that became too much trouble, he let the fringe grow. If nothing else, he was a rarity because of his incurable hair loss.

His face was unremarkable, as were his brown eyes. His ears stuck out a little bit, but it wasn't very noticeable. In a crowd he would be ignored, if not for his bald head. That would draw some stares.

He wasn't a big man, but was well proportioned. He was dressed in the standard coverall, but it fit him better than most. It looked as if it had been tailored to fit, but of course it wasn't.

He said, "I was going to call you in the morning. Got something here."

Nancy Vores, the grad student who was in the room, stood up and moved to a point where she could look at the monitor. She smiled brightly, showing the nearly perfect teeth that had cost her parents so much money years earlier. Genetic manipulation wasn't all that cheap.

She was a dark-haired woman of twenty-five, who had dropped out of college for a couple of years. She then went back, earned her degrees, and now found herself on Mars, which suited her just fine. As one of the few women on Mars, she was sought for her company. That she was very bright helped.

She refused to wear the unisex coverall, preferring clothes that displayed her. She liked shorts and T-shirts. She liked hip huggers or low riders, and she liked the stares that came with them.

To Bakker, she said, "We got it about twenty hours ago and are just beginning to get everything plotted."

"Twenty hours?" said Bakker, her voice rising, surprised at the delay.

"Signal comes and goes. Faint. Not sure what we have here," said Peters. "Might not be anything at all."

Bakker, suddenly excited, walked around the table, which held almost nothing other than a glass with a dark liquid in it. It might have been tea, or it could have been something carbonated that had long since gone flat. She couldn't tell. It looked as if it had been there for a while.

To Peters, she said, "Show me."

"Well," he said, pointing to the screen, "this is what we have. Regular and pulsing but it's not something I recognize. The source is new."

"How far?" asked Bakker, knowing that they hadn't had the time to figure that out with any degree of certainty.

"I make it something over a hundred light years. Anything much closer and we'd have better numbers," said Peters. "Could be as much as three, four hundred."

Without thinking about it, Bakker reached out and pulled a chair around so that she could sit. She leaned forward, watching the data march across the screen. To one side, in a window, was a small map of the section of the galaxy where the signal had been detected.

Finally she looked at Peters and then at Vores, grinned broadly, and said, "Last time this happened I felt like dancing around the table and shouting to everyone standing nearby. I wanted to run up and down the hall screaming. Adrenaline. But now, after so much time, after all that has happened since that first discovery, I'm thinking that we might have found the answer to our question."

Peters leaned back and laced his fingers behind his head, smugly. "That's what I was thinking too, but it's a little early for us to make any sort of judgment."

Vores laughed and said, "Blasé. You two act as if this discovery means nothing."

"Right now," said Bakker, "it means nothing. I remember when we found the first intelligent signal. Sat in a room like this, on Earth, with others telling me that it was some kind of artificial signal, which we already knew. We just didn't know if it was alien and from outside the Solar

System, and we didn't want to believe until it was verified."

"Verification has begun," said Peters. "I've asked for a plot from both the moon and the Earth. We get that, and we'll have a good idea of how far away this is."

Bakker reached out for the glass, but stopped, remembering that it had been there when she arrived, and she still had no idea what was in it.

"A hundred light years is good," she said. "Two hundred would be better."

"Lines of communication?" asked Peters.

"That's what I was thinking," said Bakker. "Keeps them out of our backyard. Means they can't get here with any degree of ease."

Vores couldn't contain herself. "You think it is intelligent? You think it's them?"

"There is still a lot of work to be done," said Bakker. But, she thought they had found the enemy again, and they knew where he lived.

[3]

HACKETT RETURNED TO HIS OFFICE, BUT BAKKER wasn't there. He wondered where she might be and then realized that she would be with the astronomers. She felt at home there, and when she seemed to have disappeared, that was where she usually was. He'd walk over and find her there.

As he was leaving the building, he ran into her walking his way, fast. He held up a hand, then stopped as he saw the look on her face.

When she was close, she said, "You'll never guess what I just found out."

"No, I guess I won't."

She looked around, but the other people were involved in their own projects or with other people, in their own conversations. She leaned close, lowered her voice, and said, "I think we might have found it."

"You mean?"

She nodded and grinned broadly. "I'm not sure, and there is work to be done, but we might have it."

Hackett looked from her face toward the astronomy building and then back at his headquarters. "We have anything definite or are we speculating?"

She leaned closer and whispered, "I didn't say anything to either Peters or Vores, but I think this is it. Same sort of signal that we had from their ship."

"Another ship?"

"Too early to tell, but given the distance, I'd say that it was planetary based."

Hackett rubbed his face and started to turn, but then stopped. He was confused. He wasn't sure what to do. "These data are preliminary?"

"Yes. Very rough."

"When will you have something a little more definite?" he asked.

"Well, I think, if we can get any confirmation from Earth and the moon, we'll have a better feel for it in the morning. For precise data, we're going to have to wait a week or more, if we can hold on to the signal for that long. It's very weak and hard to detect."

"Then there is nothing we can do tonight?"

"Well, no. Not tonight. What's on your mind?"

"Just that there isn't anything we can do tonight about any of this. The signal might not be what you think it is, right?" he asked.

"Well, no, it might not be. But neither Peters nor Vores are as familiar with everything as I am. I think they've got it nailed."

Hackett looked to the right, at the shadows, as they began to race across the city. The sun was setting, and the dome's internal lights were popping on. It was actually getting brighter in the dome. That always disoriented him.

He needed night to be darker than day, not the other way around.

"So we can eat our dinner in peace. We can go home and relax, ready for tomorrow."

Bakker took a step back, as if surprised and said, "There are things we can do tonight."

"Necessary things?"

"Well, no, not things that are necessary. But things that can be done."

Hackett suddenly understood. She was excited by the discovery, even if it turned out to be another false alarm. She wanted to do the preliminary work now and wouldn't be able to sit still until she had done some of it. She would fidget through dinner, and she wouldn't be able to sleep. There were questions that she wanted to ask and clues she wanted to scan. If she didn't start now, she would be miserable until she had the chance to study the signal and find a few answers.

"Where do you need to go now?"

She looked relieved. "I want to go back to astronomy and check a few things."

"Well, in that case, I'll return to the headquarters. Maybe let someone know that we might have something."

"Okay," she said, and then whirled. In seconds she had broken into a trot, heading for the double doors.

[4]

STEVEN WEISS HAD RETURNED TO HIS OFFICE because Linda Mitchell hadn't seemed interested in an afternoon away from work with him. He wasn't interested in doing anything other than staring out the window, or pulling something up on the flat-screen to watch. Not work related. Something of a more entertaining nature.

He wasted the afternoon watching others frolic on huge beds, kitchen tables, in the backs of vehicles, on airplanes and space craft, and finally in a sun-drenched field that made him slightly homesick. He hadn't been to Earth in years.

Finally as the lights came on outside and the sun disappeared over the horizon, Weiss decided that it was time to do something about his situation. He decided to see what had been posted to the net and if any of that would be of sufficient interest to lessen his frustration.

Just for laughs, and as he did once every other day or so, he took a look at the E-mail passed among the various offices. He wasn't supposed to be able to access it all, only that addressed to him, but the security was poor and the firewall easily defeated by someone on the inside. He could read whatever he wanted and then prepare to meet any threat be might detect. Or, he could begin to target any of the women who showed even a passing interest in him. People put a lot of personal information, confidential information, into their E-mails, assuming that they wouldn't be read by anyone other than the addressee.

He scrolled down the list, looking for anything that might be interesting to him. Out loud, and to no one, he said, "Ah, what do we have here?"

He read an E-mail that Ken Peters had sent the radio facility on Earth. It was only a few lines, and it hadn't been encoded, so it was there for anyone to read.

"So, you think you've found the signal again."

He looked for a reply but then noticed the time-date code was little more than an hour old. Given transmission times between Mars and Earth because of their relative positions, and time for someone to actually review the data, it could be another ten, twelve hours before there was a reply. He had lucked into an important bit of information. It made him forget his frustration for a while.

Grinning broadly, Weiss, closed the E-mail, exited the system, then stood up. He walked to the door, left, and headed up the stairs. He could see that some of the corridor lights were on, which meant that someone had walked down it recently. He could also see that a light was on in Hackett's office. He moved down toward it, hesitated at the door, then knocked.

Hackett looked up and said, "Yeah?"

"Got something that might be of interest, though, I suppose you already know."

Hackett waved a hand, signaling Weiss to enter. He sat back in his chair and waited.

Weiss entered but didn't sit. He said, simply, "The signal might have been found again."

"I know," said Hackett. "How do you know?"

"It's not classified or anything, it is?" asked Weiss.

"Well, no," said Hackett. He thought for a moment, wondering why it wasn't, and then asked, "How do you know?"

"E-mail. Read the query sent to Earth."

"You supposed to be reading that?"

Now Weiss smiled. "Just doing my job, such as it is. Trying to stay on top of everything."

"Who have you told?"

Weiss shrugged. "No one. Came here in case they hadn't gotten around to telling you, yet. These scientists sometimes forget who the boss is around here."

Now Hackett laughed. "Why wouldn't they tell me? I need to know that to do my job."

"I really meant that they hadn't gotten around to telling you yet, not that they wouldn't. Maybe because they're trying to make sure this isn't a false alarm or they're waiting until they have some better data."

Hackett nodded and said, "Okay. I can buy that. Why don't you relax for a moment?"

Weiss dropped into the closest chair. It was burned orange and didn't match anything else in the office. It looked to him as if there had been a meeting and they needed an extra chair and just hadn't taken it out yet.

"This could be it," said Weiss.

"Well," said Hackett, "it would be nice to have a clue about their home. Give me a little peace of mind."

"I haven't ever understood that."

Hackett stared at him for a moment and said, "You really don't understand?"

"No."

"From a military perspective: we're dealing with a potential enemy." He held up a hand to stop the protest. "I didn't say it *was* an enemy, only that the potential was there. If the enemy is operating from a hidden base, then we are at a great disadvantage because we don't know where he is. We can't attack him if that becomes necessary. Can't interdict his supply lines. Can't disrupt his lines of communication."

"But this isn't . . ."

"I know that. I'm merely talking from a military perspective. Now, if we have that information, our job is a little easier and we are less vulnerable. If all else fails, we can attack that base."

"But it's light years, dozens, maybe hundreds of light years away, and we don't have faster-than-light travel."

"All too true," said Hackett. "But then you don't understand the military mind. If we have the information, we feel better than if we don't. You've heard of military intelligence."

"Sure. An oxymoron."

Hackett's smile was weak, pained. "Not really. In this context, intelligence means, simply, information. Weather data are military intelligence. Distance from A to B is military intelligence. Size and distribution of enemy forces is military intelligence. Information."

"So?"

"So, if we know the home world of the enemy—" Hackett raised his hand again—"of the other known sentient race, then we are just a little safer, even if we can't do much about it. Or maybe I should say that we feel a little safer."

"Unless Smertz gets his ship to operate."

"Well, then, the situation changes again. Now we can make a reconnaissance of the enemy . . . alien home world. We'll know more about them, and we'll actually be safer."

Weiss grinned. "But if we don't know where their home is, then it will be damned hard to make any sort of reconnaissance."

"Right," said Hackett, "regardless of what Smertz is able to do, or not do, with his ship."

"So," said Weiss, idly, "who would go on this reconnaissance of yours?"

"I would," said Hackett. "Sarah would. Wouldn't you like to go, too?"

Weiss laughed. "No. I'd rather just return to Earth and study."

"Then you wouldn't go down in history," said Hackett.

No, thought Weiss, *and I wouldn't go down in flames either.*

CHAPTER 3

[1]

WENDELLE B. BARNETT HAD ACCESS TO MORE
than two hundred separate secure computer systems that
fed him information at an incredible rate. There weren't
enough technicians on Earth to properly analyze all the
data that poured into his mainframe based under Des
Moines, Iowa. He had selected Des Moines because the
territory around it was stable, meaning earthquakes were
extremely rare, and the water table, known as the Ogalala
Aquifer, had slipped from its original twenty-five or thirty
feet below the surface, down to about two hundred feet.
That meant the water table was low enough that he didn't
have to worry about moisture in the underground computer rooms, and given the current consumption of water,
he didn't have to worry about the aquifer being recharged
anytime in the next century.

Of course, given shielded communications, fiber op-
tics, and networking, he didn't have to be in Des Moines
to run the system. He could do that from anywhere, including the moon, if he was inclined to space flight and

the rigors of living on an airless world that was alternately baking and freezing. Barnett, who thought of roughing it as not having twenty-four-hour-a-day room service and the ability to summon anyone into his presence in a matter of hours, didn't want to live on the moon. Visit there, yes, maybe, in ten years, but not now.

Instead he lived at the top of a skyscraper where he could look out on the world and pretend that he was Alexander the Great surveying all that he had conquered. Barnett believed that he ruled the financial world as Alexander had ruled the ancient world and that his conquests were more substantial than Alexander's because his not only covered Earth, but he had toeholds on the moon and Mars as well. Alexander had controlled the known world, but Barnett controlled whole planets. Barnett thought of himself as a near god.

As he did every night, between ten and midnight, he sat in front of his flat-screen, a large monitor built into the wall, looking like a window into the world, which, in one sense it was, and studied the parading information. He flipped from program to program, searching for anything that would give him a leg up the next day. He knew that knowledge was power, and the more he knew, the more powerful he was.

Rarely was anyone allowed into the small, almost theater-like room. The screen dominated one wall and was hidden most of the time behind curtains. The lights could be as bright as those in an operating room, or as dim as those in a boudoir. There were three plush seats arranged in front of the screen, with a keyboard set on a swing-out table, if he wanted it, and a microphone built into an arm, in case he preferred voice activation or he needed to communicate with any of his lieutenants anywhere in the world.

The room was soundproof, and the door more of a vault door than anything else. It looked as if it was wooden, but it was the strongest of the latest composites, and it would take several hours to burn through. The walls were equally strong and equally disguised.

Barnett, wearing a long bathrobe and nothing else, sat in the middle chair, his eyes fixed on the screen. Crouched at his feet was a young woman, taller than he, with light hair, blue eyes, and a thin body. Had she wanted it, he could have made her a top model or even financed a movie to star her. Instead, she preferred living in the penthouse with nothing to do but wear little and entertain Barnett on the rare occasions that he desired anything other than a pleasing view.

Of course, like everything else in the room, she wasn't quite what she seemed, but then Barnett was happy, for the moment, and she didn't have all that much to do. During the day, when he was in conferences around the world, she was free to roam, and sometimes not required to return in the evening. The world was at her fingertips, and she played that for all it was worth. She did have a vital function. It just happened to be one of her own and had nothing to do with anything that Barnett might have wanted or desired.

"Well, now," said Barnett, breaking his long silence. He reached out and touched the top of her head, much like a man might pat a dog, and said, "Looks like there is something cooking on Mars." He didn't expect her to understand.

"What's happening on Mars?" she asked, looking up at him. "My brother's on Mars."

Barnett didn't really hear what she said and didn't really care that she had spoken. With his eyes fixed on the screen, he said, "They've got something new."

"What's that?" asked Catherine DeCourtenay. She had taken the name of her great-great-great-and so on grandmother as a kind of "stage" name. Her true first name was Catherine, known variously as Cathy or Kate, but her last name was the very mundane Smith. Far too many Smiths in far too many places in the world, which caused far too much confusion.

Barnett ignored the question as he leaned forward, as if that would somehow make it easier for him to see the screen. Still talking, more or less to himself, he said, "They might have gotten the home world."

"I don't understand that," said DeCourtenay, in a little girl's voice.

"The star flyers. You know. The aliens. Those eggheads might have figured out where they live." He said, surprised that she didn't even know that much.

"I don't care."

"Well, you should. This could affect everything and everyone around us."

She looked up at him and blinked slowly. "It's so hard to understand."

Barnett, without taking his eyes from the screen, said, "It means that we have information about the aliens, but more important, I have information about the aliens that no one else has."

"Where did you get it if no one else has it?" she asked simply.

Barnett chuckled, "Well, only a few people know right now. Those eggheads on Mars turned up something."

"How does it help you?"

Barnett looked down at her. She had turned around and had both her hands on his left knee and her chin on her hands. She was staring up at him, her eyes wide, looking as if she couldn't add two and two, yet had asked a very perceptive question. For a moment he wondered if she wasn't smarter than he thought, and wondered if she had some ulterior motive. He dismissed the idea rapidly because he had seen her struggling to figure out how to open a tamperproof medicine bottle. The medicine had been an illegal substance packaged like its legal counterparts. He didn't worry about a drug raid, because he had enough money to prevent that from happening even if she was using something illegal.

He said, "Well, it has to do with the ship we're building

and what I can do to raise my profit margin and what demands they might make in an attempt to alter the terms of the contracts based on additional and new information. Any alteration, or exertion of pressure by outside, say public influence groups, increases my percentage or provides me with an opportunity to increase my percentage. It relates to tax liability, corporate profits, and making the bottom line on one side agree with the bottom line on the other, as long as all the pluses and minuses align."

"It's all so complicated," she said.

"Yes it is. But if I can manipulate public opinion and change the terms of the contract to my benefit, then I can make more money."

"But don't you have enough already?"

Barnett laughed and reached down to touch her cheek. "My dear, there is no such thing as too much money. You must keep making it, or it erodes rapidly. Now, if you'll allow me, I'll get back to earning some of that additional money that keeps you happy."

She turned so that she could see the screen. She understood a great deal more than Barnett thought she did, which was what made her so dangerous.

[2]

HACKETT FINALLY GAVE UP WAITING FOR BAKKER, figuring she would be busy all night chasing the signal, or, at least busy while the source was still in the sky. Then, she might be able to switch her search to another telescope on Mars, or the moon, or Earth, though the distances began to complicate the task. She was now completely and totally absorbed in what she was doing and had probably forgotten everything except the radio noise directly in front of her.

Hackett walked out of the building, down to the street level, where he joined the crowd. On Earth, in many cities, the streets would be nearly deserted . . . or rather, there would be very few pedestrians. Everyone would be in a car, on a bus, or in the subway, but not walking from one place to another. Why walk when you could ride?

On Mars, in the domes, internal combustion engines were not allowed because of the problems created by their pollution, not to mention the difficulty in getting fuel. Electric cars and buses were the rule, though there were few of those. The distances simply weren't all that great. People could walk everywhere if they wanted. No need to ride when the destination was so close.

Hackett walked along the street, which was not hardened concrete, but more of a greenbelt that helped generate oxygen inside the dome. They had been so successful in planting the greenbelts that they had to monitor the oxygen levels to keep them from getting too high.

It was as bright as day, brighter, with people enjoying themselves outside the buildings. Hackett sometimes thought that the society growing and evolving on Mars was more reminiscent of something out of the late nineteenth century than the more modern world. Entertainment, piped into the apartments of what were Martians, even if most of those Martians had been born on Earth, could only sustain humans for a while. They needed to mix with other humans, so they were often outside, mingling. The dome was set up to facilitate societal mixing, though those with few or no social skills could remain inside forever. They didn't have to interact on a personal level.

Hackett nodded to those he recognized as he walked toward his apartment. Two or three people he knew well tried to ambush him and buy him a beer, or a beer and pizza, but Hackett begged off, keeping his destination in mind. He was tired and just wanted to get home. Besides, he hoped that Bakker would finish early, even though he knew the chances of that were as remote as the polar cap.

He came to his residential building, one that rose from the street to nearly the top of the dome. It was a gigantic complex that filled a couple of blocks. It was made of a white material that almost looked like marble, making it unique in the dome. It was stepped so that there were areas where plants could grow and people could congregate if they wanted. The very top seemed to touch the dome, though Hackett knew it was actually fifty feet short.

He entered, nodded at a woman he recognized, and walked up the steps to the second floor. There, outside the glass, was one of the first of the *parks*. He couldn't think of another term to describe them. The premium apartments were those that opened onto that space.

He thought about walking out, but decided to just get to his own place. He took the elevator up to the twelfth floor, and then walked down the hall. The apartment would have been called an "efficiency" in a different time and on a different world. It had a large room that served as a living room, dining room, and bedroom. There was a small kitchen and a small bath. There was no bathtub, only a shower, and everyone was encouraged to shower together to conserve water. Hackett didn't understand that because the water reserves, frozen into the Martian soil were as large as the Pacific Ocean on Earth. The small population would never be able to consume all the water, but, conservation would mean that there would be plenty of water to support the future growth of Mars.

He took off his uniform jacket and dropped it onto the single chair. He sat on the couch, which faced the flatscreen that served as the computer monitor, communications center, and entertainment area. Everything he needed to see could be seen on that screen. It dominated the room and too often, dominated people's lives.

For a moment he just sat there, suddenly too tired to move and too tired to think. He sat, staring at the composite floor, which looked like hardwood but had been created out of the natural materials found on Mars. He heard the quiet sounds of the building as the servos clicked and moved and the air conditioning circulated and filtered the air, and the far away noise of people around a swimming pool. He almost grinned at the thought because they had trouble keeping the water in the pool. The kids could make splashes that rose to dizzying heights, and the water rained back almost in slow motion.

Finally he forced himself up and walked into the tiny kitchen alcove. He took a plastic dish from the freezer, put it into the microwave, and set the timer. He touched the button and turned to make himself something to drink. Just as he poured the 7Up into a glass, the timer chimed quietly. His dinner had cooked.

He took it from the oven and dropped it on the little table near the wall. He wasn't hungry, but the food smelled good. He sat down, peeled the plastic out of the way, and looked at the food. All he really wanted was for Bakker to return. He hated to eat alone.

When he finished, he walked back to the couch and sat down. He reached for the remote, pushed a button, and watched the screen blossom. He flipped through the channels, looking for something that was interesting. Something that he wouldn't have to watch carefully to understand. Something that would allow him to fall asleep easily.

He stretched out, the remote in his hand, flipping from channel to channel, stopping to watch for only moments. Finally he found an old movie. He put the remote on the floor and closed his eyes.

It seemed like only minutes had passed when there was a noise at the door and Bakker burst through, looking as if she had just gotten out of bed, refreshed. She was alive with excitement and ran over to sit next to him.

"We've got it," she said.

Hackett, for a moment, didn't understand what she had gotten. He blinked rapidly, glanced at the flat-screen where the movie had dissolved into something he didn't recognize, and back to her. "You've got what?"

"The alien home."

Now he sat up, pushing her to the side and swinging his feet to the floor. "You're sure?"

"This signal matches the last we had. It's based in a system. It's stronger than that from the ship."

The information was coming too fast for him, and Hackett didn't understand it all. He would have thought that the enemy, the alien, signal would have been found much sooner. He said, "I thought we would have already found it." He was confused by all she was telling him.

Bakker waved a hand and stood up. She nearly danced around the room. She touched the flat-screen and knelt near the couch, picking up the remote. She turned off the flat-screen and faced Hackett.

She said, "It's a question of distance and knowing what to look for. We assumed that because the enemy ship operated in a certain place and in a certain range that all communications would be operating in the same way. That just wasn't true."

Hackett was still slightly groggy. He wasn't following all that she said. He walked into the kitchen alcove, found something cold to drink, and poured a glass. He took a swig, shook his head as if throwing off water, and walked back to the main part of the room.

"Now, tell me why we didn't find this before."

"Two good reasons and a bunch of little ones. First, we have spent a great deal of time searching around what was known as the watering hole. It was a radio band that we assumed that anyone who wanted to make contact across the vastness of space would use. Well, these beings aren't broadcasting in that range because they really don't care to make contact with any other civilization. Second, the frequencies they routinely use are lost in the star noise around them, which might be one of the reasons they selected them. We have lots of radio sources in the sky, and unless we're looking for something specific, we have a hard time picking it out of all the noise around us."

"But we knew where to look . . . what frequency they used," said Hackett.

"No we didn't. We thought we did, based on what we learned from the alien ship, but that seems to be only a frequency used by that ship for its communications. Other ships would use other frequencies, or rather we think they would, and the home world is broadcasting in an area we simply didn't expect them to be using. We found this by accident."

"They were trying to hide this?"

Bakker sat down for a moment and then stood up, moving about. She shook her head. "No. I think it was just the way they evolved their communications. We did it one way, based on the chronology of discovery, but had we made some discoveries before others, our evolution might have been different. Hell, the best example is the development of the commercial bands and how that was patterned from one country to the next. And we all lived on Earth."

Hackett was struggling with this, but only because he had been in a deep sleep. He decided he wasn't all that interested in theory. He said, "You're telling me that you're sure. You've got them."

"I'm about ninety percent sure," said Bakker, grinning.

"How far?"

"Just over two hundred light years. Off toward galactic center."

"Which we always expected."

"Yes," she said.

"We should report this to Earth."

"Done," she said.

"On whose authority?"

"Standard protocols," she said. "The documentation lays out who we tell and the order in which we tell them."

Hackett waved a hand to shut off that avenue of discussion. He didn't want to hear it. His head ached, and he felt as if he had been awake all night drinking. It wasn't fair that he should feel hungover when he hadn't been drinking. All the punishment and none of the fun.

Bakker, still enthusiastic, said, "We have our target. We can set off whenever we want, now that we know where they are. We can go look at the enemy."

"No we can't. Our ship exploded."

"We have another," said Bakker. "We know where they are, and we should go look at them."

Hackett knew that she was right, and he knew that Smertz would have another test ready in days. If it worked and the ship didn't explode, then he would be ordered to outfit an expedition for a reconnaissance of the alien home world. At the moment, it was more than he wanted to think about. At the moment, he felt as if he was going to be sick. Of course, when he learned the truth about faster-than-light drive, he would be more than sick.

[3]

ONCE THE SHUTTLE HAD DOCKED, AND ONCE IT had off-loaded passengers and cargo, the crew took a standard eight hours for rest and relaxation. Then with Joe Douglas and Sally Wilson strapped in the back as passengers, the shuttle pushed away from the station and began its long, complicated descent to Mars.

Douglas hadn't thought he was tired and figured that he would stay awake, looking at the sliding landscape of Mars, seeing if he could spot the city domes or see where they were in attempting to recreate one of the Martian seas. Machinery was attempting to remove the soil and sand from the huge ice sheets that were buried just under the surface. They would be melted and then kept heated and in a liquid state. That, at least was the plan, but Douglas didn't believe they could keep the seas liquid without extraordinary amounts of heat. He thought they were creating a gigantic glacier on the surface that would crawl forward grinding down everything in its path. If they could keep it from freezing over, then the sea could alter the climate, creating a different type of environmental disaster. It was an interesting, but to Douglas overly ambitious, plan that hadn't been thought out.

But the quiet vibration of their passage through the thinning Martian atmosphere and the lack of anything that was startling, new, and surprising conspired against him. Although he had expected to entertain Wilson and watch the show, he found his eyes closing. He wasn't aware that he was falling asleep, until he woke with a start as something changed.

Wilson was looking at him grinning. She said, "What's wrong?"

"I don't know."

The sound came again, and Douglas relaxed, grinning in turn. "Attitude adjustment."

"You should have seen the look on your face as you woke up. Confused. Scared."

Douglas kept on smiling. "You'd be scared, too, if something woke you and you didn't know what it was."

"I wasn't sleeping," she said piously.

"There is nothing wrong with sleeping," said Douglas. "I can do that back here because someone else is up front flying this thing."

The hatch to the flight deck opened like a dilating iris, and a tall, thin man stepped through. Douglas recognized him as Charles Wedemeyer. He had been a copilot on a number of flights and had finally been assigned as the pilot-in-command for this one. He had been very careful with his docking, the unloading of the equipment, and supervised the loading of the equipment and material to be returned to Mars, and of the passengers, though Douglas and Wilson were the only two passengers.

He dropped into the seat next to them, took a deep breath, and sighed. "We're about an hour or so from touchdown."

"So, Chuck," said Douglas. "How's it going?"

"Routine. Everything routine, thank God. And don't call me Chuck."

"Anything interesting?"

"Radio has been busy. Asking about when we plan to arrive. Asking if I have you two on board. You suddenly become famous and not tell me?"

"I have no idea what that could be about," said Douglas. "I'm just the guy on the station orbiting Mars, and that's all. I don't know anything."

"Well, someone is interested in your getting down to Mars this morning."

"That cause you any trouble?"

Wedemeyer smiled. "Nope. I'm just doing what I'm supposed to be doing. We're on schedule, and we'll land in an hour, as we're scheduled to do. Someone will meet you at the spaceport. And that's all I know."

Douglas glanced at Wilson, who shrugged. Douglas said, "Well, I don't get this."

"It's nice to be important," said Wilson.

"Just thought I would let you know about the ride into town," said Wedemeyer. "Thought you'd want to have everything ready when we touch down."

Wedemeyer pushed himself out of the seat and made his way forward, disappearing up, onto the flight deck. When he was gone, Douglas said, "That was nice of him."

"What do you think they want?" asked Wilson. "You think we're in trouble?"

Douglas hesitated, then said, "Nah. They've got something going on, and it's our expertise they want."

"You sure?"

Douglas nodded. "Of course."

But the truth was, he didn't know for sure. Being ordered out of the station was slightly unusual. Once it happened because the man in charge turned out to have a psychological problem that had somehow been missed by the screening committee. The routine background check discovered a history of psychological treatment, and they thought it best to get him onto the surface of a planet where it would be more difficult for him to cause trouble.

So, Douglas worried a little bit about what was waiting for him. He looked through the tiny window, at Mars, and waited. He saw the surface of the planet coming up to meet them, and he felt the nose of the shuttle raise as they flared to slow their forward speed and rate of descent. He sat quietly as he lost sight of Mars and felt them falling slightly, toward the surface of the planet. He felt the bump as the wheels touched down, and if asked, would have said that he heard the chirp of the tires as they touched the concrete of the runway. He hadn't, of course, but he thought that he had, which was sort of the same thing.

They rolled to a stop near a one-story terminal building that gleamed white in the dim of the sun. What had once been called a Jetway, was extended, and then attached itself to the side of the shuttle with a loud, metallic clang that echoed through the shuttle. Douglas, had anyone asked, would have said that he felt a vibration as the Jetway connected to the shuttle.

Without waiting for a word from the flight deck, Douglas stood up and grabbed his duffel, which held his spare clothes, shaving gear, and an old paperback that he carried for luck and not because he read it anymore. Had he wanted to read, he could call up anything on the station's computers, and if it wasn't stored there, he could have had it transmitted from Earth in a microsecond burst that cost nearly nothing. Topic didn't matter. Everything was available.

With Wilson following him, Douglas walked along the Jetway, a clean, white, nearly antiseptic hallway that reached into the terminal building. They exited into a waiting area, but there was no one standing there. No one waiting to get back on the shuttle and head up to the station. No one anywhere around them, and even the snack bar across the building was closed down. Unlike its

Earthly counterparts, there was no steel mesh over the snack bar to keep vandals and thieves away. Although there might be vandals and thieves on Mars, they didn't get that deep into the terminal. There wasn't much crime on Mars, because so few were allowed to travel there.

Douglas laughed as he turned to the reception area where they could arrange transportation into the dome. They walked out into the center of the terminal, where the roof seemed to be thirty or forty feet above the floor. They were heading toward a large circular desk, crowded by people waiting to ask questions or get information, when a man dressed in dark gray separated himself from the crowd.

"You Douglas?" he asked.

Douglas looked at him, but didn't respond. Wilson took a deep breath and said, "Douglas and Wilson."

"You're to come with me."

"No," said Douglas. "I don't think so. I want to sit down for a moment. I would like something cold to drink. I want a chance to get used to the gravity and the air and the wide open spaces."

"My orders are to take you to headquarters as soon as you've arrived."

Douglas walked away and sat down on a long bench. He leaned forward, elbows on his knees, and stared at the floor. It was a ceramic tile that had a shiny cast to it. He wasn't sure if he liked it or not.

The man walked over, stood looking down, and said, "I have my orders."

Douglas looked up slowly and said, "Which are your orders, but they aren't mine."

"I could call for backup."

Douglas found himself laughing. "Call for backup? What are you? SWAT?"

Wilson, who was standing by the man, said, "Come on, Joe. It's not that important."

Douglas ignored her and asked, "Who are you?"

"Sergeant George Towles."

"Well, Sergeant, I'm sure that whoever sent you out here didn't have it in mind for you to drag us screaming and kicking into the city. I'm sure that they thought you would escort us, not order us. So, sit down for a moment, relax, and once I catch my breath, we'll head into the dome."

Towles glanced over his shoulder at Wilson, but she said nothing to him. So Towles sat down to relax. "I'm sorry about the misunderstanding," he said.

"No misunderstanding at all, Sergeant. You have your job to do, and I'm making it a little more difficult. But you have to remember, we just got off the shuttle. We need a little time to get used to everything down here."

"Yes, sir."

"Now, do you know why someone down here has his panties all in a bunch?"

"Sir?"

"Do you know why we're down here?"

"No, sir. All I know is that I was told to escort you into town without letting you get lost."

Douglas, after resting in the heavier gravity of Mars, said, "If you're ready then."

Together they walked through the terminal, though slowly, because both Douglas and Wilson were having trouble with the thicker air and heavier gravity. They finally entered the train station, and both Douglas and Wilson were glad for the chance to rest.

The train didn't run on tracks, as those on Earth had done, nor did they use an internal combustion engine. On Mars, there simply wasn't enough free oxygen for that, and there was the problem of what to do with the waste. The train ran through an almost clear tube that was a closed system. An electric engine running on a bed of magnets eliminated many of the problems. People could ride in comfort without worrying about poisonous gases seeping into the train to kill them.

The run from the terminal to the city dome was just under an hour long. Douglas sat near a window, watching the landscape from an altitude of three or four feet rather than the several hundred miles he had been used to. He couldn't see much difference, other than the rocks he could see were much smaller than anything visible from space.

Wilson tried to talk to him once or twice, but gave up when she got nothing other than one-syllable answers. She leaned back and closed her eyes. Their escort, Towles, was content to sit quietly, reading an e-book.

They reached the train station in the dome without incident. Douglas wasn't ready for the ride to end. He would have gone onto the next dome had Towles not stood up and told them it was time to get to work. They walked through the city, stopping frequently to rest. Douglas was impressed with the progress that had been made, surprised at how much had been accomplished and how many people now lived on Mars. It all seemed so natural. It was hard to believe that half a century earlier they were arguing about the cost of sending the first crew to Mars.

They finally reached the headquarters building. Both Douglas and Wilson were worn out, though the walk hadn't been all that long. They made it up to Hackett's office and were invited inside. Hackett grinned at them, waved toward the chairs, and said, "Please have a seat."

"Thanks," said Douglas.

"You look tired."

Wilson smiled. "They made us walk from the train. We're not used to all this gravity and then physical activity on top of it."

Hackett rubbed his chin. "You know, I should have thought about that. It wouldn't have been all that difficult to arrange for some vehicular transportation from the station, but everything is so close and everybody walks, I just didn't think about it."

Douglas waved a hand, almost like a drowning man

trying to attract attention. He said, breathlessly, "We're here. What's so important?"

"Yes," said Hackett. "There's the rub. It wasn't all that important to get you both here right now this minute. I think someone misunderstood his or her instructions. We wanted you here, need you here, but just not right now."

"Great," said Douglas.

"Don't get me wrong," said Hackett. "We can use you here, but you're just a tad early. They could have put you up in the transient quarters, gotten you a good dinner, and had you come in tomorrow morning."

Douglas pushed himself up. It was a struggle. He grinned and said, "Then, if you don't mind."

"Sit down," said Hackett a little annoyed. "People jumped through hoops to get you here. The least you can do is listen before you go running off."

"Sorry," said Wilson, "but Joe doesn't have good manners. He believes the world revolves around him."

"I do not."

"Okay," she said, grinning. "Our space station revolved around you."

"Only because my quarters were in the center."

Hackett thought about staying annoyed and then decided it really wasn't worth it. Both Douglas and Wilson had been inconvenienced by someone misunderstanding orders. So, he smiled at them and their attempted jokes, and said, "If you've completed the comedy routine."

"Sorry," said Wilson, not sounding all that sorry.

"Okay. Why don't you two find quarters and alert the office as to where you'll be . . ."

"You don't have something here for us? You said something about transient quarters," interrupted Douglas.

"I was giving you the option to find something a little nicer, but check in with the TQ master and take what they have available. Either way, let someone know where you are and then relax for a little while. Check in once a day, morning, and we'll get things set up."

"That's it?" asked Douglas.

"Well," said Hackett, a little embarrassed. "Next week would have been better for us, but this way you get a little rest and have a chance to get used to the gravity and the atmosphere."

"Okay," said Douglas. "We'll let you know where we are."

Hackett turned his attention back to his desk. He wondered why Douglas and Wilson were there already and wondered if someone wasn't screwing around with the computer again. Sabotage was beginning to look like a real threat.

CHAPTER 4

[1]

STEVEN WEISS WAS SITTING IN HIS TINY OFFICE, his eyes on his flat-screen as he watched the scrolling information that suggested the next test of the star drive, the faster-than-light drive, would be made soon. He was surprised that they had managed to get the ship ready and the components installed as quickly as they had. He didn't realize that there had actually been three ships. One that explored, the one that would be tested soon, and a third that was being readied for testing and launch, but not as quickly as the others had been.

He heard something at the door and looked over at it. The woman standing there was tall, thin, blond, and had blue eyes. She stood with one hip shoved out, as if impatient, or bored, and waited, staring at Weiss.

He started to stand, then thought better of it. He dropped back into his chair, and in a voice that was almost hostile, asked, "Can I help you?"

She smiled but didn't move. "I'm looking for Steve Weiss."

"I'm Doctor Weiss."

"So you are. You look like your picture."

"That's an incredibly stupid thing to say. Why wouldn't I look like my picture?"

"Lighting. Angle. Weight loss. Or in your case, weight gain. Change of hairstyle. Growth of facial hair. Removal of facial hair. Change of hair color . . ."

"Okay. I get the point."

"So, you look like your picture."

"What do you want?" He reached over and shut off the flow of information to the flat-screen. He watched it fade, stared for a moment, then turned to face the woman.

He noticed that she wasn't a Martian. Her skin was tanned, suggesting she had been on Earth recently. She wasn't wearing the Martian uniform of coveralls. Everyone, when they arrived, tried to stay in their Earth clothes, but they always eventually yielded. The Martian semi-official uniform was too comfortable to avoid. No thought about what to wear, or worries that someone would be in a later style. Just the coverall that matched, other than color, that which everyone else wore.

The woman wore a skirt that came to mid-thigh, a long-sleeved blouse, and long boots. She was dressed like someone from the last century, or like one of the ultra-modern women of high fashion on Earth. Weiss didn't know which, but he appreciated what he could see. He let his eyes wash over her slowly, aware that he was annoying her.

The woman straightened up and took a couple of steps into the office. Without waiting, she closed the door behind her, grinned, and sat down opposite Weiss, in the only chair that was available. The other held a stack of papers, books, computer disks, and a torn shirt.

She crossed her legs slowly, keeping her eyes on Weiss's, whose dipped to watch, and said, "I have a mission here. I have a job to do and thought you might be able to help me do it."

"Depends on what it is," he said.

The woman said, "I know that you are on Mars against your will and that your father, tired of your activities, has refused to provide the private funds you need to get back to Earth. I know that you have received your doctorate here and that many on Earth think degrees conferred at a distance are the same as a mail order degree, especially when they are received on Mars. I know that you'd like to change that situation with a good assignment on Earth."

The look on Weiss's face changed from bemused to annoyed to angry. He interrupted to say, "You have missed the point."

"I have missed no point. You are not trusted by your colleagues, and you can expect no help from your father. You might just spend your career here and never get a chance to return to Earth, unless you are brighter than you look. I can fix that."

Weiss was suddenly interested, but had learned long ago that to express interest was to change the equation. The best thing he could do was pretend anger and let the woman talk. He could learn more that way.

"We're interested in the progress made on the faster-than-light ship."

"Isn't everyone, given the recent circumstances," said Weiss.

"I need information for my employer, and he is prepared to make certain arrangements . . . either financial or employment, for those who assist him. He can be a very generous man when the mood moves him."

Weiss nodded but didn't say anything.

The woman sat there, watching his reaction, looking for anything that would show interest, but Weiss had assumed a poker face. He was as readable as a statue. As open as a locked vault. He was going to reveal nothing.

She slowly recrossed her legs and noticed a flicker of interest. She said, "I take it that you are interested in some kind of a proposition?"

Weiss, who in years passed would have made his interest readily known because he had a cushion, now sat quietly because his cushion was gone. His father had jerked that clear, and he was on his own. He found himself being cautious now, so he said nothing.

She shrugged and started to rise, then said, "I guess I was misinformed."

Weiss let her stand and begin to walk to the door. As she reached it, he said, "I am always interested in new and different propositions."

She looked at him and said, "I think I need something a little more definite than that."

Weiss shrugged. "I'm interested in listening, and that is all that I'm interested in."

She smiled and fingered a button on her blouse as if she were nervous. She looked down at it, then raised her eyes slowly.

Weiss was watching her every move and thought that he understood what she was communicating to him. He just wasn't sure that he wanted to receive that message.

"So what do we do now?" she asked.

"You sit down and tell me why you're here."

"Is that all you want to know?"

"I guess you could start with your name."

"Catherine DeCourtenay."

[2]

HACKETT WAS NOT COMFORTABLE IN THE AS-tronomy building. He always wondered if the people there were making fun of him because his background was military while theirs was science. He had studied engineering in college, and he had continued those studies after graduation and after commissioning, but the Army required that he take any number of military oriented courses, and that study interfered with his pursuit of engineering. In the

end, he was a soldier first and an engineer second. Almost
no one on Mars knew of his true background. They just
saw him as a soldier who needed to be tolerated because
of the power he held.

So, he didn't like the visits to the astronomy building,
even when Bakker was with him. He sometimes thought
that she sided with the astronomers and joined the fun. He
didn't actually believe that. It was just an impression he
sometimes had.

When he got to the small conference room, which
looked more like a kitchen with the refrigerator and stove
removed, but with a table and chairs from a 1950s breakfast nook, he found he was a little late. There were three
people waiting for him, including Bakker.

Ken Peters was standing to one side, looking out the
window at the people circulating only a few feet below
them. Nancy Vores was sitting at what might be considered the head of the table. She looked relaxed, almost as
if she was about to fall asleep.

"Nice of you to finally join us," said Bakker, grinning
broadly.

Hackett dropped into one of the chairs and waited until
everyone was seated. He turned, looked at the flat-screen
mounted on the wall opposite the window, and asked,
"What have you got for me?"

Bakker said, "Shouldn't we have some preliminary
greetings. Small talk to take the edge off?"

Hackett shot her a glance and said, "I saw you half an
hour ago."

"But we've moved."

Hackett hesitated, then nodded. "Okay. Hello all. Isn't
this lovely weather we're having. Typical for this place in
the dome. Hope it doesn't rain today and spoil all the outdoor activities. Happy?"

"Your personal warmth is truly overwhelming," said
Bakker, grinning.

"Come on, Sarah. I'm on a short schedule today."

"Then enough of this light banter," she said. "We've got everything worked out now and thought that you'd want to know what we found."

Hackett just waved at the flat-screen but didn't say anything about it.

Peters stood up and walked to the screen, almost as if it was an easel holding a static display. He touched the edge, and the colors that had been dancing across it dissolved, spun, and coalesced into a star field with one star glowing brighter than all its neighbors.

Peters said, "Given what we know and given our most recent discoveries, we believe that this star, just over two hundred light years from Earth, is the home of the other intelligent, space-traveling race."

Hackett studied the star field but recognized nothing in it. He had expected to see something that resembled the night sky with constellations in it so that he could orient himself, but this looked as if someone had splattered paint on black cloth.

Peters continued quietly. "The signal strength is quite weak . . ."

Hackett held up a hand to interrupt. He looked at Bakker and said, "Why don't I recognize anything?"

"We've corrected the display to reflect the actual size and brightness of the stars, not how they look from here. This is a representation of the real sky, not the artificial construct that we made."

"This bothers me," said Hackett.

Bakker nodded and touched a button. The scene shimmered for a moment and then steadied.

"Ah," said Hackett. "I recognize this."

"Gives a false impression," said Bakker. "Makes some stars look larger or closer than they really are."

"But I see some things that I recognize."

Peters stood patiently, then asked, "Any other questions, Colonel?"

"Well, since you brought it up . . . why did it take so

long for us to find this?" He knew that the search for the signal had been long and difficult, given the strength of it, and the frequencies used by the aliens. What confused him was that a race that could travel interstellar distances had probably developed some form of radio long before they developed faster-than-light.

Peters looked at Bakker. She said, "We have a couple of theories about that. My favorite is that these beings didn't enter into a technological society all that long ago. Radio signals, as you know, travel only at the speed of light, which means these signals are two hundred years old."

"I know that," snapped Hackett, annoyed. "Everyone understands that."

"Take our own history as it relates to radio. At the turn of the twentieth century, we had just begun to use wireless radio. The signals were very weak and couldn't even travel the Atlantic without relay. Such weak signals, although radiating into space, are probably below the threshold of detection. They're just too weak and too vulnerable to radiation in space, not to mention that they were probably lost in the radio noise generated by the sun and Jupiter."

"So you're saying that these aliens developed radio only about two hundred years ago?"

"Well, not exactly, but their signals reached a point about two hundred years ago that they were strong enough to cross space, and our technology has grown to the point where we can detect them, no matter how faint they might be now. These two things had to happen before we were able to detect anything at all."

"But, from what you're saying, these aliens aren't all that much advanced on us."

Bakker closed her eyes as if in deep thought. "I'm not sure that's a safe assumption."

"Why not?"

"Well, maybe radio was never as important to them as

it is to us. Maybe it was left to the kids to develop while the adults worked on something superior to it. Maybe they've developed way beyond radio, but now it's become a hobby to them and that's why we're beginning to receive the signals. Sort of like the reenactors we have on Earth. Men and women pretending they live in Civil War America or during the Revolution. That sort of thing."

"Their ship was using radio."

"True," said Bakker, "but that might just be for relatively short, sort of ship-to-ship communication, rather than anything else. We really can't draw anything from this, other than the radio signal we have matches the signal we picked up from the ship, so we are assuming, at the moment, a connection between the beings on the planet and that ship."

Hackett said, "Something else strikes me about this. The first real sign of other intelligent life in the galaxy comes from a star system very close to us."

Bakker nodded. "I've thought about that. If that is their home world, then it would suggest the galaxy is teeming with life."

"Then why haven't there been more of them here?"

Bakker had to grin. "You remember the UFO guy we used to work with. Travis? He'd have told you that they are here, we just don't seem to acknowledge them."

"Do we want to attack from that direction? That UFOs are real?" asked Hackett.

Bakker said, "We believe that the galaxy is what, four times older than the Earth, which means that intelligent life should have developed elsewhere, and it should have developed the capability to travel interstellar distances long ago. Since we have no evidence that such is the case, other than a single accepted example, and rejecting all the UFO data as unscientific, it would suggest that intelligent life does not fill the galaxy."

"So we have a paradox," said Peters, just to get back into the conversation.

Bakker looked at him and shrugged. "I don't know what it means. We know that there is other intelligent life, we just haven't found many examples."

"Maybe the distances do limit the possibilities," said Hackett. "Even with faster-than-light drive, it still takes a long time to travel across the galaxy. Maybe faster-than-light isn't as fast as we think."

"Well, we don't know that," said Bakker. She looked over at Peters who was standing patiently by the flat-screen. "If you would like to continue."

Peters said, "Thank you." He turned his attention to the star chart. "There are some things that we can tell about this star, even at two hundred light years. It is of a size and class that matches our own sun. It seems to be slightly larger and a little brighter, but all that means, in terms of astronomy, is that the biosphere will be slightly farther away from their star."

"Biosphere?" asked Hackett.

"The area around a star in which we believe life as we know it could exist. Not too hot or bright, but that produces conditions that match what we find around Earth."

"And Mars," said Hackett.

"Now there's an interesting point," said Vores, speaking for the first time. "Mars really isn't in the biosphere, because we can't live on the surface without the protective domes, yet we can live on the surface, which we can't say of Jupiter and the outer planets. Does this mean that the biosphere includes specific planet types, too? And we can't live on the moon without protection, but it's in the biosphere."

"I think we're getting off track," said Bakker. "Ken, if you would continue."

"Yes, well, there isn't much to tell. The star has planets, at least fourteen of them. The majority are gas giants, not unlike Jupiter, at least according to our observations. There seems to be five smaller planets, all the size of Earth or larger that circle closer to the star. That solar system is, more or less, a duplication of ours, which means small planets close to the star and larger ones far out."

Hackett looked at his watch. "So, you've found what you believe to be the home system of the aliens, and you believe their technology is what, a hundred, hundred and fifty years ahead of ours?"

"Given the limited clues we have," said Bakker, "that seems to be a fair assessment." Now she grinned. "But, think where we were a hundred years ago and while we were moving into a more enlightened age, if we traveled back in time, we would overwhelm the people with what we now consider commonplace. Cellular telephones that have a hundred different uses and that can still make telephone calls. Little silver disks that contain huge amounts of data. Computers held in the palm of the hand. Aircraft that touch space and that can fly at ten, twelve times the speed of sound without creating sonic booms. People traveling to Europe or Asia for lunch and home in time for the evening news. Holograms that put you into the center of the action so that you can experience events that you missed the first time around. Thousands of people living on Mars as if it is just another city on Earth, and the creation of a ship that travels faster than light . . ."

Hackett held up a hand. "I get the point. Anyone a hundred years ahead of us makes us look primitive. Even ten or twenty years puts us at a significant disadvantage."

"So we have a destination for our first flight into deep space," said Hackett. "It's two hundred light years away." Of course, he didn't know as he said it that events would overtake him.

[3]

PROFESSOR WILLIAM BRUCE SMERTZ WAS angry. He was angry with his staff, with those putting pressure on him, and with the government in general, which didn't recognize the problems of science. These bureaucrats seemed to believe that when they ordered something, the task would be completed because they had ordered it to be so. They didn't seem to realize that the laws of physics and the abilities of humans might limit, or even prevent, the completion of a task, no matter how enthusiastic the bureaucrat might be. So, he was angry, but if anyone had asked why, he couldn't have told them exactly what had set him off.

He turned and looked back at Weiss and DeCourtenay. He didn't like either one of them in the communications room with him. He didn't want them watching the preparations or listening to his instructions to the crew on the ship. But he couldn't throw them out. Weiss worked for Hackett, and be had vouched for DeCourtenay, not realizing that DeCourtenay worked for Barnett, who was controlling everything about the project. There were wheels in wheels, and it wasn't clear that anyone understood them all, even if he or she knew of them.

The communications room they were using was one of the smallest on Mars. It was only ten or twelve feet wide and about twenty long, with everything in the room oriented toward the flat-screen hanging on the far wall. It was huge, making it look almost like an extension of the room. Or maybe a mirror hanging there reflecting everything.

Near it were other, smaller screens that provided a series of views that could be easily changed. Unnoticed were several camera lenses so that those at the far end, meaning outside the room and at the end of a microwave, could see what was happening in the communications room. Had they wanted to, they could have arranged a conference call that had fifteen or twenty participants, depending on how they split the screens and set the cameras.

Smertz got out of his chair, moved to the right, and looked down at the display concealed in a desktop. He didn't have to move. He could have called it up on his own computer screen, but he wanted to walk around. He didn't like to sit still for long periods.

He pushed past the woman, whose name he refused to learn and said, nastily, "Please stay out of my way or get the hell out of this center."

DeCourtenay jumped back and said, "Sorry."

Smertz dropped into the chair, then looked up at the main display. He watched as an astronaut, he couldn't tell if it was a man or a woman, floated to the right, into a bright light and then stopped, holding a tool in one hand.

"When need to calibrate there," said Smertz.

A moment later, a disembodied voice that sounded female, said, "I've got that."

"Someone needs to hook up the inline generator now," said Smertz. "I got no reading on that."

A different voice said, "That'll take ten minutes, maybe a little more."

"Damn it! That should have been done half an hour ago." Smertz's voice was angry. He slammed a hand down on the hollow tabletop for emphasis.

The response was the model of professionalism. "Yes, but we've had a couple of problems here. Coupling didn't fit, and we needed to make an adjustment."

Smertz turned his attention on Weiss and then the woman with him. He said, his voice tight with anger and more than a little hostility, "I thought you people had all this figured out and had assembled everything once to make sure it all fit together properly."

"These things are subjected to some extremes of temperature as they travel here. We're going to lose a little of the precision because of that . . ." She didn't realize that her cover as an airhead was being exposed. She wasn't there to defend the manufacturer, but to seduce Weiss at Barnett's order.

"Bull," snapped Smertz. "There shouldn't be any extremes. Everything is heated and pressurized. You're making excuses for bad manufacturing."

DeCourtenay looked to Weiss for some support, but he just sat quietly, watching. She said, "We're dealing with very precise tolerances here so that the shifting temperatures or pressures, or even the accelerations might be enough to throw things off ever so slightly. You have a problem with that, don't yell at me about it. I didn't have a thing to do with it, and I didn't make it."

"You are here representing . . ."

DeCourtenay interrupted. "I am not here representing anyone. I am just here observing."

Smertz looked at Weiss.

Weiss said, "She's here with me, and she has the proper clearances."

"I don't understand this," said Smertz. "I don't need a lot of observers in here cluttering up the arena. Maybe she should get out."

Weiss took a deep breath and said, "We are not going to compromise your work in any fashion. We are not going to get in the way . . ."

"You are already in the way, and you have distracted me," Smertz said.

"You distracted yourself," snapped DeCourtenay. "If you would just concern yourself with your mission and not worry about anyone else, this would all go more smoothly."

Over the closed circuit, one of the astronauts had faced the camera, the gold of the helmet keeping those on Mars from seeing who it was. The voice, again sounding female, said, "We're set up here."

Smertz turned his attention back to the screen. "You have everything set now?"

"We're set up here."

"Then let's check out the new systems starting with the generators."

"Roger that."

Smertz turned his attention to the main flat-screen, having forgotten the nasty fight. He concentrated on what he saw there and waited as the astronauts fired up the generator, which sent power toward the star drive.

Now he was watching as the power settings lighted, one after another, showing various systems coming on line. None of them were at full power, but he hadn't expected them to be. All the levels were right where he wanted them.

He let the systems run, watching for signs of trouble, something that would indicate the ship would explode once they decided to try to break the light barrier again. He still didn't really understand why the first ship had blown up, because there was nothing in the telemetry to indicate a problem that would result in a catastrophic failure and then an explosion. Nothing at all.

Satisfied, he said, "Let's shut it down."

A few moments later the systems began to drop off line, one after the other. When everything was shut down, the astronaut's helmet appeared on the flat-screen.

"We're secured here."

"Then you are cleared to return to the station. Keep an eye on the ship."

"Roger that." The image on the screen disappeared.

Smertz, feeling better than he had in a long time, leaned back and laced his fingers behind his head. He said to Weiss, "Next time, you ask permission to bring someone in to watch the experiments. You understand?"

Weiss just smiled, because he knew that he didn't have to ask, and he knew that DeCourtenay had the power to make them all miserable, if she was offended. He didn't bother to tell Smertz that. Let Smertz get himself in trouble.

[4]

HACKETT HAD WANTED TO WAIT IN THE OFFICE for a report from Smertz about the new tests. He had wanted to be reassured that everything had worked the way it was supposed to work. He had wanted to make sure that nothing had blown up, because, if it had, he would have to send that information to Earth, where there would be a number of very unhappy people, and he would then receive his orders for Utah. It wouldn't take long for them to arrive either. Somehow those angered at him would be able to send the orders faster than light, even if they couldn't get the ship to function that way.

Bakker entered the office and dropped into the closest chair. She hooked one leg over the arm and leaned back. She grinned and said, "Let's get out of here."

"I thought I would watch Smertz."

"We can do that at home. You don't have to be here, and he won't get anything arranged for an hour."

Hackett hesitated, then said, "Yeah. No need to be here as my career ends."

Bakker stood up and opened the door. She waited until Hackett joined her, then stepped out into the hall. She said, "I don't feel like eating out tonight. Can we stay in?"

"I don't care one way or the other," said Hackett.

Now Bakker smiled wickedly. "I can change that attitude. I can make sure that you don't want to go out tonight and probably tomorrow."

They left the building and walked along the street. The sunlight was fading, and the streetlights were coming on. The shadows danced around them as people moved from work toward home or toward the meeting spots. There were only a few vehicles, electric, that were part of the mass transit system.

They reached the apartments, climbed the stairs, and Hackett opened the door, letting Bakker enter in front of him. As he closed the door, she reached a hand up to the throat of her coverall and pulled it down with a sound of ripping cloth as the velcro separated.

"See," she said coyly, "I told you I could change your attitude."

Hackett smiled. "But you need to let me check the status

of the work and to alert Smertz where I am. I want to know if anything has gone wrong."

Bakker shrugged her shoulders, letting the top of the coverall fall away. She wiggled her hips, and the garment pooled around her ankles, giving Hackett a good view of her body with very little covering it.

"Are you sure?" she asked.

Hackett stepped to her and touched her shoulder gently. He looked down, at her, and then back up, into her eyes. "No, I'm not sure."

Now she laughed. She stepped to the side, out of the coverall, and then bent to pick it up. She retreated toward the bed.

"Why don't you make your calls, and I'll just wait here. I think I need a shower . . . well, I don't need one, but I would like to take one."

Hackett, still watching her, sat down on the couch and touched the arm. The flat-screen on the opposite wall brightened, and Hackett saw a sergeant sitting behind a desk. He was in charge of quarters, responsible for taking care of details when the staff had gone for the day.

He said, "I'm going to be here the rest of the evening. Have Doctor Smertz call me when he's completed his work. If anything comes in, let me know."

"Yes, sir. I think Smertz has finished. Do you want me to see if I can find him?"

Hackett glanced at the bed, but Bakker had disappeared. He rubbed a hand through his hair and said, "Yeah, I suppose so. Have him call me here as soon as you can."

"Yes, sir."

Hackett leaned back and relaxed. He closed his eyes for a moment, and when he opened them, Bakker was standing in front of him, a glass held in her hand. She had not yet showered, nor had she bothered to get dressed. She wore only her panties, which were nearly invisible.

"Why are you sleeping here?"

Hackett sat up and rubbed his face with both hands. He almost didn't want to speak because he was afraid his breath would offend. He took the glass and drank deeply, hoping for something containing alcohol, which would cover bad breath. What he got was 7Up, which, at least, washed the bad taste from his tongue.

"Didn't mean to fall asleep," he said. "I thought Smertz was going to call me right back."

Bakker sat down next to him. "I didn't know you were that tired."

"Comes from worrying all the time and from waiting for my orders to Utah."

She took the glass away from him and took a sip. As she handed it back, she asked, "You really worried about Utah?"

Hackett tried to grin and failed. He said, "In one respect, I am. I have been given the assignment to get this FTL working and the ship ready for an assignment. Now you know, I can't build the ship, and the physics of it are lost on me. How many people in the Solar System understand this faster-than-light stuff, anyhow? I know engineering, but I don't understand this, so I have to rely on Smertz and his crew and a couple hundred others. If they don't know what they're doing, then it's going to be my ass."

"But why?" she asked.

"Because I'm the man in charge. Because I'm supposed to figure out if this approach is crap or not. Hell, not long ago, just a couple of years, really, we would have argued about the possibility of faster-than-light, now we know it works. We just don't know if our approach works."

Bakker said, "It works. The experimental ship did cross beyond the speed of light. The problem was mechanical."

"So you say. And I believe that. But that doesn't change the fact that the ship blew up. If the next one does, someone is going to figure that I don't know what I'm doing and bring in someone who does."

She said again, "That's not fair."

"But it happens all the time. The team performs poorly, the coach is fired. Might be his fault. Might not, but he gets the ax. The military works the same way. The man in command is responsible for everything, even if he doesn't personally do everything. I understand the rules."

"I could let my bosses know that there are problems that are not the fault of the team here."

Now Hackett smiled in earnest. "I got to tell you, I could pay more attention to this discussion if you weren't dressed like that. Or rather undressed like that."

"I can put on clothes if you want me to."

"Don't get dressed on my account. I'm just saying that my concentration is slipping."

Bakker stood up as the flat-screen chirped. Hackett said, "That's probably Smertz now."

Bakker retreated toward the bed once again. "I'll give you five minutes, and then I'm really taking my shower, with you or without you."

The incoming message notice was flashing. Hackett touched the armrest, and Smertz appeared on the screen. "What have you got for me, Doctor."

"This preliminary test was successful."

"When can we expect the next attempt to jump to light speed?" asked Hackett.

"Three weeks at the outside. Probably more like ten days. I want to check everything very carefully."

"I can't blame you there."

Smertz looked down at something that was out of camera range. Notes, maybe. Or someone prompting him. He said, "I don't like how some of this is going."

"You'll need to tell me a little more," said Hackett. He heard water begin to run in the bathroom, but it shut off quickly. Bakker letting him know that she would make good on her threat.

"Some of the couplings didn't fit as well as they should have. I was told that the extremes in temperature and the forces of acceleration might have been responsible. I'm not sure that such is the case."

"Just what are you suggesting here, Doctor?"

Smertz looked down again, and then back up, directly into the camera. "That someone might not want the ship to be completed and is attempting to prevent it."

CHAPTER 5

[1]

WEISS HAD GOTTEN USED TO SEEING DeCourte-
nay around. She seemed to always have a question or suggestion for him. She made it clear that she worked for
Barnett, and if Barnett's agenda was followed carefully
and religiously, then Weiss could expect a reward, not the
least of which would be first-class transportation from
Mars back to Earth. Once Weiss landed on Earth, he could
expect to find a job doing what he wanted, where he
wanted, for more compensation than he needed to meet
most of his desires.

DeCourtenay wouldn't stay with him, at his apartment,
insisting that she needed her privacy and her space, but he
suspected it was because she really didn't like him all that
much. She avoided social contact, unless she wanted
something specific, and then she manipulated him in the
most transparent ways. The problem for Weiss was that he
couldn't help himself. He fell for it every time, even when
he knew what she was doing to him and why she was
doing it. What he couldn't figure out was if he was re-

sponding to her because of her personality and body or
because of the promised riches when he returned to Earth.
Sometimes he thought it was for both. For a clever and
manipulating man, he was very confused.

So now he sat with her in one of the quieter pubs, well
away from the headquarters building, where they could
talk to one another without having to shout over a live, but
poorly trained band or the canned music. It was a dark
room, much longer than wide, with a long, narrow bar on
one side and booths for the patrons on the other. Food was
served, but it wasn't all that good. It was hot, and there
was plenty of it, but food service was not their mission,
and that was evident. Selling expensive booze, both hard
and soft, meaning beer rather than soda, was their main
mission. They made the most money that way, and it was
what the owner wanted to do. Food meant that people
came in earlier and stayed longer. Eating inspired drinking, so he put up with the requests for food, because they
helped line his pockets.

DeCourtenay leaned forward across the table and
asked quietly, "Why didn't the connectors fit?" When she
saw him trying to stare down her blouse, she smiled.

Weiss stared back at her, not wanting to talk about
the experiment and trying not to look at her chest, but fail-
ing. He said, "I don't know. Maybe it was as you said
earlier."

"I just didn't want Smertz to go off on another tan-
gent," she said. "He was drifting away from the topic and
what was important."

"And that would be?"

"Getting the ship ready for the next test. That's what
we need to do."

Weiss decided that he didn't want to hear any more
about the ship and tests of it. He was interested in how
DeCourtenay had gotten to Mars and how she had been
able to penetrate the security, such as it was, around the
mission so easily. Even Barnett shouldn't have been able

to penetrate security through a third party—he shouldn't have been able to get DeCourtenay on the inside as easily as he had, yet here she was.

He said, "What are you going to report to Earth?"

"That everything is progressing."

"But that's not a good report. Or much of a report."

"It's an accurate report," she said with finality. She picked up her glass and drained it. "I think it's getting to be time for me to head home."

"The night is young," said Weiss.

"But I'm not. At least not as young as I used to be. I need my sleep, and I want to go to bed."

Weiss started to say something, but looked up at her and stopped suddenly. He smiled weakly. "I hope you sleep well, then."

"Thank you." DeCourtenay got to her feet, seemed to hesitate as if she expected something from Weiss, but when nothing happened, she walked out of the bar.

Weiss finished his drink and sat there, watching the people circulate and wondering if this was what it had been like in the frontier of the American West. Conditions on Mars were crude compared with some areas on Earth, but they were certainly better than anything from the nineteenth century. The housing was better, cleaner, safer, drier. There was the best of modern medical care, though it was sometimes a little remote or a little slow in arriving. There was more home entertainment than most could imagine, but many people still liked to get out and circulate.

The people on Mars, hell, the whole human race, were on the fringes of the first real steps into deep space, but they had to make some sacrifice. It took a great deal of energy, money, and trouble getting everything and everyone to Mars. Personal freedom was restricted because of the hostility of the environment both in space and on the Martian surface. Sometimes there were restrictions on food or drink, but all that was an outgrowth of the situation on

Mars that changed with the circumstances. It was all an inconvenience rather than a real sacrifice.

He sat there, wondering what had triggered those thoughts, and then looked up as two women entered. Both were scantily dressed, defying the convention of coveralls that seemed to be worn by everyone else. They were obviously working girls, another throwback to the nineteenth century frontier and one that was winked at by those in authority.

Weiss half stood up and waved a hand. One of them spotted him and walked over. She leaned forward, her hands flat on his table, looking down, into his eyes. He didn't look up into hers, but let his gaze focus on her chest. She was letting him see down her open shirt, where her breasts were unrestrained.

"You looking for a date?" she asked more than a little sarcastically.

Weiss wondered, for just a moment, how they had gotten to Mars. Surely those computer geeks on Earth wouldn't just sign up girls to work the domes of Mars as prostitutes. They must have had another job description when they boarded the ships for the flight to Mars.

But here they were, in an environment where the men outnumbered the women by a good margin. They provided a service, and suddenly Weiss wondered if it wasn't strictly regulated by the government. It would be a way of generating capital for public projects that might not be funded in any other way. A tax that few knew about and fewer complained about.

He grinned and said, "Why don't you sit down for a moment? I'll buy you something to drink."

She slid into the chair. "I haven't seen you around here before."

"Don't get here much. Sometimes. When I'm thirsty."

"Well, as you know, time is money."

"I don't think we need to worry about that right now, do we?" asked Weiss.

"Well, I don't have a lot of time to waste," she said, seeming to appraise him.

"No, I suppose not. What's your name?"

"You can call me Tiffany."

"Okay, Tiffany. What do you do?"

"Depends on the money and if I like the guy. Sometimes we just can't get together."

Weiss sat back in his chair and looked at her. She was a young woman with long hair that was so fine and perfect it almost had to be a wig. She had wide, bright eyes, a small, delicate nose, and a wide mouth with thick lips. The features were spread across her rounded face evenly, symmetrically, giving her a pleasing look. She wasn't beautiful, but she was pretty. She didn't look delicate, rather she looked as if she could hold her own. A strong woman used to getting her way, and that made Weiss leery of her.

The waiter brought her a drink and set it on the table in front of her. "Who's paying for this?"

Weiss said, "I will."

The waiter said, "Got it," and retreated. The cost of the drink would be automatically deducted from Weiss's account in the local, Martian branch of his bank, which, in reality was little more than a computer terminal. The process saved having to deal with any sort of currency.

When he was gone, Weiss asked, "How'd he know what you wanted to drink?"

"I always have the same thing. He just brought it over when he saw me sit down."

Weiss suspected a scam. She'd claim the drink was something expensive, the bartender would deduct that from Weiss's account, but the drink would be tea or colored water rather than something expensive. It was a trick as old as civilization itself.

He watched her for a moment, but she looked like a girl on a date more than anything else. He wanted to ask the timeworn, clichéd question, but restrained himself, doubting he would get a straight answer.

Finally he said, "So, you'll come home with me?"

"If you like, but that costs so much more."

Weiss decided that he was tired of the game. She was what was known as a sure thing, and he just wasn't that interested in the sure thing. To him most of the fun was in the pursuit and the mystery of the final moments. In this case he knew what would happen, and if she was a good actress, he would feel as if she was having a good time. She would consent to anything he wanted as long as the money continued to flow. But he just couldn't generate any real interest in the game. Not tonight anyway.

"Why don't I buy you and your friend . . ." He looked around and found the other girl engaged with someone else. He grinned and finished with, "Why don't I buy you another drink? I've got a lot of work to do back at the office and really should get back to it."

She looked disappointed.

When she started to protest, Weiss held up a hand. "No. Let's not spoil it now. Let's just pretend that this never happened. Thank you for the company."

The waiter appeared with a drink, Weiss confirmed his willingness to pay for it, and then stood up. When he was clear of the club, outside of it, where the air was the same temperature but the humidity was lower, he took a deep breath, now unsure if he should have passed on the date. He didn't know when he'd get another chance. As it turned out, it would be quite a long time.

[2]

HACKETT AWOKE BEFORE THE ALARM WENT OFF. He laid in bed, staring at the window, but the shade was drawn, and he could only see the border of brightness that was there day and night. He felt as if he had slept for hours, maybe days, but when he finally glanced at the clock, he saw that he hadn't been asleep very long.

Trying not to disturb Bakker, Hackett pushed back the covers and got up. He walked out of the bedroom alcove, wishing he had a larger place. He stepped to the couch, sat down and turned on the flat-screen, and cycled through the programming, thin though it was so early in the morning. He then checked the incoming messages for anything that would create havoc later in the morning, and finally, bored but wide awake, he set the screen saver.

The door of the bathroom opened, and Bakker came out wearing a short robe and nothing else. She looked sleepy, only half awake. He hadn't seen her get up or go into the bathroom. She asked, "What are you doing out here?"

"Just sitting."

"Why are you up?"

"Don't know. Just couldn't sleep, so I thought I'd take a look at the flat-screen. Nothing to watch."

"Any interesting mail?"

Hackett grinned. "Now how would you know that I looked at the mail?"

"Because it's the first thing you do every morning and nearly the last thing you do every night. You're very predictable."

Hackett shrugged. "Just routine stuff."

She walked across the room and sat down close to him. "Do you mind if I check mine?"

"Go ahead."

She leaned over and touched the controls. The mailbox appeared, and she scrolled down, looking at the subjects. The usual fare. She found one from the radio astronomy group and opened it.

"What's that?" asked Hackett.

"Stuff from the latest observation of the alien's home system."

"Anything interesting?"

"I don't know," said Bakker quietly. "Seems that the level of the transmissions have picked up. More radio noise and now stronger than it was."

"Meaning?"

"I don't know." She leaned back, her head against the wall but her eyes on the message.

She said, "If someone had looked at Earth as a radio source a hundred and fifty years ago, they wouldn't have seen much. Had they looked a hundred years ago, they would have seen us like a beacon, and had they looked fifty years ago, we would be brighter than the sun from a radio wave standpoint. If it was simply the evolution of our technology, I would understand it."

"But."

"We have an explosion of radio signals, not only in number but in intensity. Much stronger, and it developed over the last few weeks."

"They turned on their radios."

"Okay," said Bakker. "Why?"

Hackett smiled, "Thinking strictly as a military man, the radio traffic increases when an operation is about to kick off. More radio traffic because there is more that has to be coordinated."

"What about radio silence?"

"That comes later, as the forces move into position. Then the radio traffic would drop off. Any military planner, or rather intelligence officer, knows this. They might not be able to read the messages, but the volume of messages alone provides some information."

He laughed. "I remember reading, and I don't know what operation it was or how long ago, but the news media tumbled to the fact that something big was in the air and began asking lots of questions."

"Because of increased radio traffic?"

"No, increase in the number of pizzas bought by the headquarters. They noticed that people were working later than usual, ordering pizza for dinner because it was quick and easy. The reporters knew that something big was being planned. Something that had a short fuse."

"Well," said Bakker, "I just don't know if this is even

important. Might be a coincidence, might be that they brought something on-line that created more and stronger radio signals, or it might mean nothing at all."

"If nothing else," said Hackett, "we have a destination for the first long-term mission."

"Meaning?"

"We go look at the home world of the aliens," he said, looking at her.

"I thought that was understood."

"It was," said Hackett. "I'm just saying that now, with what you've got, we can make a good case for this, unless you've found another intelligent race."

Now Bakker laughed. "I've found one already and now you expect me to find another."

"It's just that I would expect there would be other alien races out there. And we've found someone very close to home," said Hackett.

Bakker turned serious. She knew that she had said it before, but she wanted to say it again. "That bothers me, too. I would have thought that a space-faring race would come from much farther away. I mean, I would have expected some sort of contact before now if we had another intelligent race as close to us as these aliens are and they had the ability to travel interstellar distances. That they're so close suggests to me that there is lots of life in the galaxy and that someone else would have discovered faster-than-light travel before now. I find it hard to believe that we're number two and we're not all that far behind number one. Someone should have developed the capability before now, given the size and the age of the galaxy. We should have seen some evidence of it."

Hackett shook his head. "It's awfully early for such a deep discussion, and you're not exactly dressed for it. I find my mind wandering." He reached out and put a hand on her bare thigh, feeling the warm, soft skin.

"You're not exactly the epitome of high fashion either," she said sarcastically.

Hackett held up his hands in mock surrender. "I mean nothing by it. I just appreciate the costume."

Bakker stood up and said, "I'm tired. I'm going back to bed. You coming?"

"Are you real tired?"

She smiled. She hesitated and dropped her robe. "Not all that tired."

They didn't know that circumstances would dictate the mission when it was finally designed and no one would realize that the biggest problem was not the alien radio transmissions, but something that had been predicted by Earth science long before there was even space flight.

[3]

IT WAS EARLY WHEN JOE DOUGLAS AWAKENED. He had fallen asleep in a chair, staring at the flat-screen, and had returned to consciousness only long enough to stumble to the bed across the room. He hadn't taken off his clothes, though he had been awake enough to kick off his shoes. He just fell on the bed, pulled at the pillow, and went back to sleep.

Sally Wilson was only a little annoyed that Douglas had fallen asleep in a chair, but they had been on Mars for several days and had been staying together in the room for each of those days, so it wasn't as if they'd had no time together. She was ready for sleep when she went to bed. She just wished that Douglas had joined her.

What really annoyed her was Douglas's semiconscious stumble to bed and how he had jerked at a pillow until he got it the way he wanted it. What annoyed her further was how he had rolled to his back and begun to snore loudly, shaking the walls, rattling the window, and threatening the internal integrity of the dome. She had been unable to sleep until he had fallen silent some thirty minutes later as she pushed at him, trying to either wake him or get him to roll over.

But now Douglas was awake, and Wilson was asleep. Douglas didn't know why he was awake, only that something had changed in the room, and that had caused him to wake up. It was something that he had done on the station. He was sensitive to the environment around him even when he was asleep. The slightest change, even when it wasn't threatening the station would awaken him.

He rolled to his side and listened carefully, wondering what had awakened him. He could see the clock, which told him it was very early in the morning. The light coming in the window seemed to be more artificial than natural, and that told him that the sun had not come up. Or more precisely, that the sun hadn't reached a place where its light would enhance that from the dome. Having been in the room for a number of days, he knew that sun could be seen in the morning, but not very early and certainly not very brightly.

There was a quiet noise at the door. It sounded as if someone had slipped an electronic key into the lock and the lock had responded. It sounded as if someone was trying to enter the room quietly and secretly.

Douglas reached out to the floor and let himself slide out of bed, almost like a snake slipping from a tree. He slid to the right, away from the bed, toward the wall and the big chair. It was a dark shadow. He couldn't see detail, but he could make out the shape.

He crouched there with his eyes on the door. The door opened slightly then hit the safety lock, which could only be worked from inside the room. There was a flash of light, and part of the lock glowed brightly and broke, falling to the carpet with a soft thump.

"Wass that?" asked Wilson.

Douglas didn't respond. He waited, watching.

"Joe? Where are you?"

The door closed quietly.

Douglas sprang from his position near the chair, fumbled with the broken door lock, and threw open the door. He stepped out into the hallway, and at the far end, saw a flash of orange coverall that disappeared as someone ran around a corner.

"Joe? What's going on?"

Douglas looked down at the floor, but there was nothing there. No clue about who had been trying to open his door, or why.

"Joe?" Wilson had gotten out of bed and was standing in the center of the room, away from everything, looking small and frightened. The lights were now all on. She was wearing very little, which made her look all the more vulnerable.

Douglas closed the door and looked at the broken lock. Laser cutting tool. A good one, too. It had cut the metal quickly, without creating too much heat and with little in the way of a glow.

"What in the hell is going on, Joe?"

"I don't know," said Douglas. "Someone was trying to break in to the room."

"Why? We don't have much here."

"I don't know."

"You going to call the desk?"

Douglas walked to the chair and sat down, his eyes on the closed door. "I think maybe I should call headquarters security instead."

Now she was confused. "Why? It was just an attempted burglary, wasn't it?"

"I don't know. Pretty sophisticated for a burglar. High-tech, expensive equipment. I think maybe we should call security rather than the desk."

"Okay, Joe. Just call them."

"What I don't understand," said Douglas, "is why that guy would try to break in here. We have nothing he could want."

Douglas, in that instance, was wrong.

[4]

BACK ON EARTH, WENDELLE B. BARNETT WENT over the financial statements one more time. It was clear that his engineers, who had structured the cost of the project, had badly miscalculated nearly everything. They had underestimated the costs of materials, shipping to Mars, costs of analysis, costs of research and development, and the costs of building three ships to travel faster than light. They had blown it completely, missing by nearly a billion dollars, and then advising him that the best move, financially, was cost plus 10 percent. Even with the overruns, they believed that the corporation would make some money.

Which, of course, would have covered everything and made a tidy little profit for the company, except for the penalty clauses. That was what was going to kill them. That was going to force them into bankruptcy inside of twelve months, unless he thought of something fast. At that point, Barnett would no longer have the private jet, the condominiums, town houses, and penthouses. He would no longer be a captain of industry, but just another CEO who had driven his company into bankruptcy, and who would be on the outside looking back in. He would be ruined, and he would have thirty or forty years of life left in which to contemplate his failure. Unless he solved the problem himself, he would be working for someone else, making a tenth, maybe a hundredth of his current salary.

And he would be powerless.

There was a way out of this. He had to fail. If the project collapsed, meaning that it failed because of unforeseen problems, whatever those problems might be, the contract would be canceled. With the government canceling the project, the corporation would be able to maintain their profit. It wasn't their fault that faster-than-light travel was technically beyond them.

If he were to succeed, the penalty clauses would kick in. He would be forced to bring on line a dozen other aspects of the project and they just couldn't do it.

Barnett sat at the top of the building, in a penthouse that looked more like a palace, and realized he didn't want to live in a regular apartment, have waiters ignore him, have to fly commercially rather than in a private jet. He didn't want to live like normal people. He had tasted the sweet fruit of success and would no longer be happy with the ordinary. He just could not go back.

He touched a button, and the curtains that covered the plate glass windows opened rapidly. The view was breathtaking as the city turned from night to day. There was a paling of the sky, a beginning of brightness on the horizon, but with the twinkling of the lights of the city. It was a beautiful sight.

He walked to the window and looked down toward the streets. Cars were moving, some people were walking around, and vendors were setting up to begin their days.

He turned and said, "I want Davis in here."

He spoke to no one. He expected the computer to translate his words into binary, make the appropriate decisions, and then automatically alert Davis. He expected Davis to arrive within five minutes, because Barnett was a man who didn't like to be kept waiting.

There was a knock at the door, and Barnett was sure that Davis had arrived. Instead, a waiter pushed in a cart and began to set up the table for breakfast. It was brought up automatically each morning. He had the same basic breakfast most days, and if he wanted a change, Barnett would tell his secretary to change the order.

Barnett didn't speak to the waiter. He was just one more piece of furniture, there with a single function, and once that function was accomplished, the furniture would be removed. There was nothing that the waiter could say that would interest Barnett in the least.

As the waiter finished, there was a second knock at the

door. The waiter looked up at Barnett, then finished what he was doing. His job wasn't to answer doors, but to set up the breakfast, make sure it was done right, and to get out as quickly as possible.

The door opened, and Davis walked in. He was a short man. Stocky, with dark hair and wide-set, dark eyes. He wore a fresh suit, a gleaming shirt, but no tie. The shirt was buttoned up to the collar, with a bit of gold holding the collar together. Or maybe the gold was just decoration.

When Davis started to speak, Barnett waved him to silence. The waiter finished, hesitated, and, when Barnett made no move toward the table, pushed his cart to the door, pulling it shut behind him.

Barnett sat down at the table and pulled the lid off his plate of fried eggs and hash brown potatoes. There was another plate with pancakes, one of toast, and a little basket of jellies and jams. Spare plates and extra food were always included in case Barnett had a guest for breakfast but hadn't told anyone about it. This wasn't the waste that it appeared to be, because Barnett often ate the extra food, not because he was hungry, but because it was there.

Barnett gestured at the chair opposite. "Have you had your breakfast?"

"Just coffee and a roll."

"Then sit and have something more to eat. And pour me a glass of orange juice."

Davis poured the juice and sat down. He pulled a plate close, took a couple of pancakes, put two fried eggs on top of them, and poured on the syrup. He took a bite, then picked up a napkin to pat his lips.

Barnett picked up a piece of toast, buttered it, and spread it generously with jelly. He waved the toast in the air as he spoke. "Anything new in the overnights?"

"Nothing of interest."

Barnett raised an eyebrow.

"I believe that he failed to conduct a proper test, though I don't know why," said Davis.

"And the installation?" Barnett was talking about installing the new equipment.

"As near as I can tell, they were able to make the fittings work with a little effort. We made the tolerances too close, so that it wasn't the problem we had anticipated."

Barnett dipped the point of his toast into the soft center of his egg. He took a bite, chewed, and swallowed. "What have you on tap?"

"The last time we had to be crude, and we got away with it. They still don't know exactly why the ship exploded, and I doubt they will ever know. Wreckage is too far away and scattered over too wide an area. It's just debris in orbit around the sun. They suspect a manufacturing error, but they don't have any evidence."

"I didn't ask you about the last mission. I want to know about the next."

"We have operatives on Mars. The equipment has been manufactured with subtle irregularities that can be blamed on the shipping. False information is being fed into the various systems, all of which looks like simple mistakes. Taken together, it will stop the project. That is what you wanted, as I understand it."

"Yes," said Barnett. "That is what I want. But don't be so subtle that these efforts won't bear fruit."

Davis sat for a moment, studying the food in front of him, and said, "They'll never get the ship to jump to light speed. That I guarantee." He sat quietly, looking at Barnett, and added, "Even if it kills them."

CHAPTER 6

[1]

HACKETT SAT IN HIS OFFICE AND LISTENED AS
Douglas described the situation at the hotel. He didn't
make notes and didn't record the conversation himself,
aware that a video recording was being made.

When Douglas, who sat in one chair wearing the standard coveralls—this pair a dark green—stopped talking,
Hackett asked, "Did you talk to the desk?"

"No. I called security, but by the time they arrived,
whoever it was had plenty of time to disappear. Security
probably checked with the desk."

Hackett looked at Wilson, who sat in the other chair
dressed in bright red. He asked her, "You have anything
to add?"

"I didn't hear anything and didn't see anything. I was
asleep."

"Either of you have enemies on Mars?"

Douglas shook his head. "I don't know all that many
people, and I haven't been down here that long."

Wilson just shook her head.

Hackett said, "Okay. Check in with security. And then take the rest of the day off. We'll get serious tomorrow."

Douglas stood up. "Yes, sir." He retreated with Wilson, closing the door behind him.

Hackett turned and faced the window. He said, "I want Trask up here as quickly as you can get him. And I want him to bring everything he has on this."

He didn't listen for a response, because there would be none. He'd know that his orders had been received when Trask showed up at his door.

While he waited, he called up information on the flat-screen, I watching it scroll. He didn't know what he wanted and hoped he would spot it when it showed. But the information just paraded along, in a seemingly never-ending stream that gave him no clues about the situation.

There was a quiet chime, telling him that someone was approaching his door. Trask looked in and said, "You called?"

"Come on in and have a seat. Wanted to know if you had anything new."

Trask looked around uncomfortably. He shrugged as if he hadn't understood what Hackett wanted.

He gestured. "Close the door if you want. This is a secure office."

"You have recording?"

"Of course, but I can deactivate it."

"If you don't mind."

Hackett rubbed his face in irritation, leaned forward, and touched a button. "The system is off now."

"I don't mean to be a pain in the ass, but the one thing that is drilled into us is security. If the system is active, it can be accessed, and the recordings are always available if you know where to look."

"I understand, but we're going to have push forward with our tests, and we can't stand another major accident. We have to be fully ready to launch."

Trask sat quietly, looking beyond Hackett, out the

window and into the domed city. Finally he said, "At the moment, we're at a dead end. We have been unable to trace the messages back to a single source. Whoever is doing this has been able to hack a number of systems so that the messages come from widely scattered sources."

"Has there been an increase in the traffic?"

Trask pulled at his bottom lip as he thought. Finally he said, "Not really. Message traffic goes up and down, but nothing I would consider significant."

"Have you broken any of the codes?"

"Simple ones, sure, but then we don't know what the phrases might mean. Same problem as I told you about before."

Hackett stood up and turned so that he could look out into the city. He needed a moment to think. Finally he turned back around and said, "Is there a corporate umbrella over all those various sources? Maybe someone owns everything, but it's hidden in the layers.

The question stopped Trask. He looked at Hackett and shrugged. "I don't know. We haven't been looking for a single corporate entity, but, given the laws of various countries on Earth, and given the way much of the information is distributed, I wouldn't be surprised to learn of a connection. We'll have to see if we can trace any of the corporations."

"Don't waste your time on that. I'll have security look into it."

"All right."

"The one question that I have at the moment," said Hackett, "is if you have any idea how many people are on Mars? How many are involved in this?"

Trask scratched his head. "I don't really know. Fewer than a dozen I would think. At least the traffic doesn't suggest more than that."

"And you have no idea who these people are?"

"Now, I never said that. I have a couple of ideas, but I'm reluctant to name names."

"Why?"

"Because all I have are suspicions. If I'm wrong, then I hurt someone unnecessarily."

Hackett finally sat down again. "Others might be hurt if we don't do something."

"If I had anything concrete, or thought someone would be hurt," said Trask, "I'd tell you."

[2]

SMERTZ DIDN'T LIKE IT WHEN THE CONTROL WAS crowded, because he found it difficult to concentrate and he didn't want to swear in front of people he didn't know. These extra people would be in the way as he tried to move around, they would ask stupid questions and expect brilliant answers, and they would be inclined to push buttons and touch equipment. They could screw up his experiment faster than light.

He sat in the center chair where he had the best view of the main flat-screen, where he could use either the voice or key input, and where he could command the operation. Now he could see the ship, orbiting high above Mars, and he could watch the relays from the orbiting station to Mars and then out to the ship. He had everything at his fingertips, and he could see everything that he needed to watch. He believed they were set.

Standing behind him were Hackett and Bakker, both who understood Smertz's discomfort and his desire not to have so many witnesses. They stood quietly watching, hoping for the best, because they also understood the significance of the experiment. Hackett truly believed that if it failed he would be recalled to count supplies in Utah.

To one side stood DeCourtenay and Weiss, who were talking quietly. Hackett shot them a glance and realized that DeCourtenay didn't like Weiss. She tolerated him for some reason, and he found that surprising.

Trask was also there, standing on the far side, watching everyone and trying to eavesdrop on all the conversations. He was there as Hackett's spy, trying to determine who had been involved in the message traffic back to Earth.

And finally, there was Douglas and Wilson, who would be involved in the first flight if nothing went wrong. Both of them were quiet, watching everything, because they knew their lives would depend on it in a very short time, if this ship didn't explode.

Bakker leaned close to Hackett and asked, "Everything been checked?"

Hackett nodded and whispered, "The astronauts have spent three days going over everything very carefully. They found no hint of a problem."

Which, of course, worried Hackett. If there was sabotage, he would have expected there to be something to find as a decoy. Make them think that they had found all that there was. But then, he wondered if that wasn't being a little too clever. If they found one thing, wouldn't they work that much harder to make sure everything was cleared? He just didn't know.

Smertz stood up, sat down, and then got up again. He walked around in a small circle, glancing at screens, readouts, and sensor arrays. Sweat beaded on his forehead and dripped. He was nervous, frightened, and he didn't want to continue. He wanted to end the experiment before it could explode as spectacularly as the last one, and he knew that he couldn't stop the test. It had to go forward.

He asked, once again, "Are we set?"

"We're waiting on word from you. Once we have that, we can get going," said one of the assistants.

Smertz looked back, at Hackett, who nodded and then turned around. Sudden calm swept over Smertz. He dropped into his chair and reached out to finger one of the buttons. He checked the scrolling information on one of the screens, looked up to see the ship centered in the main screen, and then looked at his staff. They were ready.

Without a word to anyone, without the countdown that he had used for the first test, Smertz mashed the button, holding it down, pushing on it until his thumb was white from the pressure. He just wanted to make sure the signal was properly transmitted.

They then, of course, waited. They watched the flat-screens, and read the information scrolling along on some of them, and they checked the sensors and even listened to the voice input from some of the observers stationed throughout the Solar System. They waited for evidence that the ship had jumped to light speed and that this time it had not exploded.

Smertz circulated in the room, talking with his assistants and associates, avoiding Hackett and the other observers. He was nervous because he wasn't personally convinced that the destruction of the last ship had been the manufacturing error he had claimed it to be. He suspected privately that there was some force that they had not observed that had caused trouble during the jump to faster-than-light speed, and that was why the ship exploded. It had nothing to do with the manufacturing and everything to do with crossing what was once considered to be an impossible barrier.

It would take a couple of hours before they knew if the test had been a success or if the human race would remain confined to the Solar System.

[3]

BARNETT, WHO HAD MORE MONEY THAN HE would ever need, no matter what, or who, he wanted to buy, could get information as fast as official spy agencies, and sometimes faster, depending on what that information was and if there was sunspot activity. He had sources scattered all over the Earth, in the moon colonies, on the various space stations, including those not controlled by the United States or the United Nations, and on Mars. He could learn practically anything he wanted to know, and then he could use that knowledge to make even more money.

So, as he sat in another of the penthouses that he owned, in a city that had no view of an ocean, lake or river, but that did have a spectacular view of snow-covered mountains, he was annoyed. He didn't have the information he wanted. He didn't know what was going on out beyond Mars, and he didn't know if his fortune had been reduced by 10 percent, which meant a couple hundred million dollars. He didn't like not knowing, and he was wondering who he could fire.

He sat in a huge chair, his feet up, so that he could look out at the mountain. Seated near him were several aides who fielded the telephone calls, checked the Internet, watched the sensors, and made the calls needed as they gathered information. These were anonymous people who could work the equipment or who understood some of the specialized information. They would be replaced with others in an hour. Barnett took no real notice of them. To him they were as animated as the furniture and just as interchangeable.

Drinking coffee from a delicate cup, holding the saucer in his left hand, he watched the people work. He asked an occasional question, but was content to sip his coffee, because he knew that everything had been arranged. He had taken care of it all weeks before.

"I think they've signaled the ship," said one of the male aides, a young man dressed not for business but for sport. That was the trend. Away from the more formal attire of business and into the casual clothes that relaxed everyone.

"How soon until we have confirmation?" asked Barnett.

"Fifteen or twenty minutes."

Barnett nodded and turned his attention to the view.

The sky above the mountain was a deep, nearly painful blue, with white clouds building above it. It was a post-card view. One that people would pay to see, if only for an hour, and he could sit there for days and look at it.

"I think they have sent the launch command," said another of the aides. She was younger than the first and dressed in even more casual clothes. She looked as if she were on her way to the beach, rather than in the office of the corporate CEO.

Barnett turned slightly and looked at his main display. It had a representation of the current situation on it. He could see Mars, down in one corner, the asteroid belt scattered across the top, and a bright yellow light that was the ship. It wasn't moving, in relation to Mars, though the asteroids were shifting and dancing on the screen.

Barnett set the cup and saucer down and stood up. He walked across the thick, deep carpet, and stopped five or six feet from the display. He focused all his attention on it. Finally he said, "When can I see something?"

"We have data coming in now. You want it up on the main screen?"

"No, I only want to see this visual. You tell me what I need to know."

"Yes, sir."

As he watched, the yellow dot shimmered and then vanished. Barnett asked, impatiently. "That it? Did the ship explode?"

"Don't have that information yet," said the young woman. "Little early for that."

"Damn it. What's taking so long?"

The first aide turned to face Barnett and said, simply, "Transmission times. Radio waves only travel at the speed of light."

"I don't need a lecture from you," snapped Barnett. "I want my questions answered."

The girl turned and said, "I think they made the jump to light speed. I think they were successful."

"Are you sure?"

"The information is preliminary," she said, "but we are still getting the telemetry. They jumped only a short distance. Out beyond the orbit of Jupiter."

"That's not much of a jump," said Barnett.

"Well, they don't have to travel too far. A hundred million miles in fifteen seconds tells you all you need to know."

Barnett turned back to the view and suddenly realized there was a great deal he didn't know. He wondered about acceleration and deceleration and why it hadn't taken days or weeks to get up to light speed. They couldn't just jump to it without encountering gravitation forces that should rip the ship to pieces. Breaking the sound barrier had required the aircraft to accelerate toward 700, 800 miles an hour before slipping beyond the sound barrier. There was something about the physics of the situation that he didn't fully understand.

"The ship is intact?"

"Yes, sir. It's in fine shape. What did you expect?"

Barnett looked at her, and then at the mountains outside. He couldn't tell them that he expected the ship to explode like the first one had. He could only nod, as if that was all the joy he would show for the success. They wouldn't realize that he saw it as a failure.

[4]

AS SOON AS THE SIGNAL REACHED THEM, telling them that the ship had made a brief jump to light speed, that it had survived the jump, and that there had been nothing on the ship to suggest that humans could not withstand these jumps to light speed, meaning simply that there were no huge bursts of radiation or that there was some sort of oppressive gravitational problems, cheering erupted.

Hackett looked at Bakker, grinned broadly, and said, "We've just reached the stars."

Weiss looked uncomfortable, as he watched the others celebrate. He stood alone, near a corner, his eyes on the screens, as if he expected something else, something new to explode there. Instead, he saw only the ship floating in space, and he saw the image of Saturn in the distance. There was nothing to indicate that the ship had been damaged in any way. The test had been a complete success.

Over the shouting, Weiss heard Bakker exclaim, "Looks like you won't be going to Utah after all."

"Nope. Looks like the promotion is on track. Looks like we can now answer a lot of questions."

Smertz, looking smug, strolled over, grinned, and said, "I never had any doubt. I knew it would work."

"The only thing I want to know," said Hackett, "is how fast will the ship go?"

"Faster than light," said Smertz.

"Yes, but just a little faster, or twice as fast, or ten times as fast?"

Still smiling, Smertz said, "Theoretically, now that we have solved the problem of faster-than-light, we should be able to fly at any multiple of it that we have the power to obtain. How many times faster than the speed of sound can we fly? It's limited only by the capability of the aircraft and the dynamics of the atmosphere.

One of the assistants, a young, stocky woman with short hair and dark eyes, sort of danced over, hugged Smertz, and announced, unnecessarily, "We have done it."

"Yes," said Hackett. "You have."

Smertz looked at Hackett and said, "This is a day that future generations will study and history will remember. It is the day that humanity reached the stars and ensured their survival for all of eternity."

Hackett didn't like to think in terms of future generations and eternity, but he knew that Smertz was right. This would be one of those dates, like Columbus landing in the

New World or the Allied invasion of France that ended Nazi occupation. People would remember it forever.

"A celebration," said Smertz. "I believe that when we finish here, a celebration is in order. I would like to buy dinner and drinks for the staff who worked so hard to see that we were successful today." He looked meaningfully at Hackett.

Hackett grinned and shook his head. "Doctor, this day should be for you and your staff, not for me and mine. We were responsible for very little of your success. You should enjoy as much as you can."

Smertz just shrugged and turned his attention back to his staff, who were still dancing around, hugging one another, and smiling as if there were no tomorrow.

[5]

HACKETT SAT IN THE COMMUNICATIONS ROOM and faced the general for the first time in weeks. Lieutenant General George Greenstein was in overall command of the Galaxy Exploration Team. He was headquartered on Earth, first at White Sands in New Mexico, but later, he moved his headquarters to Colorado Springs, because the communications facilities he needed were there and he preferred Colorado Springs to the oppressive environment in Houston or Florida and the bureaucratic nightmare that Washington, D.C., had become. In Colorado Springs, the weather was milder, though the winters were slightly colder than in White Sands, and the bureaucrats had trouble finding ways to interfere with his work. He was isolated, though he thought of it as insulated.

Hackett reported that the test had been a success, meaning they had passed through the light barrier and the ship had remained in one piece. He sat in front of a camera, with a screen just above it so that he could see the

general. What was making the conversation difficult was
the time delay between them. At the moment it was a
fairly annoying twenty minutes, given the travel time of
the signal, the encrypting and decrypting, and the routing
through specific satellites and antenna farms.

They had developed a system in which one person
would engage in a monologue and then fall silent. When
he had listened to the message, he would respond in detail
and ask whatever questions or make whatever comments
he needed at that point.

Hackett looked up as Greenstein began to speak. The
general was wearing his class A green uniform, complete
with all awards and decorations. It looked as if he had
come from a high-level staff meeting or some kind of formal party.

Hackett listened, took a few notes, and when the general fell silent said, "It looks as if this will work. The
questions that haven't been answered are about top speed
and how much power and fuel it will take. We need to
provide some sort of crew quarters and life support, but I
don't think those problems are any more trouble than creating the ships that moved from Earth to Mars. A few
months of flight will get us to our destination. No one has
talked about time dilation, though some have suggested
that at faster-than-light speeds it is no longer a problem.
Approach light speed and hold just under it, and time dilation creates all sorts of problems, but move beyond
faster-than-light, and a new set of rules take over. We
haven't been able to work our way through that, theoretically, yet and hope to obtain some experimental data before too long so that we night answer that questions. I'm
thinking of a flight out to the Kuiper Belt or the Oort
Cloud as a way of testing the ship, learning a little more
about it, and then planning a long flight to the enemy
home world."

Having said all that, he sat back to wait for the transmittal to Earth, the general to form his response, and then

the transmittal back to him. He could think of no way of cutting the times down.

The image on the screen changed, becoming animated rather than the static picture that had filled the space. The general looked up from his notes and said, "In no particular order, I want to respond as follows. I believe that a shakedown test out is a good idea but think maybe we could do something a little more spectacular. We have dispatched a number of generation ships. Surely we are still in communications with them. A flight out to one might provide some interesting information, and none of the ships should be that far outside of the Solar System, given their speed."

The general looked at his notes and said, "If the field generated by the faster-than-light drive can encompass one of the space stations, I would suggest one be adapted for a long-term flight. That way we're not required to build something from scratch. The life support and the storage capacity probably can be adapted to long-term flight. Have someone begin making the preliminary study now."

The general looked off camera and then back to his notes. "The time dilation problem might magnify as we pass through the light barrier. The short trip will tell us something about time dilation. Be sure that the clocks and recorders are set properly so that we can get accurate readings on that."

Greenstein grinned and said, "We still are having trouble with the civilian counterparts here, and I need to know who, on Mars, might be working to sabotage the mission. Delegate the development of the starship and get on this. I want it solved as quickly as you can. That's all I have. Out."

The image faded, and the screen went to black. It meant that Greenstein was not going to wait for a response and that he expected the orders to be executed.

Hackett stood up and stretched. He leaned toward the

console, touched a button, and said, "I assume that we have recorded all of that."

"Yes, sir."

"I'll want a transcript of the conversation immediately, delivered to my office."

"We can have it waiting on your computer before you get there. How do you want this classified?"

Communications with the general were routinely classified as secret, simply because they were communications with the general. Hackett didn't remember anything in the conversation that would require it to be classified.

"Just make it restricted."

"Yes, sir."

Hackett left the communications room still worried about security, though he didn't know why. What was discussed on Mars, in the dome, took a while to work its way back to Earth. There wasn't all that much spying going on, though those encrypted messages they had yet to identify bothered him. Still, there wasn't anyone in his immediate circle he didn't trust, with the exception of Weiss, and Weiss had done nothing for a long time.

Before Hackett reached his office, Bakker appeared. She stopped him in the hallway, grinning, and said, "We have reached the stars this afternoon."

"That we have," said Hackett, and immediately wondered if those who had witnessed the first flight at Kitty Hawk had understood the significance of what they had seen. Hackett thought he understood the significance of what they had seen because he looked beyond the immediate success. He could see the human race expanding through the galaxy rapidly.

To Bakker, he said, "Have you thought about dinner?"

She laughed. "No. I've been thinking of trips to the stars. To places we've only seen through telescopes and glimpsed with our technology. I've been thinking that astronomy is no longer an observational science. We can now go and see if our theories are accurate."

Hackett rubbed a hand on the back of his neck, still uneasy about something. Maybe he had thought things through and understood that be was going to be ordered on the very first of the truly deep space probes. Maybe it was that he really didn't want to leave the Solar System. His sense of adventure had ended with his trip to the Oort Cloud and his eventual assignment to Mars.

Bakker said, "You don't look all that happy."

"Well, I've been thinking."

"About?"

He looked up and down the corridor. The lights at the far end were off telling him that no one had been in that section of the corridor for a while. They were alone.

"I'm not thrilled with what we've learned."

Bakker looked at him, surprised. Then she smiled and asked, "You understand what happened today? Do you really comprehend it all?"

"Yes. The galaxy is ours."

"Except for that other intelligent race."

"And any other we might encounter."

Bakker thought she understood and said, "If you're worrying about us displacing that intelligence, I don't think that's going to happen. The galaxy is huge. Big enough for everyone. Besides, you don't even know if the environment they favor is one that we can tolerate. We don't know anything about them, but today's success changes all that."

Hackett decided that he didn't want to return to his office. The transcript would be there, embedded in his computer, in a secure file, when he wanted to see it. He didn't have to do anything more to protect it. He had no reason to return to the office.

"Let's go get something to eat," he said.

Bakker was puzzled, but said, "Fine with me."

Together they walked down the corridor, the lights behind them shutting off automatically as those in front of them engaged and brightened. He lead her to the escalator and then out onto the second floor mezzanine that would eventually lead them down to the street. As they walked, he wondered why they even built buildings, given that everything was inside, and decided it was because there had always been walls and buildings, and it separated one area from another for crowd control.

"You're very quiet," said Bakker, "for a man who has learned that he can travel to the stars."

Hackett tried to smile and said, "It is exciting only if you really want to travel to the stars."

Bakker stopped walking and looked at him. "Why wouldn't you want to?"

Hackett held up a hand. "I didn't say I didn't. I merely indicated that there might be people who would prefer to stay home."

"Who are these idiots?" asked Bakker.

"Probably the same people who have never left their cities for travel around the country or the world. Those happy with staying home and living their lives there."

"If everyone felt that way, no progress would be made," said Bakker.

Hackett shook his head. "I'm just saying that there are people who don't look forward to the adventure of travel."

They reached the street level and fell silent as they walked along, more or less in the direction of their apartment. Hackett realized that he wasn't hungry. He was tired, and he was in a bit of a bad mood, though he had no reason for it. His future was set with Smertz's success. All he had to do now was get a ship, complete with crew, launched for a longer voyage. It wasn't an overwhelming task. Just one that would take time, effort, and the complete destruction of his personal life.

CHAPTER 7

[1]

WENDELLE B. BARNETT WAS IN A RAGE. HE roamed the penthouse, screaming at all who came close to him. He pushed over furniture and kicked a lamp into pieces no larger than M & Ms. He could barely contain his rage, and he could not control his speech. No one could understand what he was saying, though they all knew it had to do with the success on Mars. They didn't know why he was enraged, only that he was, and a few wished they could flee to protect themselves from the mass firings that they were sure would follow. Each believed that if he or she could get out of sight, Barnett would target someone else.

Finally, breathing like a sprinter after breaking a record, his face red, and his hair soaked with sweat, Barnett dropped onto a couch. He snapped his fingers, and a waiter appeared with a large martini. Barnett took the drink, downed it, and gave the empty glass back to the waiter.

Having calmed down, with his breathing under control

and his face returning to a more normal color, at least for him, Barnett said, "Does anyone here have a clue about this test?"

No one wanted to say a word, because no one knew what Barnett wanted to hear. Barnett was famous for firing people who told the truth when it was a lie that Barnett needed. Each tried to look as if he or she was busy with some task assigned during the rage. To make eye contact was the kiss of death.

"If someone doesn't speak in the next ten seconds, then everyone in this room is fired. I'll find someone who will answer my questions."

A young woman, looking more like a high school student than a professional with two degrees, stepped forward. In a strong voice, she said, "Apparently they were able to transit to light speed without incident."

"Oh really?" said Barnett harshly. "You pick that up all by yourself?"

"Then I don't know what you want us to tell you," she said. "Is there something that we should look for? Is there some bit of information you want?"

Barnett stared at the woman for ten seconds, though to her it seemed much longer. And then he realized that no one in the room understood what was supposed to happen. They didn't know the cost of success to the company. They had all been working toward that success, because that was what they were supposed to do. If he told them anything else, then eventually, the truth would come out, and he would find himself answering questions for Congress. That was something he didn't want to do.

Getting himself under control, he said, "You tell me exactly what you know?" He hesitated, not asking her name. She understood and supplied it. "Dana. I'm Dana Campbell."

"Well, Campbell, what do you know?"

"The ship jumped to light speed. There was no physical damage as it did so, and there seems to be nothing to indicate that such a jump would be harmful to a human crew. The test was a success."

"No indications of any trouble?"

"No."

Barnett stood up shakily, realizing that he had reacted poorly to the news. He should have been elated that the test succeeded but, instead, had been angered by it. His re-action was the complete opposite of what it should have been.

"Everyone was safe?"

Campbell looked surprised by the question. "Yes. Though I don't think that anyone was in any danger at any time during the tests."

Barnett took a deep breath and said, "Then the news is very good. Everyone clear out of here now. Take the rest of the day off and report to your various departments to-morrow."

Campbell looked at the others, surprised, but she wasn't going to say anything. If Barnett saw fit to give them the afternoon off, she wasn't going to argue with him.

As soon as the room was cleared, Barnett called, "I want Davis in here. And I want him right now."

Three minutes later there was a quiet tap at the door and Davis entered. Barnett pointed at him, his finger aimed right between Davis's eyes, and said, "What in the hell went wrong? I thought we had this all arranged."

"We did not."

"Maybe you had better tell me what happened."

Davis, without invitation, walked over to the wet bar and poured himself a stiff bourbon, dropped an ice cube into it, and then turned. "I feel that I am about to be ter-minated."

"Only if you screwed up and I can fairly place the blame on your shoulders," said Barnett.

"Our security has been penetrated."

"What?" Barnett exploded. "What do you mean?"

Davis found a chair, pushed some of the debris of Barnett's rage from the seat, and sat down. He looked up, almost as if surprised that Barnett was listening to him. He said, "I have learned that someone has been monitoring our transmissions to and from Mars. They have sent some messages in a simple code, and one or two that can't be decoded, but I think they're playing with us. They're telling us that they know we're out here."

"Can they track it back to us?"

"I wouldn't think so. At least not easily."

Barnett took a deep breath and said, "Then let's shut it all down. Let the people on Mars know that they are to curtail their activities."

Davis hesitated, then asked, "Are you sure?"

"There is no percentage in it now. The situation has changed with the success of the mission. Anything we do now is only going to make the situation worse."

Davis lowered his eyes, studying the pattern of debris on the floor. He said, "There is one operation in play at the moment, and I might not be able to stop it."

Now Barnett raised an eyebrow and asked, reasonably, "What's that?"

"Final bit of trouble for the ship. Something that could make them rethink their plans to go forward."

"Anything that would be linked to me or to the corporation here on Earth?"

"I wouldn't think so. Very subtle."

Barnett smiled for the first time since he had learned that the ship hadn't exploded and that the test had been an unqualified success. He said, "Then let it go."

[2]

CATHERINE DeCOURTENAY WASN'T SURE JUST how much she should tell Hackett or if she should even bother to see him. No one had briefed her as to who really knew what. Her assignment had been clear, and she had been told she wouldn't have to consult with any of the locals. She was on her own in the matter.

Still, as she walked toward the building, she thought that now was the time to let Hackett know some of what she knew. His responsibility was to see that the faster-than-light ship project succeeded, and hers was to help him.

She walked up the stairs, to the outdoor mezzanine, crossed it without really looking at it, and entered the building. She made her way to the Hackett's office and then nearly turned around. She just didn't know what she was supposed to be doing.

Finally, she knocked on the door and was surprised when it simply opened. She entered to find a man sitting behind the desk. Without waiting for an invitation, she slipped into one of the chairs and said, "I think we need to talk."

"And you are?"

"Catherine DeCourtenay. You'll find that I came in a few weeks ago and have been working with Weiss."

"Without letting me know?"

DeCourtenay shrugged. "My job was not to tell everyone what I was doing here."

"Just what *are* you doing here?"

She looked at him, then at the open door, and finally to the flat-screen hanging on the wall. She said, "I'm trying to make sure that the tests prove we can travel faster than light."

"I thought that was my job."

She waved a hand, annoyed. "Yeah. That's your job. Mine is to make sure that there are no artificial problems introduced into the testing."

"I don't understand."

"No," she said. "I was sent by a corporation on Earth to assist people here in their sabotage of the ship. My real mission, authorized by the U.S. government and approved by your General Greenstein, is to make sure that sabotage fails. I am, in practical terms, a spy." She grinned broadly.

Hackett was surprised and rocked back in his chair. He studied her carefully, then said, "Of course, you realize that I can't just take your word."

She nodded. "Coded inquiry to General Greenstein will confirm my credentials."

"So why have you decided to reveal yourself to me?"

"It is clear that you are not working to sabotage the project."

"So who is?"

"On your staff? I'm not sure. I can tell you it isn't Bakker, and I don't think it's Weiss, though he can be bought. The culprit, I suspect, is a low-level functionary with access to the ship or its components."

"That's not much help," said Hackett.

"Actually it is, because it tells you there is an active plan to sabotage the tests and it gives you a clue as to where to look for the sabotage. It also means that you will look harder for any sort of irregularity, and it will make it more difficult for the sabotage to occur."

"Do you know the form this alleged sabotage will take?"

"No, I was unable to obtain that information, though I suspect that anything I learned on Earth would now be out of date."

"How about when?"

DeCourtenay shrugged again. "All I can tell you is that they wish to see the project fail, and from what I understand, it is a delicately balanced project. A slight nudge in any direction will be sufficient to wreck it."

Hackett was tired of the discussion. He wanted her out of his office, because he had other things to do. He said, "Well, without a little more information, there isn't a lot I can do."

"There's quite a bit, actually . . ."

"And I don't have any more time to devote to this.

Thank you for stopping by." He stood up and held out a hand.

DeCourtenay realized that she was being dismissed. She was surprised, wondering why Hackett was acting like he was. Then she realized that she had shown up without an appointment, without an introduction, and with no credentials and had begun telling Hackett that his project was in danger from sabotage. She had nothing in the way of proof, and she couldn't tell what form the sabotage would take or when it might happen. In fact, she wasn't telling him much of anything. She didn't blame him for wanting to get her out of his office. She'd have done the same thing if the situation had been reversed.

She stood and said, "Colonel, I'm sorry that I haven't been much help here. Check with the general. He'll tell you I'm who I say I am. And just watch everything carefully. If I hear anything, I'll be in touch."

She walked to the door and looked back at Hackett. He was sitting at his desk, working at something. It was as if she had never shown up. It was as if she hadn't given him any warning. She was afraid that spelled the end of the faster-than-light project. Hackett would allow it to be destroyed, because he wasn't paying attention.

[3]

DOUGLAS WAS FINALLY GIVEN SOMETHING TO do. He finally learned why he had been called down from orbit and why he had to spend time on a planet's surface. He sat in the conference room looking at the holographic display that floated above the table and wondered why a conference call, with him on the station, wouldn't have been a better solution. That way he could have stayed in space, where he preferred to be, and they could have accomplished the same thing. There was no need for him to be dirt side.

Douglas, accompanied by Wilson, met with Smertz

after the ship had returned from its quick trip out to the Oort Cloud. Douglas didn't know that Hackett was annoyed at how fast the trip had gone, because it had taken him, literally, years to travel out there and back in a conventional ship that couldn't travel faster than light. Now it was a trip of weeks, if that much. No one knew what the potential was, now that the light barrier had been broken.

The conference room was a secured site, meaning that access to it was restricted, that there was a guard monitoring who came and went, and that it was swept for bugs periodically. Since it was an interior room, with no wall or window on the outside, no one could bounce a laser off the glass to listen in to the discussions, no one could attempt to plant a sensitive mike on the outside wall, aiid no one could eavesdrop on those inside without sophisticated equipment. Not that any of that mattered, because nothing on the agenda was classified.

Smertz, looking as if he hadn't slept in a long time, looking a little gray, and more than a little hungover, sat at the head of the table. He stared first at Douglas and then at Wilson. He ignored his staff members who were also there. They were to answer his questions and provide any information that he didn't have at his fingertips.

A holographic display of the space station in orbit around Mars appeared to shimmer above the table, looking slightly anemic. The color was washed from it, and parts of it shimmered and flickered, sometimes disappearing completely.

To Douglas and Wilson, Smertz said, "I don't know how much you know about the generation of faster-than-light drive, so I will assume you know nothing. I'm going to give you the basics, so that you can begin to plan a long-term trip to the alien home world."

"We understand the concept," said Douglas.

"Well, here is something you might not understand," said Smertz. "The faster-than-light drive is more of a generator than it is an engine. Think of it this way. If we

THE EXPLORATION CHRONICLES: F.T.L.

followed conventional thought, then we would have to accelerate up toward the speed of light and punch through it.
That acceleration could take, literally, months. At the far
end, we'd have to decelerate, a process that again could
take months. We have to keep the forces of acceleration in
check, or we kill the crew."

"Obviously," said Douglas, sounding like the kid getting the birds and bees lecture long after he had begun to
have sex. He knew the basics, but not all the nuances. He
could decide the act but didn't understand the emotions or
the consequences.

"But the generator removes all that. It creates a field,
inside of which there are no gravitational forces to kill the
crew. It moves the craft and space around it, accelerating
suddenly to the speed of light and beyond. We trick space
into doing what we want it to do so that we don't have to
worry about turning the crew into a puddle of goo."

Douglas smiled at the rhyme and said, "How is that
possible?"

"The theoretical aspects of it are quite complicated, but
the math suggests it works and our tests showed us that it
worked, which explains how we could accelerate a ship to
the speed of light in a matter of minutes rather than weeks
or months."

"How large of a field does this thing generate?"

"Theoretically," said Smertz, grinning, "any size we
want, as long as we have the power. In theory, we could
accelerate Mars out of the Solar System."

"Make travel to the stars a little more comfortable,"
said Wilson.

"There are other considerations. The atmosphere
would be stripped away in a matter of minutes, and without the sun, or a star close by, the temperature would
plummet. We don't have the technology to overcome any
of those problems."

Douglas looked at Smertz, and at the representation of
the space station hovering over the conference room table.

He understood completely. "So you're going to install your generator on the station and blast it off for the alien home world."

Smertz nodded. "That's about it. Environment and life support is already installed. It's large enough for a crew of a dozen, and all we have to do is move it out of orbit."

"That's why we're here. To help plan for the trip," said Wilson.

"Oh, no," said Smertz. "You're going as part of the crew. You two know more about the station than the people who designed and built it. You're going."

Douglas said nothing. He just grinned.

Wilson had a different reaction. She said, "Oh, no I'm not. I didn't sign on for that."

Smertz was surprised. His eyebrows rose on his forehead. He said, "You don't want to go?"

"No."

"Well that certainly complicates the matter."

Douglas looked at her and saw that she was scared. Not that he blamed her. They were being asked to take a new system out into deep space, where there might be no hope of rescue if anything went wrong. They would be on their own.

And if the generator quit and they couldn't fix it, then they would be years from home. Of course, they'd never survive the trip. They'd run out of food, water, air, or heat long before they had to worry about getting back home.

"Maybe she's right," said Douglas.

Smertz turned to face him. "Are you crazy?"

"No, I think I've just regained my sanity. We'll have to do some serious thinking before we agree to this."

[4]

HACKETT ONLY WAITED A FEW MINUTES AFTER DeCourtenay's departure before he left his office and headed down to where Trask was hidden away behind his locked doors, monitored hall, and with his various computers. Hackett went through the security ritual, through the outer office, and confronted Trask in the back office that was filled with computers, flat-screens, recorders, sensors, and even a shelf of real-life, honest-to-God books.

With no preamble, Hackett asked, "If I give you the name of a person here on Mars, who would have been in shielded and coded communication with Earth, can you learn anything?"

Trask stared at Hackett and then broke into a smile. "Of course, my boy. I can learn a great deal."

"You can read the messages?"

"As long as they are not gibberish, and given the proper time, I should be able to break the code." Trask took on his college professor air and added, "No code is unbreakable. Both the Japanese and the Germans, during the Second World War, thought they had unbreakable codes. The Americans and the British broke their codes and routinely read their private communications. It was one of the closest-held secrets of that war."

"Then you can read the messages."

"If I know where to look, and if I have enough time, yes, I can read their messages."

"Catherine DeCourtenay."

"Is?"

Hackett took a deep breath, as if to settle himself, to calm himself, and said, "She came to my office, told me that she was working for us but was pretending to work for some Earth corporation that was interested in stopping our faster-than-light project."

"Religious fanatic?"

Hackett shook his head. "She's not, but I don't know exactly who she is working for. Just warned me of possible sabotage on the project. I thought, with a name, and what to look for, your job would be a little easier."

"Well, this way I don't have to wade through all the transmissions to Earth, and with a topic, I can search for strings that match, though that's fairly old-fashioned analysis."

"But you can do something?"

"Look, all message traffic going to Earth is broadcast by radio, obviously. I mean, we can't string shielded cable from here to Earth. A burst transmission, with everything cramped into a split second, is difficult to detect, but we monitor all outgoing signals across the broadcast bands, recording everything and then eliminating what's unimportant to us."

Hackett had known all that simply because it made sense. This was the first time that it was confirmed by the people doing it. He wasn't happy about it, because it sucked privacy out of the air and it made everything that he sent back to Earth an open book to anyone who could record and then decrypt it. He was old-fashioned enough to believe that the government, whoever that might be, had no right to listen in on his private conversations.

True, he understood the necessity, especially now, with the potential for sabotage to be very real, but he didn't like it. Who decided what needed to be filed and what could be ignored? Wasn't that the way the FBI or the CIA had gotten into trouble so long ago? They had decided that certain groups needed to be monitored because of a potential threat to the security of the United States, and the next thing you knew, they were delving into the personal lives of citizens for no other reason than that they could.

And now, here he was, standing on Mars, learning that the same thing was going on here. But he didn't have the authority to stop it, and he didn't like using it because it, somehow, suggested a tacit approval of the system.

Trask, who was more interested in the challenge of breaking codes and finding specific information in all the information that flowed between Earth and Mars, didn't think of it that way. To him it was just a game. With that in mind, he asked, "Who do you want me to spy on?"

"I wish you wouldn't use those words," said Hackett.

Trask shrugged his apology. "What do you need?"

"I have to know what is being said by—and to—De-Courtenay, and by Stephen Weiss."

"One of your own people?"

Hackett hesitated, then said, "Yes, one of my own. Is that going to be a problem?"

"Nope."

"And if you find anything significant, let me know right away."

"Don't I always?"

Hackett left without another word, feeling as if he had done something wrong, but couldn't really think what it might have been. He didn't know that the monitoring would produce results in a matter of hours.

[5]

WEISS HAD GIVEN UP ON LINDA MITCHELL. SHE had strung him along, hinted that she was interested in him, listened as he talked about work, about why he hated Mars and everything associated with it, and then somehow, avoided going home with him. She always had a good excuse, and sometimes there was a message waiting, or an important phone call that demanded her time. No matter what he did, what he said, or what he promised, she always ended up leaving him alone.

So, when she appeared at this office door, smiling, and wearing clothing that was not standard to Mars, Weiss was surprised. Pleased, but surprised. He sat behind his desk, not wanting to give her any clue about his reaction. He remained quiet, just looking at her.

"Mind if I come in?"

Weiss indicated the single chair with a wave of his hand. He still said nothing.

She sat down, watching him watch her. She said, "I haven't heard from you for a while."

Weiss just shrugged and said, "Busy. You know how it can get."

As she smiled, she said, "I certainly do. I was wondering if you had anything to do tonight."

Weiss realized that she had violated one of the subtle rules of dating. Never put someone in the position of having to admit that the evening was free. Phrase the question with a little tact. Suggest it was short notice and say that you hoped that any engagement wouldn't be unbreakable.

"I don't believe I have anything pressing," said Weiss.

"Well then, how about you buy me a drink?"

Weiss had to laugh. He couldn't believe that she was this inept. Maybe it was an act formulated so that he would take pity on her. He said, "Well, I might be induced to accompany you, but I think you might have to buy your own drink."

"How about this? I'll buy the first round, if you'll buy the second, and then we can negotiate dinner."

"I might be inclined to go along with that," said Weiss, "but is there a limit on spending for dinner?"

"Also open to negotiation."

She leaned forward so that her shirt opened slightly, giving him a good view of her breasts. It was so blatant and obvious that Weiss didn't even bother to look.

"If you're finished here," she said, "then I'm ready for that drink."

Weiss glanced at his flat-screen and then at his desk. He said, "I have nothing pressing."

Together they left the office and then the building, walking out into the late afternoon sun. The shadows in the dome were long and indistinct, certainly not like those on Earth. The city was dim because many of the lights had not been turned on yet. That would come a little later in the day, as the sun dropped so low that the only hint of it would be the golden highlights reflecting from the dome and the tops of the tallest buildings.

Mitchell led the way, as if she had a destination in

mind. She didn't slow to look at the sights or to study the people on the streets or sitting at the tables scattered outside the restaurants. She walked steadily, as if she had a mission and time was running out.

Almost as soon as they sat down at the table, Mitchell said, "I have a proposition for you."

Weiss nodded, his face a mask. "I wondered what all this was about."

"A business proposition," she said, misunderstanding him. "One that will make you rich."

"I'm already rich."

"Your father cut you off, which explains why you're still here on Mars, rather than Earth. You can't afford to buy your way back to Earth."

Weiss laughed. "Is that what you really believe?"

"My people have verified it."

"Your people. What people would that be?"

She looked around, saw that no one was paying them any attention, and said, "The people I work for. Those who have an interest in the faster-than-light ship."

Weiss felt his stomach turn over, and he suddenly felt lightheaded, as if he had swallowed too much alcohol a little too quickly.

"Just what is your interest?" asked Weiss.

"Steve," she said, reaching across the table to touch his hand. "This project is not going to work, and it's going to cost my employers a great deal of money . . ."

"But it already works," said Weiss, not sure if that was common knowledge or if he should be saying anything about it.

"In the long run it will fail, and in the long run it could bankrupt the corporation. If we can stop it now, then we can save some lives and a great deal of money."

"What do I get out of this?" he asked.

She smiled, leaning forward, closer to him. "Money. Power. A little fame. Enough money to get home. Enough to live well when you get there. And a prime position at a prestigious university. A position of respect where you can continue your research and where you will be able to establish a consulting service."

"I have money and a good position."

"Sure. Working for Bakker and Hackett, both no-names with no vision. Not like you."

Weiss took a deep breath and wondered if she knew just how transparent the pitch was. She was offering him everything that he wanted, including an independent source of wealth, but he didn't know if she had either the power or the authority. She could be blowing smoke for her own advancement.

"Just what do I have to do?" he asked.

"Then you're interested?"

"I'm always interested in a way of improving my station in life. Isn't everyone?"

"Well of course," she said. "I'm not really all that thirsty. I have all the makings of anything you could want to drink. And I can get us food."

Weiss was taken aback by the offer. He had tried, once, to convince Mitchell to follow him home. He had been blatant and obnoxious, and she had responded with something less than enthusiasm. Now she was throwing herself at him.

He said, "Why not go to my place? It's more comfortable there, and I have everything we need."

"I don't have any clothes there," said Mitchell.

"It doesn't matter. I wasn't planning on wearing very many clothes myself."

Mitchell smiled and said, "Then let's go."

"I have to make a call first, if you don't mind."

"Go right ahead, but why call now?"

"Because, I don't want to be interrupted once we get to my place, and there are a couple of things that I needed to take care of at the office. It won't take long."

Mitchell, still smiling, stood up and said, "I'll just

leave you alone to make your call. I need to make one of my own, anyway. Business before pleasure."

As soon as she was out of earshot, Weiss called Hackett and said, "I've been bribed. Or rather, I'm being bribed. I think there is something wrong here. I'll be at my apartment, and I think I'm going to need security."

CHAPTER 8

[1]

THE TELEPHONE CALL FROM WEISS HAD CAUGHT him flat-footed but the message was no surprise. Weiss was having a drink with a woman who was attempting to bribe him with offers of money, power, and glory, all things known to tempt Weiss. And yet, he had called, suggesting that Hackett and security might want to talk to the woman.

Hackett wasn't sure what to do. He stood up, walked around the office, looked out the window and then sat down again. He was bothered by something but didn't know what it might be. It was some sort of image of impending doom, that something was about to go wrong, but he didn't know what it could be. Everything seemed to be moving on smoothly.

Finally, he left the office, heading down to see what Trask had to say. He worked his way through the security rituals and found Trask sitting alone in the back room, his attention focused on a flat-screen.

"You got a minute?" asked Hackett.

Trask leaned forward and lowered the volume and then

smiled slyly. "Entertainment. Just relaxing as I try to decide if I want to go home or find something more interesting to do."

"Got a strange call," said Hackett. "Weiss . . ."

"Weiss?" interrupted Trask. "Why would you think a
telephone call from him was strange?"

"Mainly because he was talking about some woman
trying to bribe him and that he was taking her home to
learn a little more about it."

"You get her name?" asked Trask.

"Why?"

"Well, if I had a name, it would make my job that much
easier. I'd know where to search and who to look for in
the answers to the various E-mails and the like."

"Linda Mitchell."

Trask turned to face a keyboard and typed for a moment before breaking into a large grin. He turned his attention to the flat-screen and said, "You aware of her
apparently personal interest in Bakker's research?"

"No, but that's not significant."

"She was passing information back to Earth, to a corporation based in New Orleans but that has offices in
Madrid, Moscow, and Auckland, New Zealand."

"So?"

"Yeah, well, they are a wholly owned subsidiary of another corporation that claims a headquarters in Switzerland,
which, I know from another project, is little more than a mail
drop created for legal purposes. It moves American corporations off North America for tax purposes and to remove some
of the regulatory arms of the government."

Hackett had never cared much for business, thinking of
it as just another way to make money and to snag wealth.
He had been more interested in learning things, which explained part of his eclectic college background. Having a
good job, a career, had meant more to him than making
piles of money, though he often regretted those early
choices. He should have paid a little more attention to

who got the big dough rather than trying to create a career field that interested him.

"That still doesn't suggest anything nefarious," said Hackett.

"No, but I'll bet if I trace this far enough, I'm going to find one of the sources of those strange little encoded messages that have you so concerned."

"Really?"

"There are only so many candidates for this on Mars and most of them work in this building or know those who do. Your girl fits the profile and you said that she was trying to bribe Weiss."

"Which is what he told me."

Trask rubbed at his eye. "Well, if it was up to me, I'd try to learn what she knows."

"I need something a little better than Weiss's concern with her and your rather nebulous suggestion that she might be tied to a corporation on Earth that has connections with other companies around the world."

"Give me a couple of hours and I'll have the evidence. Right now it's clear to me that she is one of those who has been communicating, on the sly, with those on Earth."

Hackett said, "Well, I hate to have security jump on her only to learn that we were wrong."

Trask said, "We're not wrong. She has the connection. Now, understand, it might not be anything for us to worry about. It might all be innocent, but the connection is there."

Hackett stood up and said, "Thanks."

"What are you going to do?"

"That," he said, "is the question."

[2]

THE SECURITY FORCE, MEN AND WOMEN DRESSED in jet black coveralls, boots, and wearing body armor that was unnecessary because there were no guns, in the classical sense, on Mars, assembled near the elevators. Hackett stood with them, though he was dressed in a more conventional fashion without any body armor. He wore a side arm, but it was a laser rather than an old-fashioned slug-throwing pistol.

The commander of the security force, a young captain, looked at Hackett and awaited orders. Hackett glanced at his watch, though time meant nothing, then at the door, and finally back at the security captain.

"Let's hit it," he said.

The captain raised her hand, snapped her fingers quietly, and pointed at the point where the lock was. Two men, holding the handles of a long, heavy weight, stepped forward, swung the weight, aiming at the lock. The metal tore and twisted, and the door splintered, falling in.

Without a word, her weapon drawn, the captain leaped through the opening. She quickly checked out the area around her but saw no one. "Clear," she said.

Two men entered, one to cover the other as they ran across the room to the other door. One of them kicked at it and then jumped aside. As the door flew open, slamming into the wall, the other man leaped through, rolled, and came up with his pistol pointed at a startled woman wearing nearly nothing.

She threw up her hands and cried, "Don't shoot. Don't shoot."

Weiss, standing off to the side, near the bed and close to the bathroom, stood still, not moving and not talking. He just watched as more people entered the bedroom.

"Take her into custody," ordered Hackett.

"Yes, sir."

"But let her cover up first," said Hackett.

The security captain said, "That's not a good idea. Gives her a chance to grab a weapon."

Hackett said, "Linda? You don't plan to grab a weapon do you? You going to cooperate?"

She didn't speak. She just nodded her head afraid to move anything else.

"Go ahead, Linda," said Hackett. "Get your clothes on. But move slowly."

She glanced to her right, toward the window that looked out onto the city and down, toward the pool. It was more than a hundred feet to the rough concrete. The pool was only about three or four feet deep.

Hackett said, "You'd never survive the fall."

She looked at him surprised and then reached down, slowly, her eyes on the pistols pointed at her. She retrieved her clothes and began to put them on.

Hackett retreated to the door, while security watched her. Hackett said, "Steve, come with me."

"Is he under arrest?" asked Mitchell.

"That's to be determined," said Hackett.

"Am I under arrest?"

"I think that is a safe assumption." He stepped through the door and into the other room.

Weiss followed, and keeping his voice low, asked, "Am I in trouble here?"

"Why would you think that?"

"Well, you said you were going to determine if I was under arrest or not."

Hackett waved at the couch and Weiss sat. Hackett said, "Sometimes we say things for the political capital it gains us and nothing more."

Mitchell, escorted by two of the security officers, appeared. They had not restrained her but they were moving with her. If she tried anything, they would burn her. They took her to the door and then out, into the hallway, where more security waited.

The security captain entered the room and asked, "You going to want me for anything?"

Hackett looked at Weiss, as if thinking about it, and then said, "No. We're through here."

"You sure?"

"Yeah."

"Okay. I'll have her back at security in the detention area when you want to talk to her."

Hackett said, "Thank you."

As the door closed, Weiss looked at Hackett and asked, "Just what in the hell is going on here?"

"I was hoping you could tell me."

"I just warned you about an attempted bribe. I don't think it warranted her arrest. I mean, is it illegal to offer me a bribe? I'm not an official. I don't know any secrets. I can't give them anything of value."

Hackett laughed and said, "I'll have to look that up. I don't think it's illegal to offer you a bribe. It could be considered job negotiation. You have a talent or expertise they want, and they are offering you a chance to work for them."

"But you arrested her. If I can't be bribed, in the classical sense, then how can you arrest her?"

"The story takes a bit of a turn there. It's more than her offer to you."

"But you're not going to tell me what it is."

"Steven, you have never been a team player. You have looked out for yourself at every turn. You have stabbed people in the back and never thought about the consequences. Your decision-making processes have always revolved around what is best for you and nothing else."

"I called you about Mitchell."

"Yeah," said Hackett, "and that bothers me greatly. It is out of character."

Weiss looked as if he was going to respond angrily, but then didn't. Instead, he said, "So this time was different."

"My question is what's in it for you?"

Weiss stood up and walked to the window, looking down on almost the same view he had from the bedroom. He could see people playing in the pool, drinking, lounging, chasing one another. He could see people having a good time with one another. He could see friends and family. Everything he could see reminded him that he had none of those things.

"Maybe I just saw this as a chance to do the right thing," said Weiss.

Hackett, was tempted to laugh but didn't. He said, "You earned yourself a few points with this."

"For telling you that Mitchell wanted to bribe me?"

"It goes beyond that and maybe later you'll find out all that it entails. Right now we've eliminated one of the problems for the faster than light project."

Weiss said nothing.

Hackett stood up and said, "I have things to do. See you at the office tomorrow."

"You're not afraid that I'll escape?"

Now Hackett laughed. "If I worried about that, you'd be in custody, but let's say I misjudged you and you took off in the night. Just where would you go? You might avoid us for a day or two, but, eventually, we'd find you."

"I suppose."

"And now I have to go see what Mitchell knows and how that information can be put to use."

[3]

MITCHELL SAT IN WHAT LOOKED LIKE A POLICE interrogation room that had been built on Earth a hundred years earlier. Although much newer, the psychological principles were the same. Separate and isolate the subject. Provide no visual stimulation or diversion. Let the subject sit in the austere environment and contemplate his or her transgressions.

Looking through the one-way glass at Mitchell, Hackett had to believe that the psychology was working. She was fidgeting in her chair, looking from the floor of molded light plastic to the walls of molded, darker plastic to the ceiling of molded light plastic that saw a duplicate of the floor. There were no tiles to count, no nails to count, no stains that might form patterns or designs. There was nothing but a single table, without drawers or compartments, and two chairs. One was for the interviewer and the other for the interviewee.

Mitchell had to know that the mirror on her side concealed the one-way glass window. She had to know that people outside the room were studying her reactions, yet she seemed incapable of hiding them. She fidgeted, stood up, sat down, and seemed to be slipping closer to the edge with each passing minute.

"How long are you going to leave her in there alone?" asked Trask.

Hackett had asked the older man up to watch Mitchell and provide any insight he might have.

Hackett said, "A little longer. She's just building up terror in her own mind."

"Know what you might do?" asked Trask. "Take her breakfast. Now."

"Why?"

"Well, she has no idea how long she's been in that room. She believes that it has been no more than an hour. Convince her it's been several hours with breakfast. Nothing fancy. Maybe a donut. But juice. And coffee. Lot's of fluids."

Hackett couldn't help smiling. "You're an evil old man."

"Just trying to help you out. Make her a little more vulnerable. More willing to cooperate."

"How do you know she won't cooperate now?"

"Anyone brought into this circumstance is going to have an instinct to resist. Doesn't matter if cooperation will help completely. The instinct is to resist. You get her disoriented and that instinct will fade faster."

Without a word, Hackett turned and left. He found a cup of coffee and a box of donuts. He found a can of juice. He put them on a tray and carried them back to the interrogation room. He thought about having someone else take them in, but then decided he would do it. He would be the good cop. It was a role that he rarely got to play.

He pushed open the door and carried the food into the interrogation room. He set the tray on the table and said, "Sorry about the delay. I had no idea we would be keeping you here for so long. I thought a little breakfast might be in order."

She looked at the food, but ignored it. Instead she looked up at Hackett and said, "You ordered me arrested."

Hackett took the other chair and sat down. He said, "That's not exactly true. I ordered you taken into custody, assuming that you would be questioned about your involvement in certain activities. I didn't expect you to be held here through the night without food or water."

"I'm not hungry," she said.

Hackett took one of the donuts, pulled it apart and then bit off a hunk. He chewed quietly, swallowed, and reached for a glass of juice. "You sure you're not hungry?"

"You the good cop now?" she asked sarcastically.

"I think we're a little too sophisticated for the good cop, bad cop routine. I think you're too sophisticated to fall into that trap. We're all here doing a job and that's about it. No lives have been lost. No one is in danger. We're here to learn the truth and go on from there."

Mitchell eyed the food but didn't reach for any of it. She sat silently while Hackett ate.

"You sure you don't want something?"

"Just leave it," she said. "I might get hungry later."

Hackett glanced at the mirror and then back at the food. "I don't really know if I should do that."

"You think I'm going to engineer an escape with a jelly roll?" she asked.

"No, but . . ."

"What? I'll fashion a weapon out of the paper. Smash the glass and use a shard as a knife? What?"

Reluctantly, Hackett stood up. He started to reach for

the tray and then straightened. "If you get hungry, it'll be waiting for you."

"Yeah, right."

[4]

DAVIS, NOT HAPPY WITH THE REPORTS HE HAD just received, entered the penthouse of Wendelle B. Barnett, and said, "I have some news from Mars."

"Well, it had better be good or your ass is fired," said Barnett.

"Then I'm fired," said Davis, not really caring.

Barnett felt his face go white hot. He felt fire build in his belly. He stared and asked, his voice unnaturally quiet and way too calm, "What now?"

"Mitchell has been picked up."

"What's that mean?" asked Barnett. " 'Picked up'?"

"I don't have much because we've been trying to reduce the traffic between us here on Earth and our people on Mars, but what I know is that she was arrested."

"For what?"

"She was having a discussion with Steven Weiss and security broke in. She was arrested."

"What about Weiss?"

"I don't know. Mitchell is in custody."

Barnett moved toward a wall, but before he reached it, a section slipped up, into the ceiling, revealing a wet bar. He took a bottle of bourbon, splashed some in a glass, and then drank deeply. As he exhaled, he said, simply, "Smooth."

"We haven't got many details . . ."

"Close the operation," said Barnett. "Close it now."

"I'm not sure that I can do that easily. There are a number of people and we have been using coded transmissions."

Barnett walked over to a large, overstuffed chair and

sat down so that he could look out on the fading sun. The tops of buildings were bathed in a golden light. Some of them looked expensive now, with the sun highlighting them. He took a sip of the bourbon.

"I didn't ask for excuses. I told you to close it down now. If Mitchell remains silent and doesn't implicate us, then she will be rewarded. If she talks, we deny and we cut her off. I hope she understands that," said Barnett.

"I can't communicate with her now," said Davis. "I'll have to wait until they release her before I can communicate."

"Which will probably be too late," said Barnett.

"She shouldn't be saying anything."

Barnett shook his head in disgust. "We're twisting in the breeze here. I want to know what is going on and I want to know soon. If you can't do it, I'll find someone who can. I'm not going to go down in flames here."

Davis took a deep breath and said, "I'll do what I can but I don't think it will be much until she's released."

Barnett looked at him, stared at him, and finally said, "Kill her."

[5]

AN HOUR AFTER HE HAD TAKEN IN THE DONUTS, and forty minutes after they had been removed, Hackett showed up with sandwiches and soft drinks. As he set the tray on the table, he said, "I'm sorry about the delay getting your lunch in here. There is a big problem in the center of the city and most of the security force has been dispatched."

Mitchell looked up and said, "I would like to use the facilities."

Hackett shook his head. "I'm afraid we'll have to wait a few minutes with all that is happening."

Mitchell didn't move for a moment and then reached

out for half of a sandwich. She opened the bread and looked at what was a good simulation of ham and cheese complete with a spicy mustard. She put it back.

"Still aren't hungry?"

"Look, you've kept me here for hours. You bring food and drink but you don't tell me anything. I have rights. You can't hold me indefinitely."

"Well," said Hackett slowly, "that's not exactly true. This isn't the United States . . ."

"It's U.S. owned. The Constitution applies."

"I'm not sure about that," said Hackett. "It can be argued that this, meaning the whole dome, is government property and that as such, the rules and regulations that apply to government installations apply, which is not to say the Constitution."

"This is preposterous," said Mitchell.

"I'm not a Constitutional attorney," said Hackett, "and by the time one could get here to represent you, given appeals, appointments, travel time, availability of transport, you could have been here, in custody, for years."

"You can't do that," said Mitchell.

Hackett shrugged. "It's not me, but the military. They believe that you have engaged in espionage. They think you pose a danger to the faster than light project."

"That's not true," said Mitchell. "I wasn't doing anything of the sort."

"Well," said Hackett as he picked up one of the sandwiches, "you were trying to bribe Weiss."

She grinned at that and then reached up to smooth her hair. She said, "I would like to take a shower and brush my teeth. I haven't been out of this room in hours."

"I'll try to arrange something later. I did note, however, that you have attempted to avoid my point."

Now she reached for one of the sandwiches, took a bite, and said, "Is trying to bribe Weiss against some Martian law?"

"Depends on what you wanted him to do. Trying to

hire him away from his job doesn't strike me as something wrong. Attempting to sabotage the project is something else entirely."

"I was only making a job offer."

Hackett leaned back in his chair and looked up at the ceiling, as if considering her answer. Finally he said, "We have information that someone, some group, was attempting to sabotage the project and your name surfaced in that investigation."

"That's crap," she snapped.

"The evidence is fairly good."

"Yeah," she said. "You'd say that, wouldn't you?"

Hackett finished his sandwich. He looked at her and said, "Well, we've had some trouble on the project. The first ship exploded and we don't really know why."

"Sounds like a personal problem to me." She grinned and added, "Or maybe a personnel problem."

Hackett ignored the joke. "You're the first person we found who is in communication with those on Earth who seem to have taken an interest in seeing this project fail. What do you think we'd think about that?"

Mitchell stood up, as if agitated. She walked about the chair and then sat down again. "I would like to use the facilities."

"Of course. All that in a moment. You haven't answered my question."

"What is this? Some new interrogation technique?"

Hackett shook his head. "No, I'm just carrying on a conversation here. The interrogation will begin as soon as a couple of other things are completed. I think you can expect some sort of chemical regression, a truth serum, to help you recall, accurately, what you have been doing."

"You can't do that without my permission," said Mitchell.

"Again, I think we can, but the point is moot. It will be done before you can lodge a formal protest."

"This is crap," she said.

"I don't know about that," said Hackett.

"I want to go to the bathroom," she said.

"Why do you want to see the project fail?"

She stared at him as if she couldn't believe he was speaking to her. "I don't give a crap about the project," she snapped. "I have never cared about it."

"Then why try to destroy?"

"Because that's my job. I was paid to do it."

Hackett raised an eyebrow. "By whom?"

"By the Ragsdale Corporation." As soon as the words were out of her mouth, she realized what she had said. She knew that she had gone too far. She should have sat quietly, ignored Hackett, his food, and his laid-back interrogation. She hadn't been prepared for what had been done to her. She had expected an interrogation that would include light shined in her eyes and men screaming at her, demanding answers. She hadn't expected the Hackett with his "let's talk" attitude.

Hackett stood up and knocked on the door, though that wasn't necessary. It opened and he said, "Let Linda use the facilities, but do not let her out of your sight."

"Yes, sir."

[6]

WHEN HACKETT LEFT THE INTERROGATION room, Trask caught him and said, "We know now exactly what to look for. We'll have no problem building a case based on the E-mail and other transmissions between here and Earth."

"I'm more concerned with this idea that some kind of sabotage will be tried."

Trask grinned. "Don't be. We have the clues there, too. We just review everything that came from them, check the areas where their people had access, and make sure the components they manufactured meet specifications."

Hackett wiped a hand over his mouth in thought. He glanced at a chair and then dropped into it. Looking up at Trask, he said, "That's not going to be as easy as it sounds."

"Won't Smertz have some ideas along those lines?"

"I suppose, but you have to remember that the corporation is the major contractor. They've touched just about everything going into this project. It wouldn't take much of a change for it to blow up."

"Which, by the way," said Trask, "explains the first explosion. Sabotage."

Hackett said, "Now that Mitchell has spilled her guts . . ."

"I wouldn't characterize it as spilling her guts. She slipped up under your questioning."

"Whatever," said Hackett. "What I mean is that she might be inclined to help us uncover any sabotage directed at the latest phase of the project. We won't be going into this blind."

"So, you're going to make a deal?"

Hackett smiled. "We can turn her into a double agent. Hell, you've got what you need to undercover everything at the other end. We can build a good case against her and her corporate bosses. Maybe they'd be inclined to a new attitude if they were protected from prosecution. As long as they fulfill their obligations to us, we sort of forget what they attempted to do."

Trask said, "You're a little shortsighted here."

"Meaning what?"

"You've got them dead to rights but you don't know the motivation. If they've got some religious conviction against interstellar flight, they're still going to be against anything we do. If the reason is financial, though I can't see a financial advantage, then you have a different set of problems."

"I don't think learning the motivation is going to be that difficult, now that we have the information," said

Hackett. "And we can get to work without having to worry about the ship exploding again."

Trask nodded and moved toward the door. He said, "I'll get to work on it. If I learn anything that impacts on the mission, I'll let you know."

"Thanks. Now all I have to do is pick a crew and head off into deep space."

"Easier said than done."

"And probably a little more dangerous," added Hackett.

CHAPTER 9

AS HACKETT WALKED FROM ONE SECTION OF
the station to the next, ducking down to pass through the
small hatch, he was astonished at how large the ship actually was. Since it was assembled in space, made of materials refined on Mars, the cost, in terms of energy and
national wealth, was small. They could add a few "frills,"
which were private cabins for the crew, a large communal
area, and extra space for food supplies. There was a re-
cycling plant designed to recapture water lost through the
process of living and to purify the air because it would be
difficult to resupply it.

Compared with the ship they had used to journey out to
the Oort Cloud so long ago, this was luxurious. People
were not crammed together in makeshift compartments.
Room for a large meeting area, room for privacy, and
room to spread out. Hackett was stunned by the size.

And in this case, size didn't matter. With only a slight
increase in power, the generator could expand its field to
encompass the whole ship. Had they wanted, they could

have boosted an aircraft carrier into space and then generated a field around it that allowed them to move the whole thing faster than the speed of light. The only factor inhibiting the size of the ship was getting it into orbit.

So Hackett was impressed with the size. And he was impressed with the lack of complexity. Four people could run the ship without much strain. Someone had to be alert at all times, searching surrounding space for anything that the defensive shield couldn't repel. Hitting a baseball at a speed faster than light would create an explosion that would light the heavens for millions of miles. If it happened close enough to Earth, those on the ground would be able to see the flash, hear the boom, and wonder about it.

Once they had completed the tour, which included the flight deck, or cockpit, they returned to the conference room. It was another of the luxuries that Hackett found impossible to accept. Always there had been a desire to keep the weight down, especially when everything had to be boosted into orbit from Earth. That was no longer a real consideration, so the room was elaborate.

Hackett stepped into the conference room, where Bakker, Joe Douglas, Sally Wilson, Steven Weiss, and even Linda Mitchell waited. This was going to be the core of the crew. No one had thought much beyond these people.

Hackett took the chair at the head of the table. It looked as if it had been made out of solid, heavy wood, but in reality, everything in the room was plastic, light weight, and stronger than the outer hull of that aircraft carrier.

"Okay, I've seen the ship, and I have to say, it has impressed the hell out of me. Douglas, you have any comments about it or the shakedown cruise?"

"We took it out to Pluto. Looked at the planet and its moon. I'm not sure which was which. Tiny worlds of drab colors. The sun is the brightest star, bigger than any star we can see from here, but a star nonetheless. Orbited for a day or so, took pictures, and then came on back. We were gone just a couple of days."

"And?"

"Everything worked fine. No noticeable effects when we jump to light speed. No bump. No sudden roar. Views on the screens change and everything looks weird, shrinking toward one corner, but no ill effects on the crew."

"Then we are prepared to make a longer jump," said Hackett. "A real test far outside of the Solar System."

Douglas looked at the others at the table, but only he and Wilson had been on that first trip. He said, "The only way to test this thing is to take it out. It performed perfectly on the short hop, and I can see nothing that will go wrong on another, longer hop. We're good to go."

Hackett said, "What about life support? Supplies?"

Wilson took over. She consulted a flat-screen and said, "Our calculations suggest that we have sufficient life support, food, and water to last for two years in space. That's a hell of a long time for us to be traveling faster than light."

"How fast can we go?" asked Hackett. "No one has ever given me a good answer to that."

Bakker spoke for the first time. "Theoretically, there is no top limit. Once we've defeated the problems of traveling faster than light, traveling ten, twenty, fifty times faster shouldn't change the equation."

"Except we outrun our capability of spotting danger," said Douglas.

Hackett waved a hand as if to wipe a slate clean. He looked at each of the people in the room and asked, "Are we ready to launch?"

"If you are asking if we are prepared for a long-term mission," said Douglas, "then I have to say that we are. We know the life support works, we have the food and water loaded for a long-term mission. We have the latest in sensor arrays and detection equipment. We are prepared to go."

Wilson looked first at Douglas and then to Hackett. "I think we're prepared to go."

Hackett turned his attention to Mitchell. He stared at her and asked, "Is there anything that we need to know?"

"I have told you everything that I know. I have given you everybody who was on Mars and who was involved. At least all the names that I knew."

Now Hackett grinned. "Well, here's the deal. I don't know if we can trust you. I don't know if we have sufficiently eliminated the motivation of your corporate bosses by suggesting that a destruction of this ship will result in penalties so severe that they'll be lucky to spend eternity in jail. But I will tell you this. You're part of this crew. You'll be on board for the next flight. If there is anything you know, now is the time to tell me about it."

"I've told you everything I know," she said quietly without looking directly at him.

Hackett looked around the table. "All right then. My orders are to launch within the week. I want one more check of the systems. I want a complete inventory of everything we have on board. I want to make sure that our libraries have copies of everything we'll need."

"We have a mission, then? To the alien home world?" asked Bakker.

"Ultimately," said Hackett, "but their home is two hundred light years away. We're going to try for something a little closer to home. Alpha Centauri at a maximum." Now he grinned. "But we're going to try to rendevous with one of the generation ships we launched years ago. Should be somewhere between here and Alpha Centauri."

"Can't be that far out," said Bakker.

"Light year or two. Something like that. Then on to Alpha Centauri."

"Why?" asked Bakker. "It's not that interesting of a system. Triple star with little chance of a planetary system that could produce life."

"I'm tempted to say because it's there. Or because we

can. But mainly because it's only four light years away. Far enough to give us a good chance to evaluate our systems, but not so distant that the trip will take decades."

"And then we'll head on to the alien home world?" asked Bakker.

"We return here to evaluate and plan and then on to the alien home world. Let them know that we have star flight capability, that we know where they live, and that they are now vulnerable to us."

"All that should be easy," said Weiss.

Hackett looked at him but didn't say he was frightened by it all. Frightened because it was the first time that humans had taken such a large step. Frightened because they would be on their own if something went wrong. Frightened because this was an adventure into the unknown. Yes, humans had done such things before, but they had done them on Earth, a friendly, often forgiving environment, with help always a possibility. Now, they were venturing into an unfriendly environment with no real possibility of help. He didn't know what they would find, and that frightened him.

[2]

HACKETT WALKED BACK TO WHAT HE THOUGHT of as his cabin. It was a ten-by-ten-by-ten cube. As he stepped through the hatch, he was disoriented, because they didn't think of the walls as walls or the ceiling as the ceiling. Every surface was thought of as floor space. Gravity would be so light, so nearly nonexistent, that his desk was on one wall, his locker on another, and his sleeping area suspended on the third.

He couldn't think of the sleeping area as a bed, because it was little more than a series of ropes that formed a cocoon that would keep him from drifting around as he sleeps. A long, narrow cage that had soft ropes rather than bars. A sleeping cage.

He "walked" up to his desk on the wall and sat down in the chair. He slipped the arms over his legs to hold him in place as he reached out for the keyboard. He sat there, staring at the flat-screen, wondering what he was going to write, what he was going to say, and actually wondering what he was supposed to be doing.

The hatch cycled and irised open. Bakker stuck her head in and asked, "You real busy?"

"No."

"I think we've got another problem. One that no one has really talked about but that should have been obvious to everyone involved in this project."

Hackett pushed the keyboard away and turned to look at her. It was a disconcerting picture with her looking up from the hatch. Given the position of his desk, it seemed like she was entering through the floor.

He said, "Why don't you come on in and tell me what the problem is."

Bakker entered and stepped up on the wall where the desk was. Suddenly they were both oriented with a single bulkhead as the floor. She was standing next to the desk, her feet on the wall that was now the floor.

"Time dilation," she said. "We haven't talked about that at all."

"Einstein," said Hackett.

"Yes. He suggested that as a body moves toward the speed of light, time, relative to that object slows. A journey that would last for a few days for the crew might, on Earth, last several years. In theory, a crew could live long enough for a trip across the galaxy at relativistic speeds, but time on Earth would still pass. The question becomes, would there be a civilization that remembered the crew when they returned from that journey?"

Hackett rubbed his chin and realized that he needed to shave. Ignoring his beard, he said, "What are you suggesting? That our little journey to Alpha Centauri could take hundreds of years?"

"Well, what I don't know is how pushing through the light barrier will alter the equation. No one has thought much about it, because science has suggested that the speed of light is the limiting factor. In fact, Einstein suggested that we couldn't travel faster than the speed of light, because mass became infinite . . ."

"What's on your mind?"

"Just that the trip out to Pluto took, according to the records on Mars, just about a week. For those on the ship, the trip was much shorter. What I don't know is if the discrepancy is the result of powering toward the speed of light or if there is a similar problem beyond it. I don't know if time dilation is relevant once we punch through the light barrier."

Hackett smiled. "Well, that is certainly going to complicate matters."

"For more than a century we've known how to build a time machine, based on the experimental data we've held . . ."

"Time machine? Are you crazy?"

"It's a one-way trip. You could say that we are all moving into the future at the same rate of speed. Time dilation allows some of us to move forward faster. We can, in essence, travel forward in time. Of course, there is no way to return. It's a one-way trip, but then, it always has been."

"So what are you suggesting here?"

"That we haven't factored in the problems of time dilation. I don't know how much time is going to pass on Mars before we can return, though the time will seem to pass at a constant rate for us on the ship."

"You don't know how much time will pass on Mars . . . or on the Earth?"

"No. We have almost no experimental data to answer the question. I just don't have the information I need to extrapolate an answer."

"So, what do we do?"

"Well, there are a couple of things, but neither work all that well. First, we could ask that time hacks be sent to us on a regular basis, but going out, that's going to do us no good, because we'll be outrunning the speed of the signals. They won't be able to overtake us."

Hackett nodded. "But coming back, we'll be able to pick them up."

"Yeah, but they won't mean much by that time."

"So, I ask again, what do we do?"

"Shorten the trip. Rim out to the Oort Cloud, or to one of the generation ships. That's a light year or so. When we return, we'll have some better data."

Hackett scratched his head and asked, "Why not just go on out to Alpha Centauri and let it go at that?"

"Because the trip might take us a few weeks or months, but time back here might be centuries."

"I still don't understand the problem."

"What would we come back to?"

[3]

LINDA MITCHELL SAT IN THE COMMUNAL AREA, now known simply as "The Pit," and watched as others worked. Or rather, as one person used a computer. Mitchell didn't know if that person was actually doing any work or not.

She sat quietly, wondering if she had known everything that was being planned to sabotage the mission. There was no reason for her to know the details of an operation in which she would not participate. She could tell all that she knew, and she could finger all those who had similar missions. But there was no way for her to know everything and no reason for it. There could be, and probably were, missions planned that she had not known about. She could be sitting in a ticking time bomb and never know it.

Weiss, looking thin, wan, tired, and frightened, entered The Pit. He looked at Mitchell. "You busy?"

"Just thinking."

"About?"

"Why don't you sit down?"

Weiss moved as if he was going to drop to the couch, but he didn't get close to it. He sort of hovered over it in a sitting position, until Mitchell reached up and grabbed his hand. She pulled him down.

Finally sitting on the couch, he asked, again, "Thinking about what?"

"Who might have done what to the ship or any of the components to make us fail."

The little color that was left drained from Weiss's face. "What are you talking about?"

"We were supposed to stop this trip. We were supposed to convince everyone that faster-than-light travel was not possible by creating problems for the ship. How many disasters will the public stomach before they decide that it won't work?"

"But you're here. On this ship."

"Yeah. I didn't count on that. I didn't count on you ratting me out either."

"Life is full of surprises," said Weiss.

She turned to face him. "Why did you do that? I mean, I'm standing there, nearly naked, and you call security."

"I called security long before we arrived at my apartment," said Weiss.

"Yes. But why?"

Weiss turned so that he was looking straight ahead, at the bulkhead that could be a deck, given the arrangement of furniture on it. Sort of an abstract art form, except that the orientation of the people on the ship changed it into a functional conversation area. He pulled his eyes away.

"Because I was tired of being on the outside. Because I was tired of having everyone on Mars hate me, thinking of me as a small, calculating individual who thought of nothing but himself and how to advance himself. I wanted to have a few friends just to see what it would be like."

"So you ratted me out."

Weiss took a deep breath and smiled. "Nearly everyone on Mars would see my last statement as cynical and insincere. It's just the way they see me."

"So why didn't you take the deal? You'd have gotten back to Earth and been given a good job."

"But everyone would have known how I got it, and they'd just be waiting for me to betray them when the opportunity was right. I was getting sucked down, and I wanted out."

She smiled. "So now you're on the ship with me, and we don't know if it's going to blow up or not."

"I hope you're joking about that."

"I'm hoping that Hackett and his team are a little better at security than I think they are." Now she laughed. "Though Hackett did a job on me. Had me convinced that I had spent hours, maybe days in interrogation. Had me so confused that I didn't know what to make of it, and all he did was disrupt my sense of time. Convinced me that breakfast had been hours earlier when it had been forty minutes. Brought in food and drink but insisted on nothing. Just tried to engage me in conversation, and the next thing I know, I've spilled my guts."

"You told them everything?" asked Weiss.

"Everything that I knew. Told them who was going to do what to sabotage the systems. Told them how to fix the things that we had broken. Gave them the names of others doing the same thing."

Weiss visibly relaxed. "Then they found everything?"

"Everything that I knew about," said Mitchell. "I suspect, given what I knew, they could get to everyone on Mars who was a part of this. That's what I believe."

Weiss grinned and said, "Then there really isn't much to worry about."

Mitchell shrugged helplessly. "There is always the possibility that another team was sent in to back up the first, unknown to the first. If I wanted to ensure that the mission was complete, I'd have a backup in place."

"You told this to Hackett and his people?"

"They should have been able to figure it out for themselves," said Mitchell.

"Yeah, but you told them?"

"I didn't think it was necessary."

[4]

TRASK SAT IN THE BACK ROOM OF HIS OFFICE, behind the closed and locked doors, and tried to understand what he was seeing. All the radio traffic, television signals, and all the communications between the operatives on Mars and their corporate sponsors on Earth had ceased after Mitchell had given up everything she knew.

He watched as the message scrolled out once more, though seeing it again did nothing to decipher it. He sat back, his fingers laced behind his head and stared. This was something that he hadn't expected to see.

Trask leaned to the right, so that he could see the closed door and shouted, "Monica!"

The door opened and Stone looked in and said, "You bellowed?"

"I want to make a comparison between this latest transmission and those we've intercepted in the past. I think we've uncovered a second cell here."

She walked in and looked at the screen. "You think it's more of the same?"

"I think so."

"Then they didn't get everyone in the roundup. This going to present a problem?"

Trask rocked back in his chair, his eyes still on the screen, and said, "I don't know what it means. All I know is that someone initiated a sequence that is reminiscent of those messages we were watching."

"Then you have to alert Hackett."

Trask grinned. "No. He's on the station preparing for the first long-term-trip using the faster-than-light drive."

"You still have to alert him."

"I don't know what we've got here. Until then, I don't see any point in causing trouble."

Stone pulled a chair close and said down. She leaned forward, her chin in her hand, looking at the scrolling information. There was something vaguely familiar about it, but she wasn't sure what it was.

"How long have we had this?" she asked.

"An hour. Maybe a little more."

"Well . . ."

Trask stood up and walked around his chair, his eyes still on the screen. He was at a loss as to what to do. This could be some kind of automatic report that had nothing to do with the ship or faster-than-light. It could be a mundane report by someone whose function was not evil or dangerous. Or, it could signal a new round of sabotage.

"We're going to have to do something," said Trask. "I just don't know what it is."

[5]

"THEY'RE ON THE STATION AND READY TO MAKE the first of the long-term jumps using faster-than-light," said Davis. He stood near a wall of glass, on the top floor of the tallest building in the city. The lights were sparkling as they made the transition from day to night.

"And that affects me how?" asked Barnett.

"Limits what we can do now that they had people on the station. We don't want to kill anyone."

Barnett walked across the room, toward the wet bar, and found a bottle of bourbon. He poured two fingers, swallowed it in one massive gulp, and then nearly filled the glass. He didn't bother with ice or water.

"What we want is to end this project," said Barnett.

Davis turned from the window. "I have to ask you this. There something else going on here? Something beyond corporate policy and finance?"

Barnett grinned and took a healthy swallow of the bourbon. "Two things you should know. No one has ever thought to ask that question, and two, I'm not sure that I should allow you to ask it."

Davis walked to a chair and sat down. He looked up at Barnett and said, "You know that I know where all the bodies are buried."

"Are you attempting to blackmail me?"

Davis shook his head. "Just reminding you what I have done for you in the last five years. I have kept you in power. I have found the corporate disloyalty and told you. I headed off the attempt to remove you from the board and as the CEO. I have earned the right to ask some questions, and what I want to know is what is going on here right now? Why are you pushing to end this project? And I don't want this corporate finance mumbo-jumbo."

Barnett now walked over to the window so that he could look out on the city. It was dark enough that the structures were dark, but the windows were bright. Lights lined the streets far below. It was the vision of the future that had played out in a dozen movies, and now he was looking at it. The difference was that there wasn't horrible overcrowding, there wasn't a breakdown of society or governmental welfare, but a vibrant, alive city that had an undercurrent of poverty and extremes of wealth. It was a future of promise that was somehow different than the one seen by so many prophets.

He said, "I'll tell this truth just once, and then I will never mention it again. If it leaves this room, I will have you killed. Do you understand me?"

Davis couldn't help grinning. It was all so melodramatic. "Of course. I have yet to betray a secret."

"God does not want us traveling to the stars. He does not want his chosen to pollute themselves by contact with inferior and alien species. He wants us to remain pure and grow toward spiritual enlightenment. We can't do that if we are flying all over the galaxy."

For just an instant, Davis was going to laugh. But just for an instant. He realized that Barnett was serious. He realized that Barnett would do anything to keep the faster-than-light ship from leaving the Solar System, even if it meant killing the crew and the destruction of the company. In that instant, Davis realized that Barnett was insane, and he was the only person in the world who knew it.

CHAPTER 10

[1]

To Hackett, it seemed to take forever for the ship to leave Mars's orbit. It seemed that each time he looked out the windows, the Martian landscape was no different than it had been the last time he looked. He could feel no pressure from acceleration and heard no rumbling of chemical or atomic rockets as they pushed the station out of orbit and moved it up, out of the plane of the ecliptic. It was as if they would never move.

But he understood what was happening. The ship was moving away from Mars and away from the debris left over from the formation of the Solar System, out to where it would have a fairly uncluttered path to jump beyond light speed. There would be fewer asteroids, remnants of comets and other junk to hit. Planning now had to be a little better because the speeds were significantly higher.

So Hackett sat, not reclined as they had when the chemical rockets lifted from Earth, or stretched out in beds of foam rubber, as they accelerated to seven or eight times the normal force of gravity. Here, they were accelerating, but they didn't need to reach the speed necessary to push them off the surface of the Earth.

And, he could watch the whole thing, not only through the tiny porthole, but on a flat-screen. Cameras were mounted around the station, giving him a view of Mars, of the pencil point of light, with a pinpoint near it representing the Earth and its moon, or a large, colored ball that was Jupiter. It was an amazing sight, even more so when he remembered that he was seeing it, not from the surface of a planet using a telescope, but from the deck of a ship about to flash out of the Solar System.

He was a little surprised when the hatch to his office cycled and Bakker stuck her head in. For no good reason, he had assumed everyone would be sitting down and strapped in as they began the journey. Thinking about it, he realized that he wasn't necessary at all.

"Aren't you bored stuck away in here?" asked Bakker.

Hackett grinned and said, "I was trying to think ahead. I remember periods of acceleration where we could do nothing but wait. I tried to plan it so that I would be able to watch the show."

"Well, we're not accelerating very fast," said Bakker. "Just don't fall down. You could break something."

"Why don't you come on in and have a seat?" asked Hackett. "Maybe we can think of something to do."

"I have lots of ideas," said Bakker, "but none that seem appropriate at the moment."

Hackett said, "I was just looking at the Earth and Jupiter. It's quite a sight."

Bakker laughed. "I would guess since they're on opposite sides."

"I meant one and then the other, not both together, though I bet I could figure out a way to get both images, live, on one screen."

"I suppose so."

Hackett looked up at her. "You have something on your mind?"

She entered and sat down. "I'm a little bothered by Mitchell, and by Weiss, of course."

"How so?"

"Well, it's not like Steve to operate in an altruistic mode. He works for himself, and all others be damned."

"So?"

"Well, here he is on the ship, and there really is nothing for him here," said Bakker. "He should be on Mars scheming with someone to get off Mars."

"This does gain him quite a bit of credibility. He's on the first faster-than-light ship to leave the Solar System."

"Could be said he's on the first ship of any kind to leave the system," said Bakker. "All depends on your definition of the Solar System and how far out the generation ships have already gotten."

"Look," said Hackett, "He's on the ship with us. He's not going to do anything."

"No, but I'm not so sure about Mitchell."

"She spilled everything she knows," said Hackett. "This is as safe a vessel as we can make it."

Bakker shrugged.

"You have something you want to say?" asked Hackett.

"What if she's a fanatic. Sacrifice herself for her cause, whatever it might be."

"Psych people said no. Said that she is dedicated, hard-working, loyal, but not suicidal," said Hackett. "If she thought there was a chance this ship would explode, she wouldn't be here calmly waiting for the end."

"Then we have nothing to worry about," said Bakker.

"Didn't say that. Just don't think that either of those people will do anything to us. We're safe from them."

Bakker stood up to leave, but Hackett waved at her. "You in a hurry?"

"No," she said.

"Then stay here for a while. Let's watch the show."

Bakker was about to say that she had seen it all before, but then realized she had never been in the middle of it before. Now it was something to see. Something to amaze. She sat back down and said, "Show me what you've got."

[2]

JOE DOUGLAS SAT ON WHAT HE CONSIDERED the flight deck. Next to him was Sally Wilson. They were watching the forward screens as they moved ever faster away from Mars. The scanners and sensors were reaching out a hundred thousand miles, searching for anything that was in their path. The calibrations were set so that anything larger than a softball would be detected. They could find nothing of consequence.

Douglas was relaxed, his feet up and his fingers laced behind his head. Though he was watching the screen, he didn't expect to see anything before the sensors detected it and alerted him. He could be in the galley eating, he could be in his cabin sleeping, he could be with someone else engaging in a little intimate conversation, and still get to the flight deck in time to respond to the threat if he had to. But there would be no threat by that time. The ship would have made the various moves to eliminate the threat by altering course if it didn't expend much energy, or much more likely, creating a situation so that tbe threat altered its course.

Wilson tapped the screen. "There's something."

Douglas glanced at it and grinned. "Basketball sized. The field will push it aside."

"You sure you want to trust the field with this?"

"The theory's good, and on our first jump we didn't have any trouble."

Now she laughed. "I have to tell you. I keep having pictures of those old science fiction movies, those in black and white where they run into the meteor shower. Cause all sorts of trouble, but they weren't traveling as fast as we do."

"Poor writing," said Douglas. "Long trip to the moon

or Mars, or wherever they're going, and they had to toss in something for excitement. Throw in an unscheduled meteor shower for five minutes worth of excitement."

"Yeah, well, space debris can create trouble."

Douglas said, "What is this all about? You looked at the theoretical work, just as I did. The field pushes crap out of the way."

"To a point," said Wilson.

"Yeah, and everything beyond that point is big enough for us to see in plenty of time to react."

"At four times the speed of light. At ten times?"

Douglas dropped his feet to the floor and turned to look at her. "What's really on your mind here?"

"I don't know. I'm still thinking about what we've agreed to do, jumping into basically uncharted territory. Something happens out here, and there is no one to save us. We have some kind of trouble, and that's it, if we can't fix it."

"Well, it's a little late now. I thought we talked all this out."

She looked at him and said, "This isn't like our little jump out to the Oort Cloud. We'll really be on our own."

Douglas could see that she was scared and that she wanted him to say something to comfort her. She wanted some reassurance. But he had nothing to tell her. The dangers were real, just as they had been for any human advancement. Someone had to take the risks, and those who were successful found their names in the history books. Those who failed, unless they failed spectacularly, were lost to history.

"So," he said cheerily, "we'll just have to make sure that nothing goes wrong."

"You really want something to worry about? How about this? The field generated is more powerful than we believed, and suddenly we find ourselves on the other side of the galaxy. Nothing would look right. We'd have a hell of a time finding our way home."

"If we're just letting our minds wander," said Douglas, "then how about this. Nothing looks right because we're not in the Milky Way anymore. We're in a different galaxy."

"That'd be one hell of a trip."

Douglas nodded and said, "That has always been something I wondered about. We talk of life in the universe, but we're really talking about life in our galaxy and really about life in our section of the galaxy. Get too far afield, and even with faster-than-light drive, the distances are just too large. At ten times the speed of light, we can cross the galaxy in ten thousand years rather than a hundred thousand."

"And a trip to Andromeda would take what? Two hundred thousand years?" said Wilson.

"So even if we could survive such a trip, what would we come back to? Take a protohuman, one of our earliest ancestors, pluck him out of his environment, and bring him forward to our time."

"He probably couldn't understand anything," said Wilson. "They were little more than animals."

"For the sake of argument," said Douglas, "let's say he is as bright as we are. Unschooled. Ignorant. Good at surviving in the harsh environment of the savannah two, four hundred thousand years ago, but with no knowledge of much beyond what he needed to know to survive."

"Okay."

"He has nothing in common with us, really. Yes, he was born on Earth, but his society is long gone, and the little we know about it is based on bones and bits of artifacts found. He would be as alien to us as a creature from another world."

"Your point?" asked Wilson.

"Well, it's just that I've been thinking about this traveling interstellar distances, and it just seems to me that under the current state of technology, we're limited in what we can do, how far we can go."

"So what?"

Douglas looked at her as if she had just sworn at him. Then he realized what she meant. Today he couldn't think in terms of a trip across the galaxy, but that didn't mean tomorrow there wouldn't be a way to do it. Science had a way of proving that today's impossibility was tomorrow's routine. Once humans couldn't fly, and now they were about to take a trip out of the Solar System. It hadn't taken long to get from those first primitive flights at Kitty Hawk to the point where they were exceeding the speed of light.

Changing the subject, Douglas said, "Be about an hour before we' re ready to cross to just beyond light."

"Nothing for us to do," said Wilson, "other than wait."

"You mean wait to explode?" asked Douglas, grinning.

"I had hoped you would come up with something a little less frightening."

[3]

HACKETT WAS WITH BAKKER IN HIS CABIN, WITH the hatch locked, when the announcement came. Bakker had slowly removed her clothes, letting them fall, though that wasn't quite the right word. They didn't fall to the deck beneath her feet, but drifted toward one wall that indicated where the engines were and which direction they were accelerating. It was interesting to watch the small, delicate garment slowly drift away from her hand. Hackett didn't know where to look. At her or at her underwear.

She turned her back on him and stood straight, her ankles crossed and her heels slightly raised. That defined the muscles of her calves and thighs. She glanced at him, over her shoulder, and smiled.

"This is certainly better than looking out the window at Jupiter," he said.

She turned around and scowled. "That's it? That's the best you can come up with? I do what might be the first striptease in space, and you come up with something that lame."

"I was trying to keep from insulting you," said Hackett.

"And what exactly does that mean?"

He laughed at her indignation. She was standing in front of him naked, and suddenly she was angry. For some reason he couldn't take her anger seriously, given the circumstances. But rather than say something inept, he kept his mouth shut.

"Well?"

"It means that I respect you as a woman and a scientist and a colleague."

Now she laughed. "I get naked, and you want me to know that you respect me as a scientist."

Hackett was flustered. He didn't know what to say. Everything he could think of sounded patronizing. He had a naked girl in his cabin, and it was clear what she had on her mind. All he had to do was remain cool and not say something stupid. He wondered how he had gotten to this point where he had to dance carefully so he didn't offend her. Normally things went smoother.

She stepped closer, staying just out of reach. She said, "You know, you have on way too many clothes."

In that instant Hackett understood what he had to do. He stood up, walked up one wall, in relation to where she was standing, and slowly, carefully, began to peel himself out of his clothes.

"The first male striptease in space," he said.

"But not the first," said Bakker. "I now have that honor."

As he tossed his coveralls to the side, he moved toward the computer. "Maybe we should log on and make the claim. I'm sure the scientific world will be set on its ear."

She sat down in the chair near the keyboard and crossed her legs. She sat there as if fully clothed, unaware that he was watching her every move. She seemed natural, at ease, and fully comfortable.

"I'm not sure where to register this," she said.

Hackett said, "So, I begin the first male space striptease, and you have your attention diverted to some claim that you don't know how to register."

She turned and waved a hand. "Sorry. I don't know what I was thinking. Please continue."

"I'm not sure that I care to."

"Okay. I'll just climb right back into my clothes, and I'll find a way to register this first." She looked around. "Just where are my panties."

Hackett said, "You win."

"Then strip."

Hackett finished, releasing his shorts, letting them drift away. He felt a little uncomfortable, standing around naked, but he tried to hide it. Women, he decided, were more at home in their bodies.

"Before we begin," she said, as if lecturing a class, "I think we should register our claim first. Make a claim so that the space agency knows what we have accomplished today."

"Is this a smart thing to do?" he asked.

"Meaning?"

"Won't our colleagues believe that we are a little frivolous, trying to capture credit for this?"

"I seem to remember a documentary that made a big deal out of the first 'dirty' photographs, taken, I think, about ten minutes after they discovered photography. Hundreds of years from now, if we're not famous for making the first sustained faster-than-light journey, we'll be famous for the first striptease in space."

"I certainly can't argue with logic like that," said Hackett shaking his head. "But I think you should take complete credit for it."

"Oh no," she said. "Your name is going up there right next to mine. I'm not going to hog all the credit."

She put her fingers on the keyboard, thought, and then typed quickly. When she didn't get what she wanted, she tried to refine the search. Striptease had, of course, brought up too many sites and too many pages. She added *space* after *striptease*, and when that didn't work, she reversed the order, thinking that the more she refined it without results, the more likely that no one had ever thought of it.

Finally she just said, "Damn!"

"What?"

"Well, I should have thought of this. Of course someone has already performed a striptease in space. Those trips to Mars, twenty, thirty years ago took a long time. Someone would have thought of this to break up the monotony."

"So we weren't the first," said Hackett, not sounding disappointed.

"Well, I could point out that this record was established inside the Solar System and we could wait until we get into deep space and try again. And we can always claim the honor for the first faster-than-light strip."

She laughed then. "I like that. A faster-than-light strip."

"I think this is getting out of hand."

She pushed the keyboard away and stood up. She stretched, slowly, tensing all her muscles. "I guess we'll have to find some other way to amuse ourselves."

A quiet bong sounded, followed by the announcement. "All personnel, we are going to make the transition to faster-than-light drive. Please restrain yourselves for the next ten or fifteen minutes."

Bakker laughed out loud. "Given our circumstance, I think they could have come up with a little less provocative announcement."

"You have some ideas?"

Bakker clasped her hands behind her and said, "I can think of a couple of things, but we'll have to wait, I guess."

[4]

BARNETT HAD GROWN TIRED OF THE CITY AND had opted to move to the beach. His house sat on top of a hill maybe three hundred yards from the beach and probably four hundred from the water. He had an unobstructed view that had been arranged by his real estate firm. They had bought the two houses between him and the beach and then had them demolished. Now that he owned that land, no one could build anything that would take away his view.

He stood on the deck, a cold drink in his hand. He was wearing a light jacket, no shirt, and pale khaki shorts. His belly hung over the top of this shorts, and his legs were short, chubby, and almost hairless. He looked, from the neck down, like the fat kid who was never chosen for the baseball games. From the neck up, he looked old and worn.

Behind him, at a round table that had an umbrella and that was stuck away in a corner out of the sun, sat two of his advisers. Both of them were women, and both were dressed in small bikinis. One of them had been tempted to remove the top, but decided it might send the wrong signal.

Standing near the table was a male adviser wearing a European cut swimming suit, which meant that he was practically naked. He did not have the body for the suit, and both the women tried not to look at him. They found the sight disgusting.

Without turning to look at them, Barnett said, "Do we have a status on the ship?"

No one had to be told what ship he meant. The only ship that mattered was the faster-than-light ship.

"Latest word is that they have begun to maneuver away from Mars," said one of the women.

"How long ago was that?"

"A day."

"Damn it!" snapped Barnett. "I wanted to be kept up to the minute."

"They haven't jumped to light speed," said the woman. "I thought you wanted to know when they made the transition."

Barnett turned and stared at her. She was immediately uncomfortable. She knew she had made a mistake. She should have never said anything about when he might want information. She should have suggested it was merely the latest communication.

"If they've jumped to light speed it might be too late," he said.

"Too late for what?"

Barnett snapped his fingers and pointed to the man. For an instant Barnett was disgusted. "Put something on."

"Yes, sir."

"And then come with me. You two stay out here. Catch the last of the sun."

"Yes, sir."

Barnett walked through the sliding glass doors, through the living room, kitchen, and into another room that looked like the bridge of an aircraft carrier without any of the steering equipment. Barnett dropped into a chair and said, "I want to communicate with our people on Mars."

"Could take thirty minutes to establish contact. Maybe more. Probably more."

"Why?"

"Distance. Signal only travels at the speed of light. Speed of light there and back. And I don't know if our people on Mars will be monitoring the equipment."

"Crap," said Barnett. "Can we initiate the sequence from here?"

"Certainly, but distance is going to degrade the signal. We can't boost it too much without causing the FCC to jump into the middle of our shit."

"One time accident. FCC isn't going to cause us any trouble," said Barnett.

"It'll take a few minutes to get everything ready. I need to make a couple of adjustments if that's the direction you want to go with this."

"Do it," said Barnett.

The man worked quietly, finally pulling a keyboard around. He typed for a moment and then pushed it away. He looked back at Barnett. "That's got it."

"Then send the signal."

The man hesitated, then quietly said, "I'm not sure that I can do that."

"Why the hell not?"

"Well . . ."

"Oh, the hell with it. What do I have to do?"

"If you are sure this is the course you wish to pursue," said the man, "then all you have to do is type in *execute* and then click on the *send* icon."

"That's it?"

"Yes."

"Then get out of my way," said Barnett.

He sat down, typed the word, and then sent the message on its way. He expected to hear something immediately, actually thought he might hear the detonation, but that was, of course, fantasy. An explosion in space would be very quiet. As quiet as death. As silent as a plague.

[5]

DOUGLAS NOW SAT ON THE FLIGHT DECK, HIS feet flat on the floor, or rather the bulkhead that was acting as the floor, his eyes dancing along the various screens and sensors. There was nothing in front of him. Just a few indications of space debris, none of it larger than a golf ball. That which wasn't repelled by the field, would be sucked into it and dragged along, preventing any collision with the station. Once they had activated the faster-than-light drive, they would be, more or less, immune to any of that small space debris.

At least that was the theory, and Douglas was willing to bet the theory was right. If it wasn't, then faster-than-light drive would have to wait for a detection system that ranged out far enough that they wouldn't fly into the obstacle before they could spot it. So far the theory had proved sound.

Wilson, sitting next to him, wasn't quite as thrilled with the theory, but then, she had no choice. She had been assigned to the project and had been unable to figure out a way to keep her name off the roster. So now she waited, more than a little concerned that they would soon join that floating interstellar debris. Just bits and pieces of humanity's first real attempt to reach the stars.

With the station aimed, more or less, in the direction they wanted to travel, Douglas allowed his fingers to play first across the keyboard, typing in commands, and then over a panel that looked as if it had been created by a science fiction movie set designer a century earlier. It was as out of place as an old time cork with a magnetized needle floating in a shallow pan of water would have been.

Douglas touched a button and then flipped a switch, initiating the transition to faster-than-light speed. He rocked back in his chair and waited, knowing full well that there would be no sensation. There was no sudden lurch forward, no bump or pressure as they accelerated. There would be no increased engine noise and no increase in heat. The transition to faster-than-light speed had no outward or noticeable effects. The only real change was that the stars as seen from the cameras began to slide down toward one corner of the view screens.

Douglas looked at one of the instruments and said, "We're moving just a little faster than light."

Wilson turned her attention to the indicator. "Feels just the same as it did the last time."

Without a word to her, Douglas leaned forward, his lips close to the microphone and announced, "We have slipped past the light barrier and are now traveling at about one and a third times the speed of light."

"So now we have nothing to do until we reach our destination?" asked Wilson.

"Well, we need to keep a log, but of course, the computer will do that automatically. And we need to broadcast information back to Mars, but then, the telemetry is being relayed automatically. We'll have to make periodic checks of our health, to learn if there are any long-term problems that develop from exposure to the field generated to travel faster than light. So, no. There really is nothing for us to do, other than watch the instruments once in a while and see if we can spot a hazard that the sensors have overlooked."

"What you're saying is that at the moment we're safe from outside hazards."

Douglas shrugged. "What I'm saying is that we're now traveling nearly one and a half times the speed of light and we'll continue to accelerate for a while."

"And that we're safe."

"As safe as if we were sitting in a dome on Mars."

Except it wasn't that safe. A destruct sequence had been sent to stop the ship.

CHAPTER 11

[1]

PROFESSOR WILLIAM SMERTZ, WHO NO LONGER had any responsibility for the ship or the development of the faster-than-light drive, was still interested in everything that surrounded it. He knew that they were about to make the first sustained flight, and he was in his control room to watch. There was nothing for him to do other than watch, but he wanted to see that everything moved forward smoothly.

Sitting near him were Trask and two of his assistants. All others had been given the day off. There was nothing for them to do. Command and control had shifted to the ship and all decisions would be made there.

Watching the screen that displayed the station as it moved through space afforded no real indications that the station was in motion, because there was nothing in the view against which to measure movement. The station had moved out of its Martian orbit and had accelerated upward, as the direction related to the Solar System and the Plain of the Ecliptic. The station had reached a point where it was, more or less, out of the Solar System, if the system was thought of as on a plane rather than as a sphere.

Smertz said, "They should be jumping to light speed at any moment."

Trask grinned, nodded, and waited. To him, this was the same as standing on the dock as Columbus sailed over the horizon. It was the same was sitting in the bleachers in Coco Beach as Apollo 11 was launched. It was a historical event that marked humanity's first real trip out of the Solar System.

He wanted to say something great. Some words that would echo throughout history, but nothing sprang to mind. He wondered if those who had uttered greatness had planned their words beforehand, or thought of them later and added them to historical accounts. Not every great line in history could be the result of spontaneity.

"Any moment now," said Smertz, his eyes fixed to the screen.

"Won't this have happened fifteen, twenty minutes ago?" asked Trask.

"Of course. But we'll be seeing it for the first time. We'll learn if they succeeded for the first time."

Trask nodded and thought about that. It bothered him that the events had taken place earlier and there was no faster way to learn of their success. Radio and television could broadcast events as they happened, the delay only seconds. But now, in space, with the distances as vast as they were, it took minutes for the radio or television signal to reach them. As those distances increased, the delay became longer.

"There," said Smertz. "Something is happening."

They could see some kind of a golden glow that expanded from the station and engulfed it. The chemical reaction engines were pushing it, but faded as the glow wrapped around them. It shimmered and the station seemed to momentarily pick up speed and then it faded from sight. Or rather it seemed to blur as it headed off, out of the Solar System.

"Faster-than-light," said Smertz.

"What?"

"That glow, I think, is the faster-than-light drive kicking in. It all looks fuzzy now, because the station is moving faster than light. It'll fade away as the distance increases. Take the light longer to get here, because the station is moving so fast. Incredible."

"Then they're now beyond the light barrier?"

Smertz laughed. "I'm afraid that terminology is a little misleading. There is no single barrier."

"But they're traveling faster than light now."

"Yes. If they double their speed, then our recording of the craft will shift to the point where we won't be able to detect it. It'll be there but it'll be sort of like trying to see a bullet come out of the barrel of a rifle. It moves out, we just can't see it."

"But it's there," said Trask.

"Yes, it's there. We're going to have to invent some new sort of sensors and detection equipment to cover this problem."

Trask nodded. "Well, that's your problem now. They're flying faster than light."

"That they are."

A woman entered the room and walked straight to Trask. She crouched near him and showed him the screen of her Palm Pilot. He looked up at her and asked, "When'd you receive this?"

"Four, five minutes ago."

He turned his attention back to the flat-screen, but there was no longer anything to see. The station was gone, traveling faster than light.

"Did you decode it?"

The woman shrugged. "It doesn't seem to contain a written message. It is just a signal."

"To do what?"

"We don't know. All we do know is that it was directional, it had a huge power boost behind it, and it was of limited duration. That suggested to us that it was a signal to either activate a system or shut one down."

Trask took the Palm Pilot from her and studied the signal. It had originated on Earth. He was certain, given the frequency and the short duration, that he knew where it came from. He suspected he knew what it was for.

"The station still out there?" she asked Smertz.

Smertz laughed. "How in the hell would I know? It's traveling faster than the speed of light. It's gone, but I can't prove where it went."

[2]

CATHERINE DECOURTENAY WAS ANNOYED. SHE had thought Hackett would invite her onto the station and she would be a member of the first crew to travel outside the Solar System. Her name might be little more than a footnote in history, but she would be there, along with her great-great-great-twenty-times-removed grandmother. The original DeCourtenay was more than a footnote, though few had ever heard of her in the modern world, even if she had been eighth in line to the British throne.

The headquarters building was nearly deserted and only a few people were on the station crew. The others had taken the day off to watch the launch on closed-circuit television. True, they could have watched from the office, but why do it there, when no one cares if you do it at home. So, DeCourtenay was wandering in an almost deserted headquarters building.

Her job on Mars was finished, and there was no job to go back to on Earth. Or rather, the job she had held, as an adviser to Wendelle Bruce Barnett was long gone. Barnett had to know that she had betrayed him and lied to him. She wasn't the blond bimbo he had thought she was. She had listened carefully, remembered everything, and then had used it to help Hackett and his people close down the operation on Mars. Barnett had to know that she had been involved in that. He had to know that she was a spy, and though she had heard nothing, she was sure he would have her killed if he found an opportunity.

So, given all that, she was stuck, for the moment, on Mars, without the prospect of a good job. Spying didn't pay all that well, and contrary to the James Bond legend, it wasn't all that conducive to long life and good health. Enemies were made, and sometimes those enemies had no conscience.

Hackett's office was open, and she walked in. The view out into the Martian dome was interesting. She wouldn't say it was spectacular, because she had seen spectacular views from offices on Earth. Long-range views of giant cities sparkling with light, or huge, snowcapped mountains that dominated the sky.

Given who she was and what she knew, it took her no time to crack the system and log on as Hackett. She scrolled through the files, looking for anything that might be of interest and of help to her. She looked at the new, incoming messages, just so that she would know what was going on.

There was a file that detailed electronic correspondence from Earth bases to various receivers on Mars. There she found some of those messages that Barnett had sent to his people on Mars. A couple of them had not been decoded, and DeCourtenay grinned at that. These were gibberish, sent to confound and confuse anyone who intercepted them. She noticed that Hackett's people had spent almost no time attempting to crack them, almost as if they knew the truth about them.

She glanced at the latest, seeing that not every cell on Mars had been identified. She realized that Barnett still had a dozen or so people who were loyal to him and who had not been arrested during the roundup. She wished that

Hackett had told her of those plans. She might have been able to help.

She decoded the messages herself, because she knew the system of encryption. None of the messages told her anything she didn't already know, except that they identified two of Barnett's agents on Mars. That might be useful information at some future date.

She looked at the latest message and realized that it was not a text message. It was an encrypted code that was supposed to activate specific equipment. It was a radio signal that would detonate a minute amount of strategically placed explosive, which would cause the destruction of a larger craft.

"My God!" she said out loud. "I didn't think the bastard would do it."

She jumped up and ran to the door. She hesitated there, not sure where she was going, and then sprinted down the corridor. The automatic lights that came on when they detected motion lighted, but always just behind her, because she was running.

She reached the stairs and stopped again. She thought for a moment and then remembered that Trask had a lab in the building. She took the steps as fast as she could, went through the open door at Trasks floor, and ran down the corridor. She found Trask's lab and slid to a stop. She banged on the door with her fist, and yelled, "Open up!"

There was a barely audible click and a metallic voice asked, "What in the hell is going on out there?"

DeCourtenay looked at the speaker and saw the tiny glass eye of a camera lens. She said, "I need to communicate with Colonel Hackett. I have important information."

"We have no means of communication," said the voice. "You have the wrong office."

DeCourtenay shook her head. "No. Colonel Hackett brought me here once. I need to talk with Doctor Trask."

"There is no one here by that name."

Now she was beginning to get frustrated. "I must communicate with Colonel Hackett immediately."

"I wish you good luck," said the voice. It was followed by a click, indicating that the communication had been terminated.

DeCourtenay stared up at the lens as if she expected it to do something. She rubbed her hands over her face. She had to do something, and there wasn't much time. The signal had been received on Mars, which meant it would be at the station in a matter of minutes.

She whirled and ran back up the hall. She stopped at the stairs and wondered if the astronomers would be able to communicate with Bakker. That would be nearly as good. She ran down the stairs, out of the building, and across the plaza, toward the other building. She was barely aware of the people milling about, taking in the little sun available, relaxing, talking, and staring at her as she ran.

She got inside, ran up the stairs, and found two people standing in a hallway. She didn't know who they were. She stopped near them and then, almost breathlessly, asked, "You know Doctor Bakker?"

One of them, the male, smiled and said, "Of course."

"Can you get in touch with her?"

"I suppose. If I want to. But she's on the space station at the moment."

"I know where she is. I have to get a message to her."

The man shrugged. "I guess we could radio her something. I don't know how quickly she'll find it though. They're pretty busy."

"We've got to try," said DeCourtenay. "We can do that, can't we?"

"All right. Come with me." The man turned and began to walk up the corridor.

DeCourtenay tried to follow along, but she was nervous. She finally snapped, "Can't we move along a little faster?"

The man looked surprised. "Sure," he said, and began to walk faster.

They reached a door, and the man opened it. He allowed DeCourtenay to walk through before him. They walked through a lab that looked as if an electronics factory had exploded and no one had bothered to pick up the pieces. They came to another door, and the man opened it, too.

"After you."

Inside looked like a radio room, but something from the last century. It looked slightly out of place, as if it should have been in a museum. DeCourtenay turned and looked back at the man, the question in her eyes.

"Yeah, pretty neat, huh? We wanted something that would be of visual interest even if the mission was mundane. I kind of like it this way."

"Bakker," said DeCourtenay.

"Of course." The man sat down and reached over and flipped a couple of switches. One of the panels on a radio moved, revealing a screen. It flashed bright, darkened, and then coalesced. There were star fields in the background, one of Jupiter's moons, and in a low corner just a slight smudge that might have been an arc of the gigantic planet.

"This is strange," he said.

"What?"

"I don't see the station. It should be right there. In the center."

"What happened to it?"

"I don't know."

[3]

BARNETT SAT AT THE CONSOLE FOR SEVERAL minutes after he had sent the destruct signal but realized that he would not know the results for hours if not a day or two. He wouldn't see anything, and there would be no immediate return signal. He could only guess about his success. He could only wait to hear.

So, he had gotten up and walked back through the living room and out onto the deck. There was the noise of the surf, birds wheeling in the area at the edge of the beach, swooping in for something near the high tide line, and music drifting on the wind from one of his neighbors. A distant party. On most occasions he would have been annoyed at the intrusion, but tonight, at that moment, it seemed natural.

The two women had not moved from the table. They were still drinking, and Barnett noticed that the speech of the one he thought of as cute, who wore the red bikini, was beginning to slur. She was slightly drunk, and Barnett wasn't sure if he liked that or not.

She looked up at him and asked, "You get your work done?"

"Of course, my dear. And it looks as if you have been doing what you were told to as well."

She held up the glass and said, "Well, I'm doing what I can while here."

Barnett pulled out a chair and sat down. Suddenly he felt horny. Suddenly he wanted to see this woman without her clothes, standing in his bedroom. The fantasy was nearly always the same. She was standing, backlit by the sun, or the moon, or the city lights, naked. Some of the lights in the bedroom were on so that he could study the woman. She walked slowly toward him, and when she reached the bed, she knelt forward. Then she walked to him and straddled him. Sometimes he was naked, and sometimes he was not. It depended on his mood and how fast he wanted to get into the main action.

It never occurred to him that the women who had participated in the fantasy had done so because of his wealth and power and not because of some burning desire to know him better. They were attempting to gain an advantage by submitting to his fantasy. If that was what it took, then they were willing to play.

Some men had tried similar games, but when they realized Barnett had no desire for men, they tried a different strategy. In the corporate world where Barnett played, everyone, male and female, jockeyed for position, trying to find an advantage. Few cared what they had to do to advance their careers.

Barnett smiled slightly as he thought of the man in the European swimming suit. Wanted to be in the big time, but wouldn't push a button. Tomorrow, that man would find himself transferred to another division. It would look like a promotion, but in reality, it would be just a move to get him out of the main headquarters. If he wouldn't do what needed to be done, Barnett had no more time for him.

He picked up a pitcher of fresh martinis. One of the house staff, who tended to things efficiently and inconspicuously, had made the martinis, put the pitcher on the table, and slipped away.

Barnett took a long, deep drink, letting the ice cold liquor slide down his throat. He could feel it as it pooled in his belly. It felt good. It was just what he needed.

He turned his attention to the woman, who he remembered was named Jane. Jane something. Richards? Thompson? Some man's name that was used as a last name. He couldn't remember and didn't really care.

"Do you have a curfew?" he asked her.

"A what?" she asked, startled by the question and the sudden attention?

"Curfew? Time you need to be home?"

"No. I'm working."

Barnett nodded dumbly and thought of the prostitutes he could find elsewhere in the city. Not that this woman was a prostitute, any more than the man in the wisp of cloth he called a swimming suit was a prostitute.

"Then maybe we should go inside. Talk privately."

Jane Richardson grinned slyly and stood up. "Of course. It's getting a little chilly out here with the sun gone."

They walked into the living room, which had one wall made entirely of glass, providing a nearly panoramic view of the ocean. The sun was sitting on the horizon, and everything was bathed in a golden light. Venus was blazing brightly, looking like an alien spacecraft about to land.

Barnett stopped near the windows, then turned to face Richardson. "We can get comfortable in here. We won't be interrupted."

Richardson reached around and unfastened her bikini top and let it fall away, leaving her naked to the waist.

Barnett stared at her chest, not even trying to hide his excitement. Everyone had given him everything he wanted for so long, that he had lost the ability to feel any empathy for his fellows. To him, all the world was a stage, and all the people, actors, put there solely for his pleasure.

Then his attention was distracted by the man opening the door. He leaned in to say. "There are four cars in the driveway. They have stopped, but no one has gotten out yet."

Barnett, his anger flaring, whirled and said, "Make them go away. This is private property."

"Yes, sir," he said, closing the door.

"Now, my dear," said Barnett, "is there anything that I might get you?"

"Lower the lights?"

"Why?"

"I thought it would be nice to watch the last of the sunset." She hooked her fingers into the bikini bottom, looking as if she was going to push it down.

There was a loud bang, as if someone had hit a wide, thin board with a hammer, and then a shout. Barnett turned from the woman and looked back at the door. As he took a step forward, the door swung open, banging against the wall.

A man, gun drawn, stepped into the room, followed by several uniformed officers. He looked, first at Barnett and then at Richardson. She stood, her fingers still in the bottom of her bikini, frozen. Then, suddenly, she grinned. She was not embarrassed.

The man said, "You Window Barnett?"

"Wendelle Barnett. Yes."

"You are under arrest."

"Do you know who I am?"

"Sure do, Window."

"My name is Wendelle. Not Window."

"Whatever you say. But you're under arrest, and I'll be taking you into custody."

"You are making a career decision here, patrolman."

He grinned broadly. "They all say that, Window. But here I still am, and they're sitting in jail." He looked over at Richardson and asked, "Would you like to put on a few more clothes?"

"I guess."

He turned and said to one of the uniformed police officers, "Escort her to her room."

One of the male officers moved, and the man pointed to a female. "Let her handle this."

"Yes, sir."

"Now, Window, to do this right, I'm going to tell you that you are under arrest for fraud against the government, attempted sabotage, and just being ugly in a public place. You have the right to remain silent, and you have the right . . ."

"I know my rights. I evoke them now." He fell silent.

"Okay, boys and girls, let's take him in and execute the search warrant for this place."

Barnett said, "You can't . . ."

"Oh, but I can. I have a warrant, and you have already broken your promise to remain silent."

[4]

DeCourtenay LOOKED AT THE BLANK SCREEN and then at the people gathered around it. They were either staring at the screen, or had turned to work equipment, attempting to find some sign of the space station. Their instruments were as sophisticated as any on the planet. If the station was out there, they were sure that they would be able to detect it.

DeCourtenay felt sick. It had been her job to see that all of Barnett's agents were arrested and that every plan he had put into motion was stopped. She was to make sure that the station was protected so that humanity could leap from the Solar System. It looked as if she had been a little too slow to be successful. She had failed.

The only person she recognized, Ken Peters, pulled a chair out and sat down, his hands on a computer keyboard. He stared off into space for a moment, as if thinking deeply, and then typed a quick sequence.

He turned and said, "I have tried to refine the sensor capabilities. We need to finely discriminate."

"Nothing," said one of the women.

"Okay." He typed another line. "Now?"

"Nothing."

DeCourtenay asked, "What's this mean?"

"It means that we can't find the station where it should be. We do have a time delay because of distance, but we should be able to detect something."

DeCourtenay wanted to rush forward and use the keyboard. She wanted to ask questions. She wanted to take charge to get some answers, but, of course, she would have been in the way. There was nothing she could do that would have been more effective than what was being done.

After thirty minutes, Peters turned around and said, "That's it. Nothing more to be done."

"Have you asked Smertz what happened?"

"He won't know any more than we do. I'm not sure his equipment is better than ours."

"But you can ask, can't you?" said DeCourtenay, her voice rising slightly.

"Not that it will do any good."

"But ask."

"Listen, there really is no reason. He'll tell you the same thing that I can tell you. We have all the information he has, and we have better monitoring equipment. We can see farther than he can."

DeCourtenay felt the life drain out of her. She was suddenly tired. She wanted another job. She wanted to be back on Earth. She should have stayed with Barnett. Maybe she could have done something to stop the disaster.

Peters said, "They've either been destroyed, or they jumped to faster-than-light."

CHAPTER 12

[1]

THEY ALL SAT IN THE CONFERENCE ROOM WHERE
there was a camera hookup that displayed the area around
them. There was a navigational chart, which was more of
a video display than it was an exact representation, so that
they would know where they were and where they were
going. There was also a clock that told them the time and
date. Next to it was another clock that supplied the time
and date, but it had been calibrated to compensate for the
time dilation. They would know, not only the time and
date relative to them, but the time and date relative to
friends, colleagues, and family back on Mars or on Earth.

The one thing that bothered them all was the picture of
space outside their ship. It wasn't a scattering of stars,
some brighter than others, some closer than others, but a
single, globular clump that was sliding toward one of the
lower corners. The color was not the wide spectrum expected but a faded red or light blue, depending on the
camera's orientation to the ship's motion.

Hackett, who was beginning to get claustrophobic even

though the ship was huge and the conference room was larger than his office on Mars, sat quietly, trying not to flip out. He didn't want to be confined to a ship no matter how large. He wanted the option of going outside, but that wasn't to be. At least not for several months, if the mission went as planned.

Bakker was still studying the various screens. She was fascinated by the lack of detail that was a result of their speed. She had known there would be problems, but those they were having weren't quite what she had anticipated. Standard physics seemed to shift slightly when an object was traveling faster than light.

Opposite her were Weiss and Mitchell. Both were sitting quietly, their eyes on the various screens, but neither seemed to be very interested. They let their eyes shift from one screen to the next, but it was more out of boredom than due to any real interest.

Standing, near the head of the table, his back to almost everyone, was Douglas, dressed in coveralls and sneakers. He stood with his hands behind his back, rocking back and forth on his feet, quietly studying the screens.

The last person in the conference room was Sally Wilson, who looked completely relaxed. She was dressed comfortably, in shorts, a T-shirt, and sneakers. She looked as if she had taken the day off but had been called in to the office for an important meeting.

Bakker finally broke the silence. "I believe we are now traveling at three times the speed of light. We can make the closest star system in a matter of months."

"Is there any way to find one of the generation ships we launched?" asked Hackett. "I mean, now that we're traveling faster than light."

Douglas turned away from the screens. "Well, we know about where they should be, so if we drop out of faster-than-light drive close to one, we might be able to spot it."

"There a reason for that, Tom?" Weiss asked, to get

into the conversation, but not really caring one way or the other.

"No important reason," said Hackett. "More of a test for us, I guess. We have a small target traveling among the stars. If we can find it, then we have demonstrated one more ability."

"Gives us a real mission," said Bakker.

"I'm not sure that's a good idea," said Douglas. "I would like to travel on to Alpha Centauri, look at it, and return to Mars as quickly as possible. The more time we take, the more often we drop out of faster-than-light, the more chance we have of screwing something up. Without faster-than-light, we're stuck wherever we are for decades, if not the rest of our lives."

"But if we're near a generation ship," said Hackett, "at least we have somewhere handy to go."

"Seems to me," said Wilson, "that the real point of this trip is to learn if we can do it. Travel to a distant star system and get home. No need for a lot of other screwing around trying to find one of the generation ships."

Hackett shrugged. He had the authority to give the order, but he really didn't want to make the decision on his own. For this, he wanted to have a consensus. This would be a democratic decision based on what the crew wanted. Later, if necessary, he could change it all into an order.

Bakker said, "The capabilities of astronomy have grown nearly exponentially in the last couple of decades. We already know a great deal about Alpha Centauri."

"Our observations have been over a four-light-year distance," said Hackett. "Wouldn't you like the opportunity to make some observations from inside that system? Learn if you've gotten it right?"

Bakker laughed. "We've got it right. The technology is far beyond sitting at a telescope in a cold observatory on a starlit night."

Hackett said, "This is a make-work project. It's the

final shakedown cruise. We're going to Alpha Centauri because we can, and for no other real reason. When we return to Mars, we'll set up a plan to explore the galaxy around us. But before we do that, we just have to learn some things about this faster-than-light drive we've got."

Weiss spoke up. "You mean that we've finally earned our name. We are a galaxy exploration team, not some general's pipe dream that's limited by chemical rockets and the speed of light."

"I hadn't thought of it that way," said Hackett, "but that's right. We're making our first exploration into the galaxy in person."

"Good for us," said Douglas sarcastically.

"So, are we going to try to find one of the generation ships?" asked Wilson.

"I'm against it," said Douglas. "For all the reasons that have already been voiced."

"This is not something we have to decide right this minute," said Hackett. "We can initiate a search, and if we find one, then we can decide if we want to drop in."

"Changing direction, in the faster-than-light mode isn't all that easy," said Douglas. "Right now we're headed toward Alpha Centauri. If we alter our course, we have to drop out of the faster-than-light travel, make the change, and then power up again. I just don't want to take the chance that we'll fail to achieve faster-than-light again."

Hackett nodded. "I'm aware of that. But there are some other considerations."

"Then we'll search for one of the generation ships," said Douglas, "but I doubt that we'll find one."

Hackett was going to ask why, but he knew the answer. Douglas would suggest that it was like looking for a needle in a haystack, but the truth was, Douglas didn't want to take the time. He didn't want to tempt the gods by slowing to below light speed. Although, given what they knew, they could predict, fairly accurately, where the generation ships would be, they could somehow miss them. If Hackett insisted, then one would be located, but it would be the one that would be the least favorable. It would be the one the most difficult for them to intercept and still complete the mission to Alpha Centauri. Hackett didn't think this was an issue to fight for. That might come later, but right now, it was time to let things move forward as smoothly as possible.

Hackett put his hands on the conference table as if to push back his chair. He couldn't because it was bolted to the deck, but the gesture told the others the meeting was over. He said, "We have plenty of time, and I think we can take some of it to relax. Except for the necessary watches, I'd like to see the duty schedule altered and then resumed in the morning at, say, zero eight hundred. Questions?"

None were asked. No one even thought about the time dilation clock, which, unbeknownst to them, was highly inaccurate . . . the math of FTL had tripped them up.

[2]

SMERTZ TOLD TRASK THAT THE STATION HAD moved into the faster-than-light mode and because of that, they would have trouble tracking it. If they were able to double or triple the speed of light, then any signals they received would have been sent, not necessarily hours earlier, but possibly days and maybe even weeks earlier.

"There is a lot of theory as to what happens when an object moves beyond the speed of light," said Smertz. "Yes, the radio signal is moving at the speed of light, but the object that emitted it is moving much faster than that. Think of it as a major league pitcher throwing a baseball from a jet. When the ball leaves the hand of the pitcher, it has velocity in three directions. First in the direction of the aircraft, second in the direction of the throw, and finally toward the ground, because of gravity. All three velocities are acted on by outside forces, each independent of the others. The forward motion bleeds off, because the ball is no longer part of the aircraft. The reverse motion created by the throw bleeds off, because there is no longer any force behind it, and the ball slows. Only the force of gravity remains constant. The ball falls at a constant rate once it has reached its peak acceleration, based on the force of gravity."

"That's all well and good," said Trask, "but what does it have to do with receiving messages from the station?"

"They are traveling away from us at the speed of light, or better. If they attempt to radio us, the signal, when broadcast, is moving away from us at the speed of light, which could complicate and confound any signals they sent."

"Oh."

"When we start dealing with relativistic speeds," said Smertz, "we are long on theory but a little short in practical application. We think we know the answers, but it's a lot of guesswork."

"You are not inspiring me with confidence in this experiment," said Trask.

"The equipment works, we just don't know what consequences there might be. We don't know, for example, how the human body will react to faster-than-light speeds. My gut tells me, given the method, that the human body won't know that it's traveling faster than light and therefore there will be no consequences. But we really don't know."

"All this is very interesting," said Trask, "but my real point was that we are no longer in communication with the station."

"At the moment, no."

"So, if I need to get a message to them, I can't."

"Not until the situation changes," said Smertz. "They're outrunning our signal. Until they drop below light speed, they will not receive our signal. Then, they'd have to wait right there, without moving back into light speed for the signal to reach them. Radio just won't work."

Trask rocked back in his chair and looked up at the ceiling. He thought of the short signal broadcast from Earth that had been detected. He knew that it had to be some kind of destruct order, but he could do nothing to warn the station about it. They weren't in communication.

He could, he realized, just broadcast a general warning in the clear and hope that those on the station would monitor it. That was an old trick used in the early days of radio when two-way communication hadn't been established between two stations. Just put out the message and hope for the best. But now, more than a hundred years later, he would have thought they would have been beyond such a hit-or-miss proposition.

Trask said, "I think I'll head on over to communications in the astronomy building and see what they know."

"They're not going to know any more than I do," said Smertz. "Probably less."

Trask stood up. "Can't hurt. Thanks for the theoretical physics lesson."

"Not much of a lesson. More philosophy than physics."

Trask left Smertz feeling uncomfortable and more than a little uneasy. He couldn't put his finger on it, except for the fact they didn't know where the station was and there were no immediate prospects for finding it. This faster-than-light thing left his head spinning, and all he could think of was the old joke. You're driving at the speed of light, and you turn on the headlights. What happens? Trask didn't know and decided to ask Bakker when he saw her. Then he remembered that she was on the station and he wouldn't see her for quite a while.

He left the main building and walked out onto the plaza. He glanced up and saw the dome high above him, along with a bright light that was the sun. It was dimmer than it would be on Earth because of the greater distance and because of the dome. At the very top it was tinted, which seemed to defeat the purpose of the transparent material.

He walked slowly, looking at the foot traffic around him, amazed at how people had adapted to life on Mars. They were inside all the time, even when they were "outside," but they mingled, talked, flirted, and paired off just as if they were on Earth. They gave no thought to the environment around them, but that was because the environment mimicked that on Earth. If they left the dome, they would be dead in minutes, but inside it, they were as safe as they would be on Earth.

He entered the other building, took an escalator up, and crossed over to the stairs. When he exited the stairwell, he saw a receptionist sitting at a large desk that might have been made of oak, if it were on Earth, but on Mars was probably made of some kind of synthetic material.

"Whose around in astronomy?" he asked.

The receptionist glanced down his list. "I believe Ken Peters is in. He's in room 509. Do you know where that is?"

"I would assume on the fifth floor," said Trask.

"You would think that, but it's not true. They screwed up the numbering in this building, and 509 is actually on the seventh floor."

Trask shook his head. "How'd they do that?"

"Began counting at the mezzanine rather than at the ground. Got everything in place on the upper floors and then realized the mistake. They decided it would cost too much to fix, so they didn't bother."

"Great. And thanks."

Trask made his way to room 509, which looked more like a closet than an office. It held a desk, which was shoved up against the wall so that the occupant would see an expanse of light green paint with a rather small flatscreen on it, a chair for a visitor, and a file cabinet that might have been old a hundred years ago. Trask couldn't believe they would have shipped something like that from

Earth, so undoubtedly it was of Martian manufacture, but it certainly looked out of date and out of place.

Peters was sitting with his back to the door, leaning back and watching the flat-screen. Trask didn't recognize the material displayed on it. Clearly it had something to do with astronomy.

He said, "Excuse me."

Peters turned and looked at him. "Yes?"

"Got a minute?"

Peters reached over to shut off the scrolling information. "Yes. Please. Take me away from this. I have a minute. I have an hour. Hell, buy lunch, and I have an afternoon."

Trask couldn't help grinning. He said, "I might get the impression that you don't like your job."

"Love it," said Peters, "but like all jobs, there are times when it is routine and boring."

Trask didn't enter the small office. He leaned against the doorjamb. "I have a question."

"Shoot."

"I need to communicate with the space station. The faster-than-light ship."

"You and everyone else," said Peters.

"Meaning?"

"Had a woman in here a few days ago, maybe a week, talking to me about that. About the time they made the transition into their faster-than-light drive."

Trask raised an eyebrow. "Who was that?"

Peters suddenly became suspicious. The smile left his face. He said, "I'm not sure that's relevant."

"It's a little more than idle curiosity," said Trask. "It would help me to know."

"Woman who works, worked, with Hackett. Sarah knows her."

"And I work with Hackett and Doctor Bakker both."

"Yeah," said Peters. "I thought I recognized you. Anyway, it was that DeCourtenay woman. I don't know exactly what she wanted, but she wanted to communicate with the ship."

"And where is it?"

"Don't know," said Peters. "They went to light speed, and that's all I know. We haven't been able to detect them since they made the transition."

"It's fairly important," said Trask.

"Doesn't matter," responded Peters. "I don't know how to do it. We're flying blind here. All we can do is radiate the message and hope that they have a way to detect it."

Trask thought he had heard all that before. He asked, "What is their status?"

Peters laced his fingers behind his head, closed his eyes for a minute, and said, "We have no evidence that the ship has been destroyed. When the first ship exploded, we knew about it right away. It might have made the transition, but the debris quickly dropped out of light speed. We saw the evidence of the destruction. We have nothing like that this time."

"You're telling me that they're out there, outside the Solar System, traveling faster than light."

"We have no evidence to the contrary, and we know that faster-than-light travel is possible. They're out beyond the end of the Solar System, on their mission."

Trask straightened up. "Then there is nothing we can do at this point."

"No. I'm sorry."

"Okay," said Trask. He started to go but turned back. "Are there any protocols in place for communication with the station?"

"Yes. I have a list of people to notify when we hear something, and, of course, we're searching for them."

"Can I get put on your list?"

"I'll check to see if anyone has an objection," said Peters. "That's about the best I can do."

"Okay. Thanks." Trask turned and walked down the corridor, thinking. He wasn't sure what he was going to do now, but there seemed not to be much he could do. The station would be on its own, and he couldn't tell them about the destruct signal he'd discovered. He didn't realize that it just didn't matter.

[3]

BARNETT, WEARING THE BRIGHT ORANGE COVERalls that had been the height of prison fashion a hundred years earlier, sat in the barren and somewhat cold interrogation room. His left hand was handcuffed to the chair so that he couldn't escape. There were no windows and not even a one-way mirror on the walls.

The purpose of the empty room, and the handcuffs, was intimidation. This was where first-time, or less-thanbrilliant offenders were brought initially—those who might break and spill their guts.

Barnett had been sitting alone in the room for an hour, when the police officer who had arrested him more than a week earlier opened the door. He walked in and sat down opposite Barnett. He grinned broadly and said, "You really stepped in some serious shit here. You're going up the river for a long time."

"I don't believe you know who I am," said Barnett.

The police officer reached into his shirt pocket and took out his Palm Pilot. He turned it around so that Barnett could see the color display and asked, "That you?"

"Yes. Your point?"

"I know who you are."

Barnett had to smile. "And do you know who I know?"

The officer tapped the display on the Palm Pilot. "From this, I can deduce that you probably know the governor, certainly one or both senators, probably half a dozen congressmen and -women and maybe even the president. You certainly know the mayor, the city commission, and even the police commissioner. You might know the chief, though he is low-ranking enough that he might not be on your radar. How am I doing?"

Barnett nodded throughout the recitation. "Just fine, except that I do know the chief, and I have met the president three times, each time with a large check for his party."

"Well, then, you understand that I know who you know, and you're still sitting here handcuffed to that chair. Does that tell you something?"

For the first time Barnett looked a little worried but suddenly he laughed. "All well and good . . ."

"Griffith. Andrew Griffith."

"Well, Officer Griffith . . ."

"Lieutenant."

"Lieutenant, then. I would think that once I have alerted my attorney, or rather battery of attorneys, who will in turn make various telephone calls, you'll find that this situation is not quite as black and white as you seem to think. People will begin to agitate on my behalf."

Griffith stood up and stretched. Had there been a window, he would have walked to it and looked out. Instead, he sat down again, picked at the cuticle on his thumb, and finally asked, "What makes you think that I haven't alerted the chief, who, in turn alerted the commissioner, who alerted the governor, and so on. What makes you think, given the list of crimes we have here that any of these people will rush to your defense?"

Again Barnett looked troubled, and again he covered it quickly, almost completely. "Because they owe me, and I know where the bodies are buried."

"Be that as it may," said Griffith, "I have but a single question for you. What was the content of that last signal broadcast?"

"I made no broadcast," said Barnett.

"Well, that radio transmission, then."

"I made no radio transmission."

"And we were getting along so well. Of course you

made a radio transmission. It lasted nearly a second, and we have captured it. We know that it was sent from your beach house—which, by the way, you'll probably never see again—and we have decoded it."

"If that were true, then you'd have no reason to question me about its contents."

"What was it for? You gain nothing by dodging around this. If, however, I get some solid and useful answers, then your situation here could change."

Now Barnett fell silent, a bemused look on his face. He wished he could stand up and move around, but the handcuff prevented that. Instead he pretended it didn't exist. He felt the power in the room shift as Griffith asked his questions. They had finally gotten to the meat of the interview. Griffith had ceded the power when he offered, however obliquely, the possibility of a deal.

"And just what is in this for me?" Barnett asked.

"Charges will be dropped, and this whole ugly affair will be forgotten. You'll have to resign as CEO, of course, but your pension will remain intact. There will be a fine, but I don't think it will be significant."

"I'll be free to go?"

"And do what you will," said Griffith.

Barnett could see his future in front of him. A minor setback before he began his march to the top again. Maybe seek a political office. He had the experience. He had the expertise and the contacts, and he had the money. More money than these people knew about. Money that had been carefully and slowly bled from contracts and jobs and funneled into off-shore accounts under various names. Money from various locations.

"All right," said Barnett. "What do you want to know?"

"What was in that signal?"

"It was a sequence that would activate a small explosive device on the station."

"Designed to do what?"

"Destroy the faster-than-light drive. Drop the station back into a slower-than-light mode. Not to destroy the station or kill anyone on board it. Just a charge large enough to wreck the faster-than-light drive."

"How do we countermand it?"

"I don't understand."

"How do we stop it? How do we change it so that it won't destroy the drive?"

"Oh, you can't do that. It's too late. Once the signal has been sent on its way, you can't catch it. The device will explode, and the station will drop into sublight speeds."

CHAPTER 13

[1]

TO HACKETT THERE WAS NO DIFFERENCE BE-
tween space flight at normal speeds and space flight faster
than light. The calculations that Bakker had given him
suggested they were now flying at five times the speed of
light. At that rate they would be at the Alpha Centauri system in months rather than years. Hackett had learned that
their speed was increasing, and the way it was going, they
might be able to reach Alpha Centauri in weeks, if they
didn't stop accelerating. He liked the sound of that, because it meant they could return to Mars quicker and he
could get on with other things.

The problem with this flight was that there wasn't
much of importance for him to do. Others had functions
that required their attention on a regular basis. There was
navigation, though the computers took care of most of it.
But someone had to make sure that no errors crept in. A
random charge of electricity could introduce a corruption
of the system, though they were supposed to be shielded
against spurious discharge.

Someone was required on the flight deck, and although
the watch could be incredibly boring, at least it gave the
person assigned there a purpose. It provided a short-term
goal and helped pass the time.

There were astronomical missions for Bakker and
Weiss—and Mitchell, though her knowledge of astronomy was not nearly as broad as that of either of the other
two. Still, there were observations to be made and results
to be recorded, which ranged from the mundane noting of
instrument readings to trying to decipher the images on
the screens as the ship increased its speed to multiples of
light.

Hackett had the assignment of ship's command, which
meant he made decisions when necessary. The problem
was that a flight plan had been created for the trip to Alpha
Centauri, with a possible side trip to one of the generation
ships, if they could locate one. The plan reduced the need
for creativity and left little opportunity for command decisions.

So Hackett read books that had been put on disk and
could be accessed through any of the ship's computers.
Thousands of books were available, because so much
printed data could be crammed onto the disks, and they
weighed almost nothing and took up very little space.

And there was visual entertainment, from the latest in
movies and television programs, to the classics like *King
Kong, Gone with the Wind,* and *Titanic.* There were also
technical materials that Hackett could review to improve
his knowledge of his job, of any job on the station, or of
any job he might want to consider. In other words, there
was plenty for him to do, just nothing that was required of
him. He could sit in his private cabin, in the nude and wor-
ship the devil if he wanted to. He wasn't needed for the
everyday functioning of the ship.

Hackett sat in his cabin, watching the flat-screen and
wondering what the silver dots jammed into one corner
really were. There was nothing that he recognized outside

the station, but that wasn't unusual for him. He was often surprised and confused by the real-time displays that didn't compensate for the forward motion of the ship.

Bakker tapped at the door and looked in. "You doing anything important?"

"I'm never doing anything important. Why?"

"Believe it or not, I think we've found one of the generation ships."

"Which one?"

"Don't know. What I do know is that it's more or less on our flight path, so we can intercept it if you really want to do that."

Hackett waved her into his cabin. When she was inside, he said, "Shut the hatch."

She smiled. "I don't have time for this."

"This being?" he asked.

Taken slightly aback by his question, Bakker said, "Well, you know."

"No. I have a legitimate question for you, and I didn't want to be interrupted while we discussed it. Did you have something else in mind?"

Now Bakker grinned. "Okay. You win. I did have something else on my mind, but there really isn't time for any of that right now. Especially if you want to survey the generation ship."

"How far away are we?"

"At present speed, maybe four days. We have to be careful or we're going to overshoot."

"So what do I have to do now?"

"Tell us to slow down and to divert, or we'll just continue on to Alpha Centauri."

Hackett, who suddenly found himself engaged rather than bored, pushed himself out of his chair and said, "Let's go take a look at what we have."

Bakker pointed to the flat-screen and said, "We can do it right here."

"Yes, but why? Sometimes it's just more fun to do

these things outside of a room. Get out. Talk to the people. Have a little personal contact, rather than see everyone on a flat-screen."

Bakker shrugged and gestured toward the hatch. "Whatever you say. You're the boss."

They left his cabin and walked down a short corridor and out into the large central meeting area. They crossed it and stepped up onto the flight deck. Sally Wilson was there, watching the instruments, sensors, and flat-screens, and reading the input from a half dozen computers.

"Hey," she said. "Glad for some company."

Hackett said, "I understand that we've spotted one of the generation ships."

"Sure have. You want to see it?"

Hackett glanced at one of the flat-screens and saw only the same spotty blackness with a group of silver dots in one corner as he had seen on the screen in his room. "I don't see anything."

Wilson reached up and pulled a keyboard close. She typed quickly, and the view changed. "I've compensated for our speed. The computer has redrawn the picture."

Hackett looked at Bakker. "How come we don't just do that all the time?"

"I suppose we could," said Bakker, "but it's not really an accurate representation of what's out there. It's a false picture."

"Yeah, but it's one that I can understand."

"Then we'll set a couple of the screens for this representation, but remember, it really is a computer construct that is flawed," said Bakker. But even as she made the argument, she knew it was lame. They simply hadn't compensated for their speed, because no one really cared. They had been more interested in the effects of the relativistic speeds on the flat-screens and the cameras outside. They hadn't thought in terms of changing the parameters so they had a more recognizable view.

Wilson pointed to a light near the top of the screen. "That would be the generation ship," she said.

"Is this the best image we have?"

"We have no image right now. It's too far away for our cameras and it's not radiating much in the way of light. That's a computer-generated image."

"See what I mean," said Bakker.

Hackett laughed. "Yes, but I like this display."

"We're about four days out," said Wilson, unaware that Bakker had already said that. "As we get closer, the cameras will be able to pick up some detail, but I think, until we drop out of light speed, we're not going to get a good look at this thing."

"Well," said Hackett, "at least we have a mission that won't take weeks or months to complete."

Wilson laughed. "This is going to scare the hell out of them. You just wait."

[2]

DOUGLAS WAS ON THE FLIGHT DECK, STANDING directly behind Wilson. He had his eyes focused, not on the screen that had been computer adjusted so that it showed the generation ship, but on those that showed the real view from outside the station. He wasn't sure what he was seeing there, other than a great black spot in the center of the screen.

"We're at about light speed," said Wilson, "and slowing rapidly. We should drop below light speed in about an hour or so. We'll be within about a hundred thousand miles of the generation ship."

Douglas looked around and saw Hackett standing in the rear, away from the controls and instruments. He looked for all the world like an observer—a somewhat bored observer, who didn't understand everything he was seeing.

"I would like to register my protest one last time," said Douglas. "I don't like this."

"I am aware of your concerns, but, if we fail to again achieve light speed, we will have an alternative. We can join the crew of the generation ship," Hackett said, with an edge to his voice.

Douglas took a deep breath. "Of course. We'll continue to decelerate."

Hackett noticed that the silver blobs in the corner of the screen were beginning to push their way up and out, changing colors and starting to look like real stars.

Wilson said, "We should be close to them very soon. We're just above light speed."

Douglas said, "They probably haven't spotted us yet. They're going to think we're aliens when they see us."

"We'll be able to communicate with them," said Hackett. "They'll know who we are."

Bakker stepped up onto the flight deck. "Is it too crowded here?"

Hackett said, "No."

Douglas looked back, smiled, and said, "No reason for you not to be here. Is everyone coming up?"

"Just pipe what we're doing through the computer network so those not here can watch. They'll stay in their cabins or at their work stations."

"Not like the old days," said Hackett, "when you had to belt yourself in because of the gravitational forces."

"We'll probably have to maneuver using the chemical rockets," said Douglas, "but I don't think we'll create much of a problem with that."

"We can stand here and watch," said Hackett.

"You can stand there and watch, but if we do get into some violent maneuvers, you'll probably be safer sitting down and strapped in somewhere."

"This is not what I expected," said Hackett.

"What did you expect?"

"Science fiction movies gave me a distorted view of

faster-than-light travel," he said. "They didn't know what they were talking about, but it looked like they did."

"We are about to drop below light speed," said Wilson. "We are about a hundred thousand miles from the ship."

Hackett started to ask them to tell him when they fell below light speed, but he saw it happen. He was looking at one of the flat-screens, and all of the sudden, the star fields shifted and the colors returned to normal. In the center of the screen was the shape of the generation ship, a gigantic craft that looked as if it was surrounded by satellite pods. Hackett knew those were the specialization facilities, the engines, and the agricultural areas. There were ten thousand people living on the ship.

"I don't think they've seen us yet," said Wilson.

Douglas turned to look at the ship. It had a few lights scattered around the perimeter, but those were set so that the crew could orient themselves to the space around them. They had no function beyond that. As far as the ship's residents knew, there was only one other space-faring race, and they had only come into this section of the galaxy once.

"What do you want to do?" asked Douglas.

"Continue to approach." Hackett hesitated and then asked, "Aren't we running up on them awfully fast?"

"We've dropped down below light speed and are traveling only on the reaction engines now. It'll be more than an hour before we get too close," said Wilson.

"Let's try to make radio contact," said Hackett.

Wilson reached over, touched a keyboard, and then sat back, looking at one of the flat-screens. She said, "Generation ship, this is . . ." She looked back at Hackett and said, "They're not going to understand our designation."

"Just say you' re a United States ship traveling in this sector and wait for a reply."

Wilson turned her attention to the screen and began the call again. When she finished, she sat back and waited. It didn't take very long.

"United States ship, please identify yourself." The screen remained dark. They were only using the radio and not the television.

Hackett laughed. "I thought we had done that. Okay. Tell them that we have left Mars orbit with a mission to Alpha Centauri . . . no, tell them we're on a survey mission, Colonel Thomas Hackett in command. Someone in the command authority should recognize my name. I met nearly all of them.

Wilson repeated the information. A moment later the screen brightened, and she saw two men and a woman seated in a control room that didn't look all that much different than the one she was in. She said, simply, "Good morning to you all."

The people all looked grim. One of the men leaned forward and asked, "Have we lost the war?"

"War?" said Wilson. "What war was that?"

"We just assumed that war would break out between the Earth and the alien creatures. It was why we needed to get out of the Solar System."

[3]

REGINALD CAWLEY WAS A DISTINGUISHED LOOK-ing man who often said he had been born in England about five hundred years too late. He would have made a fine lord of the manor. When the concept of the generation ships had been publicly announced, he realized that he might have been born twenty years too early. His destiny, he believed, was on a generation ship. It was the closest thing to being lord of the manor.

Had they been on Earth and had it been five hundred years earlier, Cawley would have dressed in fine, if somewhat foppish clothes, would have had long and perfumed hair, and would have been somewhat on the pudgy, if not fat, side. On the generation ship, Cawley was dressed like everyone else, in coveralls, was lean, and had his salt and pepper hair cut very short.

Now he stood, in the command pod of the ship, surrounded by the others he thought of privately as his knights, staring at the flat-screen and wondering about the ship that had just seemed to drop out of nowhere.

When the crew had first detected it and summoned Cawley to the flight pod, there had been great concern. They had never seen anything like it, and they assumed, given its sudden and abrupt appearance, that it had to be alien, and although they had weapons on board, they would be no match for a military vessel. For one thing, they couldn't maneuver without a great deal of stress to the structure. It was built for straight flight and not the sudden and radically maneuvers required by combat ships.

Cawley had decided not to alert the general population of the ship, just as the lord of the manor might elect not to tell the peasants that an invading army was forming outside the castle walls. He knew that his peasants would learn about the ship quickly, because all the various information systems were tied together, just as the feudal peasants would learn of the invaders as they appeared on the horizon, but he could work, for a while, without having to answer their questions.

They watched the alien craft for several minutes. One of his knights said, "I think they were traveling faster than light. That's why we didn't see them earlier. That's why we couldn't detect them."

Cawley nodded but wasn't sure what to say. He did know that the only space-faring race they'd ever detected, other than those mentioned in the UFO literature, had been, at best benign. They hadn't been interested enough in the human race to do much more than slow down, take a look, and return to their previous course of travel.

Cawley hadn't been scared. *Concerned* was the better word for it. He had been concerned and was wondering what to do when the navigation officer, a young woman with long, dark hair and a surprising amount of body fat, given the restricted diets they all had to eat, said, "There is some kind of signal."

"Let's see it."

She pointed at the screen, and in a moment a human face appeared announcing they were a United States ship. Cawley felt the relief flow through him as he physically relaxed. It was in that moment that he realized he had been frightened. More frightened than he wanted to admit.

With that established, Cawley took center stage and asked, "What might we do for you?"

"We'd just like to dock with you for a few hours and then we'll be on our way."

Cawley said, "Resupply?"

"No."

Cawley looked at the screen, finding that response to be wholly inadequate. He said, "This is a sealed system, and the introduction of new people might upset our delicate balance. It is a battle that we fight constantly."

There was silence from the other ship, which told Cawley, they hadn't thought about that. He doubted that the introduction of several people for a few hours would harm the delicate balance. A little more oxygen used than normal, a little more carbon dioxide emitted into the system, but nothing that would destroy the balance. In a couple of hours, a day or two at most, the system would be returned to where it was. Cawley was just throwing stones for no other reason than he could.

"We would limit our stay and bring in no more than three people."

Cawley had to fight not to grin. He hesitated for several seconds, then said, "We are not equipped to receive outside craft."

"We can dock with your shuttle bay. We have a small craft that can cross the space."

"When might we expect you?"

"In two hours, if that is convenient."

"We'll meet you in the shuttle bay," said Cawley.

The communication terminated at that point. The navigation officer looked up at Cawley and asked, "Why didn't you ask them a few questions?"

"Like what?"

"How are things at home. Do you know any more about those aliens? Is everyone still safe?"

"I suppose I didn't bother because they'll be here in a couple of hours. Everything we want to know, we can ask them then. Just seemed inconvenient now."

"We're going to have to make an announcement to the population," said one of the other men, Randy Wagner. He was young and had just joined the command staff. Had his father not been important, Wagner would never have made it.

"No," said Cawley. "We'll see what develops, but as of now we don't make an announcement."

"You sure?"

"Yes. People will desert their jobs, and production will be disrupted. We'll see what these people have to say and then decide if we should let the population know."

"That could be a bad decision," said Wagner.

"But it's mine to make, and until I say different, that's the way it's going to be."

"Yes, sir."

[4]

FOR SOME REASON, AS THEY STEPPED OFF THE small shuttle they had used to cross from the station to the generation ship, Hackett felt as if they were now on a planet. Compared with their own station, the generation ship was massive, but it was still a ship. Granted, the interior of the generation ship looked like a gigantic park, and it was more like living in a dome on Mars than it was traveling on a ship, but the point was, they were on a ship. There wasn't a solar system nearby. Their home was traveling through space at sublight speeds.

But Hackett, more than the others, felt as if they had left a ship and had landed on a planet. He felt the pull of artificial gravity, tasted an air that didn't seem to have the metallic flavor of the recycled oxygen on the station, and he could look out into the central parks that were so vast that he couldn't see across them. He felt as if he had escaped the confinement of a spaceship, and he thought seriously about joining the generation ship crew.

Bakker stretched, as if she had been sitting in a small craft for several hours, though the trip from the station to the ship had lasted less than half an hour. She walked toward the hatch and then turned to watch as the shuttle bay doors were closed. For some reason, she found that to be fascinating.

Sally Wilson and Steven Weiss had also come along. Wilson had the piloting duties, and Hackett liked the idea of jerking Weiss around. After all the trouble Weiss had caused, it seemed only right to cause him a little in return.

A tall, slender man came from the control room at the far end of the hangar deck. As he got close, he raised a hand and said, in a hail and hearty voice, "I'm Reginald Cawley. I'm considered the leader here."

"You mean the mayor?" asked Hackett.

"Sort of mayor cum captain," he said. "Welcome to our city."

"Is that how you think of it?" asked Bakker.

Cawley looked from face to face. Hackett understood and introduced the people in his party to Cawley. He then said, "We thought we'd take a few hours and see how things are going."

Cawley said, "You've come from Mars?"

"Yes," said Hackett. "We've been traveling for a while now with a final destination . . . well, a distant destination." For some reason he didn't want to tell them that he was on his way to Alpha Centauri. There was no reason not to tell them, other than normal security protocol, but the circumstances seemed to trump that. Cawley and his people could do nothing with the information, even if they wanted to. Still, Hackett felt better for not having shared their destination.

Cawley didn't seem to notice that Hackett had not told him the destination. Instead, he waved a hand toward one of the bulkheads and said, "Let's find some more comfortable surroundings. Will you be dining with us?"

Hackett hadn't thought about that and wondered what it might do to the balance of the system. They would be taking food out of the system, as they would any water that they might drink. Of course they could replace some of those elements. He grinned as he realized the value of what they could leave behind.

Bakker said, answering for Hackett, "I think it would be delightful to dine here."

"Our schedule is somewhat flexible," said Hackett. "I'm sure that we can make some time."

"Well, come along," said Cawley. "Let me show you our home."

[5]

THEY WERE IN ONE OF THE DINING HALLS ON the generation ship and, Hackett suspected that it had been modified from the generic dining halls as they had been planned. First, it was somewhat smaller, giving it a more intimate atmosphere. And the kitchen was hidden behind a new wall, so that those eating didn't have the unpleasant view of the food being prepared.

They talked about the alien ship, which hadn't reappeared. They talked about the home of the aliens, which had been learned after the generation ship had departed. They talked about the news from home, which was getting more and more difficult for the ship to obtain as the distance between it and the Solar System increased. The signals were never meant to cross interstellar distances and were weakened by that distance and everything else in space. The crew of the generation ship lucked into reception once in a while, but it was like trying to listen to a distant radio station during a thunderstorm on Earth. Too much interference.

They sat around the table after the meal was finished and drank coffee. They were talking as if they were old friends who had rare opportunities to get together. Hackett just sat back and listened. He didn't feel a need to impress his personality on the discussion as some did. He was more interested in learning something than trying to prove that he was the smartest man in the room.

Cawley set his cup down and then pushed it and the saucer away. He said, "We have, of course, been keeping careful records of all consumption and find that there is virtually no leakage in this system. There has been no degradation of the oxygen content, for example. And the water, though not as sweet as that on Earth, is still drinkable. The closed system has stayed closed."

"I would have thought," said Bakker, "that the production of heat would bleed some of the energy out of the system."

"That's where engineering has stepped in. We are able to capture hydrogen from outside and bring it in. We use that to replace lost energy."

"And the plant life recycles the carbon dioxide into oxygen," said Weiss.

Now Cawley grinned. "Actually, the plants are a little too efficient. We must watch the levels of oxygen to be sure they don't become toxic."

Hackett said, "I'm impressed. How is the birthrate?"

"We are monitoring that carefully, and we are replacing our population without expanding it. This is the one point where we do have trouble. People still believe they have the right to have children."

"In a stable environment on a planet's surface," said Weiss, "I'd have to agree."

"Except," said Cawley, "we're not on a planet's surface, and those who signed up knew the rules when they did. Granted their children, and their children's children, made no such agreement, but then we all sort of accept the society into which we are born. The considerations of the society, given the nature of it here, require a little more obedience than does a more freewheeling society on a planet."

"So you've had some trouble there?" asked Hackett.

"Well," said Cawley. "I'm not sure *trouble* is the right word for it. Discussions and demonstrations, but nothing too noisy or destructive. It's the one area that causes trouble for us."

Bakker said, "It's an area that always has caused trouble because of the human psyche. To reproduce provides, in one sense, immortality."

Hackett had turned off the discussion. It was becoming too philosophical for him. Instead he was concentrating on the earlier discussion. Someone had said something that raised a red flag. He felt it when it was said, but didn't know why. Something was wrong, but he didn't know what.

The conversation continued on until Hackett looked at his watch and said, "We need to return to the station."

No one made a real move to get up. Cawley looked from face to face and asked, "Can we expect another visit?"

"From us?" asked Hackett. "No." He was about to tell him not to expect anyone else either and then thought better of it. Faster-than-light drive had changed everything.

Finally Cawley stood up. He held out a hand and said, "It was nice of you to drop in." He grinned broadly. "It was, quite literally, the last thing that I expected."

"And it was good to see how successful the generation ships have been."

"If you get back this way," said Cawley, "please stop in to see us."

"If I do and I can, I will," said Hackett.

As he shook Cawley's hand, he tried to remember what had been said that bothered him. Something earlier, but the harder he tried, the farther it was pressed back. He'd have to give up, or he would never figure it out.

CHAPTER 14

[1]

AFTER WEEKS OF TRAVELING AT NEARLY TEN times the speed of light, as they calculated it, with no visible side effects, they were nearing Alpha Centauri. The glow of stars that had clustered near the bottom of one of the screens had changed as they neared Alpha Centauri. There were three large spots among all the smaller, silver dots. These had some color to them and seemed about to dominate the screen.

Hackett was sitting in his cabin looking at the display, as he often did, and wished he could understand it better. He then touched the keyboard and a moment later the display changed, filling the screen with stars, the center of it dominated by the Alpha Centauri triple star system. He thought he could see smaller bodies in orbit around one of the stars, but he didn't know what they were.

Bakker, who had been sleeping, rolled over and opened her eyes. "Good morning."

Hackett nodded and said, "I thought a triple star couldn't have a planet. Something about the orbital dynamics or tidal forces created by the stars keeping the planets from forming or something like that."

"Yes, I slept just fine thank you. And no, I don't want to go for breakfast right this minute."

"Sorry," said Hackett. He tapped the screen. "This looks like a planet to me. I didn't think we'd find any planets here."

"The orbital dynamics, as you say, would normally be expected to throw a planet through gravitational forces that would destroy it. But, there are ways for it to happen. And if this is not a true triple star system but a double star with a nearby companion, then the orbital mechanics are changed."

Hackett grinned. "So there could be planets, especially since there seems to be one."

"Or the remains of a star that has burned out," said Bakker. "That's a fairly large body, and it's fairly dense."

"Is this what you expected?" asked Hackett. "I mean, given the observational information from Earth."

"Well, Alpha Centauri isn't really all that interesting, from my point of view. Its proximity to Earth, being our closest celestial neighbor, makes it interesting, but it's a fairly typical star with a companion and a couple of large planets."

"Nothing suitable for us," said Hackett.

"Not really. We're here because it's the closest."

Hackett interrupted. "Yes. A good test for our capabilities. Our first trial, but frankly, I can think of a couple of other places that might have been more interesting."

"And, at least twice the distance," said Bakker.

"Well, there is that."

Bakker said, "We'll be dropping out of light drive in a little while. We'll be able to get a better look at this system then."

"How long do you want to explore this thing?" asked Hackett. "That really is up to you."

"We can gather enough data to keep researchers busy

for decades by just recording everything we can. If we stay to make a few observations, we would be able to develop an exploration plan that could keep everyone busy for the next century. This will be the first time we have actually visited a place outside the Solar System that we have only been able to observe. One of the things we can do is learn how good our long-range observations are."

"So we'll orbit out here for a while, and you can make your observations."

"What about going in closer?"

"Depends. We start flying around inside a planetary system, there is a bigger possibility that we'll hit something, and even if we can survive that, it might damage something, making it impossible to get back home."

"Do you think anything like that will happen?" she asked.

"No, but why should we tempt the fates?"

Bakker shrugged. "It's going to be an hour or so before I can begin any useful observation, and I don't have anything to do."

"And you want me to fill your time so you won't be completely bored?"

"That thought had crossed my mind. Besides, once we start observations, I don't know when I'll find myself with any more free time."

"Well, then," said Hackett, "we'd better think of something for you to do."

[2]

THEY HAD SLOWED TO NEARLY A STOP, RELA-tive to Alpha Centauri, which meant they were in orbit around the star, holding a position that was nearly constant. They were far from Alpha Centauri, it looking somewhat smaller than the sun looked from Mars. They had a good view of the system, including Alpha Centauri's companion and the four planets, all of them larger than Jupiter, which they had discovered in orbit.

Bakker was sitting near one of the flat-screens, a keyboard near her fingers. She was taking in what the cameras were showing her, making random notes, and keying those observations to time codes, so that everyone could later understand what she was seeing and when she was seeing it.

Hackett sat back, out of eyesight, watching her work and watching the scenes that were being played out in front of him. He wasn't overly fascinated by the star system, thinking of it as a rather poor solar system. Four planets, but two suns, scattered debris that looked like the remnants of other planets that had been pulled apart by gravity, and a distant, third sun that was larger and brighter than Venus, but that was not actually part of the system. Or, maybe it was, because it would affect this system, even if it was not technically part of it.

Bakker said, "Well, I can tell you one thing. This doesn't look like a planetary system that is predicted by any of the laws we've designed, but then, there are too many stars too close together."

"Life anywhere around?" asked Hackett.

"Not as we know it. None of the planets are in what we think of as the biosphere. They'd either be too hot or too cold, and I don't think any of them have any liquid water."

"The whole system is lifeless, then?" asked Hackett.

"I would say so."

"Any chance on the moons?"

"Well, I haven't surveyed the ones we can see yet," said Bakker, "but I really doubt it. They'll suffer from the same problems as the planets, though the surface gravity would be less. Still, they're all outside the biosphere."

"Maybe we should have picked a better destination," said Hackett.

Bakker turned and looked at him. "Why? You know something that you haven't shared with the rest of us?"

"No. It just seems that it's a waste of time coming here. If there was a planet suitable for life, we could alert that generation ship, and they could get here faster than anywhere else in the galaxy."

"Is there a hurry?"

Hackett shook his head. "I suppose not. The ship is functioning as it should, and they're not about to run out of food, water, air, or energy. It just seems sad that so many people will be born and die on a ship without ever knowing the joy of living on a planet's surface."

"Before we learned to drive and fly, most people lived and died almost within sight of their homes. To travel more than twenty-five miles was radical. Those people will know a closed, safe environment, not one filled with disease, foul weather, earthquakes, or other natural disasters. They'll have a good life. One that is better than thousands that came before them. Better than most who remain on Earth."

"Okay," said Hackett, "you made your point."

Bakker turned her attention back to the flat-screen. "This is really fascinating stuff."

But Hackett just couldn't get into it. He had made the discovery, just as Columbus had made the discovery of the New World. He was in command of the expedition, but he didn't understand the astronomy. Bakker would write the papers and publish the findings. In the end, his name would be in a footnote as the commander, but Bakker would shine because she was doing the real work.

And, they hadn't actually "discovered" the system, because they had known it was here all along. They were just the first humans to visit it. That added another footnote in the history books.

Hackett grinned to himself and wondered why he was suddenly so sad. His place in history was made. While he might only be a footnote, the real point was that he *was* a footnote, and there were billions who had come and gone without making a ripple. He wasn't sure why having his name recorded was important, but at that moment he knew that it was.

"Got a comet," said Bakker.

"Coming at us?"

"Nope. Falling in toward Alpha Centauri. Looks like a big one and seems to be operating the same way they do in our Solar System. Long tail."

"Is that important?"

Bakker turned and looked at Hackett. "Important? Do you know what comets are? Big dirty snowballs. There's a theory that most of Earth's water came from comets. So, if Alpha Centauri has comets, and they are equivalent to what we have at home, then we have a source of water. Frozen water, but water nonetheless."

"Life?" asked Hackett.

"Microbes frozen inside, maybe, but probably not. Still, makes this system important because a ship traveling in this sector could stop off here for water if they needed it." Now she grinned broadly. "An oasis in the desert."

Hackett thought about that and realized that as they began to seriously travel interstellar distances, there were going to be times when resupply would be necessary. Accidents, mistakes, and poor planning would create problems, but if they knew where to resupply or find what they needed, interstellar flight would become a little safer. Mapping was important.

"How long are you going to need to finish your research?" asked Hackett.

Bakker, who had turned back to study the flat-screen, shrugged. She looked at Hackett. "The more time the better. I mean we are here now, we have the resources we need for the exploration. There is no pressing need to head back to Mars, as far as I can see."

"Other than I'm damned tired of living on this ship."

Bakker focused her attention on Hackett. "What's going on here? Living on this ship isn't that much of a burden. We have some privacy, the food, while not diverse, is certainly palatable. The quarters are comfortable, and as far as I know, you have no girlfriend on Mars waiting for you, so what's wrong?"

Hackett said, "I just don't like living on this ship for a year or two. No matter what you say, it's still a ship."

"Yes?"

"I want to get out of it. Walk around. Go somewhere that isn't simply another part of the ship."

"You're claustrophobic," she said almost triumphantly.

"Somewhat," said Hackett.

"I can understand that, but is it going to influence your decision about staying here?"

"I will bow to your advice and others' about what information of a scientific value you can recover. When we reach a point where we've gotten so much that we're just refining the details, we go home. Keeping in mind that we do have limited resources on the station."

Bakker said, "With all cameras and sensors recording, we've gathered enough raw data that we could go home now. If we stay, we can refine that data, and by reviewing some of it, we can think of questions to be answered now. At home those questions might be a little harder to answer."

"Would any of this information be vital?"

"I doubt it. I think we can deduce from what we have all that we'd need." She smiled again. "Besides, with faster-than-light drive, we can get back here in weeks to make additional observations, if needed."

"So we can go home now."

"Yes, but I'd like to stay. The thought that comes to my mind is if you can be bribed?"

Hackett looked at her. "Bribed?"

"To stay a while. Let us study the system for a couple

of weeks before we leave. What would it take for you to make such a decision?"

Hackett understood that they were no longer talking about science. They had moved into a new arena. He leaned back against the bulkhead and folded his arms.

"What do you have in mind?" he asked.

"Well, I can think of a lot of things, now that you express an interest. Money, for example," she said somewhat innocently.

"Money does me no good out here. Nothing to buy and nothing to do with it except play poker, and then only for scorekeeping, because, again, there is nothing to buy."

"Well, how about food? Specially prepared food rather than the same old rations."

"And who would be cooking this food? Don't forget, I know you. Cooking is not one of your strengths."

"Okay, food is out. Any special knowledge you desire?" she asked, an evil smile forming on her lips. "I know a lot of things."

Hackett stared at her as she added, "A lot of things. Some of them I have never mentioned to you."

"There might be some special knowledge that would interest me way out here," said Hackett. "What precisely did you have in mind?"

She reached up for the zipper of her coverall and pulled it slowly down, until the garment was open to her belly button. "I have a few things in mind."

"I hate myself for saying this, but won't this interrupt your work?"

"I'm at a good stopping place right now."

Hackett laughed. "I don't think so."

[3]

THE WARNING BELL CAUGHT HACKETT IN THE middle of a dream that was taking place on Earth, on a beach, and that was filled with young, beautiful women, tan, fit men, and some kind of game that he didn't quite understand. Then he realized that it wasn't an alarm clock ringing, but an alarm bell. He tossed off the covers with his right hand and tried to sit up. His left arm was caught beneath Bakker and somehow entangled in the bed webbing. She moaned in displeasure, rolled to her left, and then sat up abruptly.

"What's that?"

"Alarm. We'd better get dressed."

Hackett pushed himself toward the foot of the bed and climbed out to stand on the deck. He found his coveralls and donned them quickly.

The lights in his cabin came on then, and he watched as Bakker worked her way out of the bed webbing and stood, naked, on the deck. She said, "I'm cold."

"Me too."

She found her clothes and put them on quickly. As she finished zipping up the coveralls, Hackett stepped to the flat-screen and touched a button. He saw Douglas's face staring back at him, looking only slightly nervous and more than a little tired.

"What do you have?"

"Unidentified object nearing us," he said. "I think it's natural, but it isn't like anything I've seen before. Do you know where Bakker is?"

"She's here with me," said Hackett.

Bakker stepped behind him and looked at the screen. "Show me what you have," she said.

The scene changed from Douglas seeming to lean into the camera to a view outside the station. On the screen was an oblong object that was barely visible in the light provided by Alpha Centauri. It seemed to be rotating on its axis.

"It's heading more or less toward us, but if it doesn't alter its course, it will miss us by a couple thousand miles. We can alter our course to miss it as well."

"How fast is it traveling?" asked Hackett.

"About half our speed. It did come out of the system, though I'm not sure that's relevant."

Bakker moved forward and bent down. She asked, "Can we get a better look at this?"

The image on the screen disappeared and then began to reappear, starting at the top. In a couple of seconds they had a closer view of the object.

"Looks like an asteroid," said Bakker, "but I would expect it to be spinning faster."

She sat down and began to use the keyboard, calling up all the information available. She compared the object to everything in the library, but nothing matched it exactly, because it was something from a different system.

To Hackett, she said, "I think it's an asteroid but its composition doesn't match those of the asteroids in our system. I wouldn't really expect it to. It's close enough that I think it's natural."

"But coming at us," said Hackett.

"Well, more or less, but I don't think it's a threat. You know, we could put a shuttle out and land on it. See for ourselves."

"Is that necessary?"

"No. Just a thought. I mean, if there are intelligent creatures in this system, they could be meeting us at the edge of their system, just as we did that first group of aliens."

"We made it clear that we were there," said Hackett, "by using our radio, infrared, and anything else we could think of."

"So they wanted to sneak up on us to take a look," said Bakker. "I will tell you this, if they had interstellar capabilities, we'd have seen them already. I mean, this is the first place we came. We could expect them to look at us as one of their first missions."

"Assuming that there is anyone on that thing."

"Assuming that, of course."

[4]

HACKETT HAD MOVED TO THE FLIGHT DECK, where he could watch the object on the big screen. Bakker had gone to the science center, where she could use the equipment to study the object. It hadn't changed course, and neither had they. Each side seemed to be watching the other, waiting for them to make the first move.

Hackett, although a military officer, was also a scientist. He wanted to gather information before he acted, but the information he had was bare bones, and he couldn't make a decision without more data.

Bakker finally pushed herself away from the sensor array and left the center. She walked slowly toward the flight deck. When she reached it, she looked in and said, "It's natural. There are no indications that it is under intelligent control."

Hackett, who was still watching the slowly rotating object said, "You're sure?"

"It has not maneuvered. Its path is predictable. There are no indications of a power source, and there is no heat signature. That suggests that it is just a naturally occurring object."

"We don't know everything about all alien life forms. We have little in the way of a baseline."

"True," said Bakker, "but we do know this. First, based on human life, we had to draw a few conclusions. For example, that a certain amount of heat would be expected. If there was life on that object, it would radiate some heat, just as we are radiating heat. Even the alien ship that we intercepted in the Oort Cloud had a heat signature."

"Okay," said Hackett. "Does that mean we're done here? We can go?"

Bakker said, "There are no indications of intelligent life anywhere in this system. If there was, I think we could have discovered it. We can expect certain things from life, and none of them are here."

"You've finished your survey?" asked Hackett.

"Of the object?"

"That first."

"Yes. It appears to be an asteroid. The composition is slightly different than those at home, but as I said, I would expect that. I mean, there is very little iridium on Earth. What we find can be traced back to an extraterrestrial source. The composition of meteorites doesn't match exactly the composition of rocks found on Earth. There are differences, so I'm not surprised by what I see here."

"Okay."

"And no, I haven't finished the survey of this system, but then, I could never finish it. We are the first people to enter this system. There is so much to learn, and we've spent so little time here."

Hackett laughed. "But you do want to go back home, don't you?"

"Of course," she said. "And soon."

"What's a realistic time frame?"

Bakker leaned back and locked her fingers behind her head. She focused on one of the screens, but wasn't really looking at it. Finally she said, "I think we've gotten everything that we need to begin our work. Give me a day or so to review, but I think we can go any time you're ready."

"Thanks."

Hackett left the science center and began a slow stroll through the station. He found Weiss sitting with Mitchell. They were both studying the asteroid, but they seemed to have lost some of their intensity, now that they believed it to be something natural and not artificial.

He didn't want to disturb them, but they didn't seem to be all that busy. He dropped into a vacant chair and said, "How goes your studies?"

"I don't follow," said Weiss.

"Is there anything you are doing here that would require us to remain in this system any longer?"

Weiss sat quietly for a moment and then broke into a large grin, understanding the question. "No. I have everything I need. I've been running the recorders nonstop since we dropped out of light speed. I have enough data that it will take years, maybe more to fully comprehend."

Mitchell said, "We have so much now that I don't know how we're ever going to wade through it."

Hackett almost said something about who he suspected was her real boss, Barnett, but bit the remark off. Barnett should now be in jail, and Mitchell was working with them, not Barnett. Instead, he asked, "Has she been of help to you?"

"More than I could have guessed. Her knowledge of astronomy is amazing, and she has provided some interesting insights into what I'm trying to do."

Hackett nodded and stood up. He continued his task, surveying those on the station. He learned the same thing from all of them. They had gathered more data than they could ever hope to review themselves. What they had would take years to fully appreciate, and there had been nothing observed that was of such a difference, or so unexpected that it warranted their remaining in the Alpha Centauri system.

He also noted that everyone wanted to go home. They had been gone a long time, and they had been under a great deal of stress during the flight. No one knew exactly what long-term effects faster-than-light travel might have on them. No one knew how well the generating equipment would hold up. No one knew whether they could survive a failure, and if they did, whether they would be able to repair the equipment so they could get home. There was too much danger and too little in the way of safety, so, the idea of going home made it feel as if a burden had been lifted.

Once he had gathered all his data, Hackett sat in his cabin, knowing that Bakker was still watching that asteroid, and made his decision. It was a relatively easy one to make, and once he made it, he pushed a button, used his keyboard, and announced throughout the station, "In twenty-four hours, we are going to head for home. If that is going to inconvenience or adversely affect any studies under way, let me know now. Otherwise, tomorrow at this time, we're going home."

CHAPTER 15

[1]

HACKETT WAS STANDING ON THE FLIGHT DECK,
when Douglas initiated the sequence to move them back
into faster-than-light drive. He watched as Douglas
worked over the controls, and having been conditioned by
years of movies, disks, videos, and television, expected
that engines would roar and that the stars would suddenly
turn into streaks of light as they flashed by. Instead there
was no noticeable change, other than that the view beyond
the ship began to shift. Some of the lag was the result of
computers that couldn't process the incoming information
fast enough to create accurate displays.

There was no real way to know that they had passed
into faster-than-light drive, other than what the sensors,
computers, and flat-screens told them. Hackett wasn't
precisely sure when they had made the transition. Nothing
on the station changed, at least from his perspective inside.

Douglas turned and looked up at him. "That's it. We're
on our way home."

"How fast?"

Now Douglas grinned. "How fast would you like to go?"

"How fast can you go?"

"That I don't know. We haven't really attempted to top it out."

"Then punch it up to ten times the speed of light."

Douglas turned back to the console and pulled a keyboard close. He typed briefly, then said, "It'll take us a little while to reach that speed."

"Let's then increase it in increments of five until we're up to thirty times. I don't want to push it much beyond that."

"That'll get us home in very short order."

Hackett nodded. "That's what I'd like to do."

"Of course, we're outrunning our sensor arrays at that speed. Hell, we're outrunning that at two times the speed of light, so I guess it doesn't make that much difference."

"There's a lot of crap in space. How come we're not hitting any of it?"

"I've thought about that," said Douglas, "and this is my wild ass guess. We generate a field that allows us to move through space faster than light. This field pulls the station with it. I think that anything that nears us is pulled into the field, regardless of the direction it originates from. So, anything that presents a danger to us is dragged along with us, caught in our slipstream, so to speak."

Hackett shrugged. "Makes sense to me. How big an object can we drag with us?"

"Anything that could destroy us, that is big enough to resist the field, is easily visible to us, and we can avoid it. No, that's not quite right. Anything that big would be known to us, and we could avoid it. Once we get close to the Solar System, we'll need to slow down, because of the Oort Cloud and the Kuiper Belt, which have comets and debris in them that could destroy us, but we know where they are, so we can avoid them."

"So you're saying that out here, in empty space, we're in no danger of colliding with anything."

"Space is not empty . . . well, for our purposes, I guess it is. Anything that is a threat would be dragged along with the field, and anything else would be so big we'd know about it."

Hackett wasn't all that comfortable with what Douglas was saying. How many airplanes had flown into mountains. They were big enough that the pilots should have known about them, but circumstances changed the equation. Still, they should be relatively safe from anything large.

"Could we drop out of faster-than-light and look around once in a while?"

"Sure. Might make some sense because no one has traveled this far from the Solar System before. We could begin the mapping of space around us."

Hackett smiled, but he wasn't confident. For some reason, he was suddenly concerned with space debris, though no one had given it much thought before this.

He said, "I suppose if we keep a good watch, then we should be relatively safe."

"Relatively," said Douglas. He turned, consulted the sensor array, and then looked at some of the instrumentation displayed on the flat-screen. He said, "We're moving at nine times the speed of light now."

Hackett said, "I don't feel a thing. I don't feel any motion at all."

He looked at one of the flat panels and saw the stars grouped down in one corner, looking like a silver mess, splatters on the screen.

"There," said Douglas. "We're at ten times."

"Hold here for a while, and then let's slowly increase the speed. If you need anything, I'll be in my cabin."

"Of course."

[2]

HACKETT WAS SITTING IN HIS CABIN, HIS FEET up and his hands locked behind his head. His eyes were focused on a flat-screen where a series of numbers paraded. He wasn't sure if he understood the significance of any of them. They were input from the flight deck, telling him that they were approaching twenty times the speed of light.

There was a tap at the hatch and Hackett said, "Come."

Bakker looked in and asked, "You real busy?"

"No. I'm trying to figure out what all those numbers mean," he said.

"They mean that we're moving at a very fast clip, and if we keep it up, we're going to be home before we know it."

"Alpha Centauri is four light years from Earth, so, at the speed of light, it takes us four years to get home. At twice the speed of light, it takes just two years."

"Yes, and at four times the speed of light we'd be home in one year. Eight times, six months, at sixteen, three months, and at thirty-two, six weeks."

"So," said Hackett, "we're motoring."

"We are moving very fast."

"You have a point?"

Bakker shook her head and said, "Not really, other than we are going to be home soon, and we have to prepare."

"Prepare for what?" asked Hackett.

"Change. We should see some change when we get there. We've been gone for a long time."

"Are you talking about time dilation?" asked Hackett.

"In a way. See, we're not traveling close to the speed of light in any conventional way. We have created a field that sort of drags us along with it, and Einstein might not apply, just as the concerns of gravity and acceleration and deceleration no longer apply. I mean, it should take us a long time to reach the speed of light, and the braking requirements should be astronomical, yet we can accelerate and decelerate on a dime. We're not dragged back by gravity or centrifugal force, but instead, I'm standing here, more or less on the deck, while the station accelerates."

"Okay," said Hackett. "I get it. We're violating the laws of physics."

"Well, I'm not sure that we are, because we are moving faster than light. We really know nothing about that, other than what we are observing here."

"Sarah, what is on your mind?"

"Just that there may be changes when we get back to the Solar System. I don't know how extensive they might be. It's just something that we should think about."

Hackett dropped his feet to the deck and said, "Okay, I'm thinking about it."

"And that's it?" asked Bakker.

"What would you have me do?"

Now she grinned. "I guess just be aware of it."

"Does our speed bother you?"

"In what sense?"

"In the sense of running into something?"

"Nope. The chances of that are really quite small," said Bakker.

"Well, if you're happy, then I'm happy," said Hackett.

"I do have one other thought," she said.

"And?"

"It would be nice to drop out of light speed for a day or two, just to shoot the stars around us. We'd be able to calculate our exact position, it would give us an interesting view of the sky from this point, and it would be a way of checking our speed calculations."

"And it wouldn't increase our trip by much," said Hackett.

"Not really. We'd also have the opportunity to check out the station to see if it suffered any adverse effects because of this high speed."

"Is that necessary?"

"Eventually we'll want to chart the galaxy. This is a necessary first step."

Hackett took a deep breath. He didn't like being in the station, breathing recycled air from someone else's lungs.

He wanted to end the trip as quickly as possible. He was beginning to wonder if he had been cut out for space travel.

Despite what flashed through his head, he said, "A day or two one way or another won't make any difference."

"And we can see if we can pick up any signals from the Solar System," said Bakker, grinning. "It might be interesting to see what sort of message we're sending."

[3]

THEY DROPPED FROM FASTER-THAN-LIGHT SPEED into normal space with no more trouble than they had getting into faster-than-light drive. There were no noticeable changes on the station as their speed slipped, other than the data recorded by the outside cameras. Space looked normal again.

Hackett sat there, thinking of down as the direction of the deck, but the station was set up so that down could, in fact, be the walls. He realized that outside of the station, there was no up or down. It was as if they had been dropped into an ocean and bounced around and there was no gravity to help them orient themselves. Up and down were based not on gravity, but on what they felt like at the moment. In relation to the plain of the ecliptic in the Solar System, they could be on their side or upside down, and it really didn't matter.

But Hackett found the thought somewhat disconcerting. He stood up and almost felt as he were falling. He grabbed at the back of the chair that was bolted to the deck. And then, cautiously, he let go. He didn't float up, didn't fall back, but just stood there.

Finally he moved toward the hatch, let it open, and stepped through. He walked in his velcro slippers, along the strip glued to the deck. There were similar strips on the bulkheads and even along what he thought of as the ceiling. They could orient themselves in the station any way they wanted.

In the main area of the station, he found Weiss, Mitchell, and Bakker. They were sitting, talking quietly. As Hackett entered, Mitchell stood and said, "I need to draw some blood."

"Again?"

"We traveled at a very high speed for two weeks. I want a sample, now that we're at a virtual standstill."

"Give me thirty minutes."

"Certainly."

He turned his attention to Bakker. He was somewhat surprised to see her there and said, "Are you getting what you need?"

"I've got several computer programs running right now," she said. "They're gathering the data. I could look out the window, so to speak, but that's not going to do me much good."

Hackett sat down on the couch. "Anything showing up?"

"Nothing unusual."

"What about radio signals from the Solar System?"

"That's a little strange. Earth has been radiating radio, hell, let's call it what it is, electromagnetic radiation, for nearly two centuries. Granted that early stuff would be nearly impossible to detect because of signal strength, and anyway, those signals would be long gone. They'd be a couple of hundred light years from here. But we should be detecting stuff from Earth and Mars. Those signals would be about two years old and should have sufficient strength, or rather some of them should, that we'd be able to hear something."

"Capabilities of our equipment?" asked Hackett.

"Well, we're not sitting on what could be considered state-of-the-art, but we've got good stuff here. On the way out, before we transitioned into faster-than-light, we were detecting stuff. When we visited the generation ship, we made some recordings of the stuff we were picking up. I just haven't had the time to get to it, because it's not that important, but it did show that we could detect the signals from far out in space."

Hackett snapped his fingers. "You know, while we were on that ship, someone said something that bothered me immensely. I just can't remember exactly what it was, or why it was important, but there was something."

"Regardless," said Bakker, "we're not getting anything from the Solar System."

"Meaning?"

"Well, we know it's still there because we can see it."

Hackett grinned. "Or see it as it was two years ago."

"Well, yes."

"Then something might have happened . . ."

"But it would have to be something so large that it would take down the capability to communicate on a planet-wide, two planet-wide, scale. If the sun went nova, for example, that would explain it" said Bakker.

"Is that possible?"

"Well, yes, but not very likely. Stars don't just blow up for no reason. We should have been able to detect signs that there was trouble, but there was nothing in the literature to suggest that. Nothing at all."

Hackett sat back and looked down at the deck. "The aliens returned?"

"You know. I've been thinking that," said Bakker. "I mean, we aren't very good at this faster-than-light travel. The aliens have been at it a lot longer. Maybe the display we made at the fringe of the Solar System scared them."

"And they invaded," finished Hackett.

"Possible." She shook her head. "No. I don't like it. There should still be electromagnetic radiation for us to detect. They wouldn't take down the communication system, and besides, the invasion would have had to happen before we left. No. That can't be it."

"But we have something," said Hackett.

"Yes. Something."

Hackett said, "Then, if you have no objection, why don't we put our observations here on hold and head home as fast as we can safely do it?"

"Tom, I don't want to create a panic here," she said. "I'm just concerned that we can't detect anything. Could be something simple. Could be a software problem, or could even be our hardware. Could even be something to do with traveling so fast for so long. I just don't know. We shouldn't panic."

"But we enter the Solar System cautiously. Maybe don't announce ourselves to the world."

"Maybe," she said. "I just don't know."

"Then it might be a very good thing that we launched those generation ships."

"Could be humanity's salvation."

[4]

THEY HAD NEVER DETECTED A PROBLEM FOR those on the station. There were no adverse effects from traveling faster than light. No genetic changes, no mutations, no new and complicated diseases. Breaking through the light barrier was no more dangerous than breaking through the sound barrier, or moving from horseback, with a speed of five or six miles an hour to a train that could travel thirty, forty, fifty miles an hour.

As they approached the Solar System, they bled off their speed, dropping from nearly thirty times the speed of light to just over one. They approached slowly, almost afraid, as returning townspeople might approach their walled city after talk of an invasion. They didn't know what they would find once they walked through the gate, but if it was bad, they needed a plan to escape.

Hackett had told them they would just turn around and try to join one of the generation ships. They would find more humans and could live out their days among their own kind. They had decided they would never tell the people the fate of Earth and the Solar System, if it was bad.

But, with weeks to develop the worst-case scenario, they had eliminated everything that would have involved a single planet. The giant asteroid that had slammed into Earth 65 million years ago had created environmental problems that took decades, if not centuries, to overcome. Such a catastrophic event would certainly have taken down Earth's civilization, but only Earth's civilization, and not that on Mars. Besides, Earth's technology should have been able to defeat an asteroid.

They knew that whatever happened had to be something big enough to take out the Solar System. It had to affect both Earth and Mars, and in reality, the outposts on the moon, in the asteroids, and those on Jupiter's moons. They could only think of two things that could do that. The sun going nova and an alien invasion.

As they approached the Solar System, they knew the sun hadn't gone nova, which suggested alien invasion. As they shed the last of their light speed and dropped into normal space, Hackett was on the flight deck. They were now in the Oort Cloud, where they hoped to avoid detection if they could. If they discovered the alien fleet, they would get out as quickly as they could.

As the cameras began to record the scene in front of them, Bakker said, "Well, the sun going nova has been ruled out."

"We're still about a light year out," said Hackett. "Could have happened a year ago."

Bakker grinned. "Not really. We know they went silent more than two years ago, so had it been the sun, it would be dark by now. Since it's not, the sun is still shining."

Hackett nodded. "Of course."

Douglas, who sat at the flight controls, such as they were, said, "So what do we do?"

"Well," said Bakker, "we'll be very difficult to spot. We're not really radiating much of anything. We'd be a big heat source, if they're using infrared, but then there are lots of heat sources to fool them. We absorb most of the light directed at us. We're not creating any disturbance in space. It's not like we set up gravity waves breaking or anything like that. So, given all that, I say that we continue forward."

"At our normal speed, it'll take years to get home," said Douglas.

Hackett, staring at the screen, looking at the sun as a very bright circle of light and the bright specks that were Jupiter and, he thought Uranus, rubbed a hand through his hair. He said, "Maybe we should take this in increments. Just into faster-than-light, drop out to look around, and then jump back."

Bakker said, "During our research, I didn't see anything to indicate that our jumping in and out of light speed sets up anything that is easily detectable. No reason not to do it."

Hackett said, "There should be something here to tell us what's happened."

Bakker, her eyes jumping from screen to screen, said, "I don't see anything. The system looks normal."

Hackett asked, "Do you have a good feel for this, Sarah, or are you just making random observations?"

"I could spend weeks looking at this stuff and not detect any change. I see nothing obvious, but then, we're still quite a ways out."

"Then let's jump in closer," said Hackett. "Maybe half a light year or so."

"How fast?" asked Douglas.

Hackett looked at Bakker. "If we move at just over faster-than-light, it'll take half a year. Two times, it takes three months, and so on, as you know. The faster we go, the faster we get home."

"They call this the Oort cloud," said Hackett.

"That they do, but it's not a very dense cloud and we can take a couple of hours to make observations along our intended path, if that'll make you feel better."

"That it would."

"Then Douglas and I will engage in mapping," said Bakker.

"Before you jump," said Hackett. "Let me know."

"Certainly."

He started to leave the flight deck, but stopped and turned back. "Do you have any idea what's going on?"

"No. I really don't," said Bakker.

[5]

THEY WERE INSIDE THE ORBIT OF PLUTO, AND as near as they could tell, inside the orbit of Neptune, still a long way from Mars and Earth, but the sun still shone, now, by far the brightest thing in the sky. Pluto, somewhere behind them, was a small, dim mass, traveling with its companion, Clarion. Without their cameras and magnification, Pluto would have been lost in the brightness of the star fields behind it. Had they looked out the window, they wouldn't have seen much of anything.

As they began to slow, dropping out of light speed, Hackett, along with Bakker, Weiss, and Mitchell, headed to the flight deck where Douglas and Wilson waited.

When Hackett approached, Douglas said, "There are spacecraft all over the place."

"What?"

Douglas pointed to one of the screens and said, "There are indications of spacecraft all over the place. I don't recognize the designs. We've detected a presence on Europa and maybe a couple other of the larger moons. I think there has been mining done in the asteroid belt. There are spacecraft all over the place."

Hackett looked at a screen but didn't see anything. "Show me," he said.

Douglass turned, pulled his keyboard close, typed, and said, "There."

Hackett leaned forward to get a better look. Centered on the screen was a small globular-shaped object. There were lights all around it, shining brightly, but these seemed to be navigation lights put there so that others could easily see the craft, rather than something put there for illumination of space. He didn't recognize either the ship or the pattern of lights.

"What can you tell me?" asked Hackett.

"It's an air breather, meaning," said Douglas, "that it has an atmosphere in it. It's warm enough for human occupation, and it is very fast. It seems to dart around. I think of a hummingbird when I watch it."

"What's it doing?"

"Chasing something in the atmosphere of Jupiter. Or rather in the upper atmosphere, but I confess that I have been unable to determine what it is."

Hackett said, "I don't recognize that ship."

Weiss leaned in and said, "I've seen some drawings, speculations, about the best design for a ship to operate inside the Solar System, but this seems to go beyond that."

"It doesn't look like the alien ship," said Bakker.

"Then whose is it?" asked Hackett. "It's way beyond anything that we've got."

"You find anything else?"

"Got something way in the distance. This one is big. Bigger than we are."

"Put it up."

The scene shifted to a point that looked as if it was somewhere inside the asteroid belt. This ship, while fat, was long, and certainly not rounded. The same pattern of lights they had seen on the ball-shaped ship repeated itself along the side of this ship. They were telling everyone where they were.

"You know, we put lights on our ships just to provide illumination for those inside. We didn't worry about traffic. All these lights suggest a high level of traffic," said Hackett.

"That would mean that there is so much traffic that they have to worry about such things," said Bakker.

Weiss looked at her and said, "Who would be looking out the window? There's better ways to see them."

Bakker just shook her head. "This is your problem, Steve. You don't think. We're looking out the window, aren't we. We saw the lights before we detected them in any other way. So, putting lights on them serves a function."

Hackett interrupted. "But whose craft are they? I've never seen anything like them."

"Got to be the invasion fleet," said Weiss.

Douglas said, "I don't know. I don't see any evidence of a battle or a conquest."

"What you getting on the radio?" asked Bakker.

"Nothing. Still nothing."

"We should be hearing something from Earth, for crying out loud," said Bakker. "They wouldn't have gone silent."

"Unless they were conquered," said Hackett. "Take away the voice, and you take away one tool of revolution."

Bakker looked at him, momentarily stunned, and then shook her head. "No. We'd see evidence of that. The enemy on patrol."

Hackett pointed at the screen. "What do you make of that? I've never seen a ship like that. Have you?"

"No, but that doesn't mean they aren't ours."

"We haven't been gone long enough for them to have developed that much."

And as he said it, he remembered what had bothered him on the generation ship. They had talked of multiple generations already. Not as an abstract in the future, but as if they had already passed. It suggested a passage of time that was longer than Bakker had predicted and meant that time dilation had reared its ugly head. They just hadn't realized what they were seeing. It wasn't a generation ship that had been flying along for fifteen or twenty years, but one that had been flying for fifty, seventy-five, or a hundred.

And Bakker, who looked at him, saw in his eyes what he was thinking and realized it, too. They hadn't been thinking about it, because it was an abstract. Einstein had predicted it, but he had not predicted faster-than-light drive in any form. Light speed was the limiting factor, but it turned out it wasn't. She had ignored it because they were ignoring so much of what Einstein had said by traveling faster-than-light.

Douglas turned toward them, surprised by the look on their faces. He pointed back at the screen and said, "You two had better pull it together."

"Why?" asked Bakker.

"Because. Here they come."

CHAPTER 16

[1]

AS THE STRANGE CRAFT APPROACHED, HACKETT wasn't happy. He wasn't scared, but he wasn't happy. He'd wanted longer to observe the enemy. No, enemy wasn't right either. He'd wanted more time to study these ships. To search for a clue as to their identity and to determine if they posed a threat to his ship.

And, he wanted to know what was happening on Earth and on Mars. They still had no communication with either planet, and he found that unsettling. Without some answers, he didn't know how to respond to the approaching ship. Military doctrine demanded that he see it as an enemy and a potential threat, but it was from inside the Solar System, and that made it friendly. Military doctrine confused him.

Douglas said, "What do you want to do?"

"We could just turn around and run," said Weiss.

Hackett shot him a glance and was about to snap at him, when he realized that the suggestion wasn't that out of line. They could run. They could probably outrun anything in the Solar System, assuming that ships operating regularly inside a system would not have a faster-than-light drive.

In the end, he just asked, "And where would we run to?"

"It might give us some time for additional observations," said Bakker.

"But right now we have a chance to end the questions with a few answers," said Hackett. "We hold our ground . . . or hold our position. Do you have anything coming through on the radios? Any attempts to communicate?"

"Negative. Do you want me to attempt to initiate communication?"

"Go ahead. Just be careful with what you tell them."

"This all strikes me as extremely dangerous," said Weiss. "We just don't know anything about them."

"They haven't fired on us," said Hackett, "and they are not approaching with a hostile attitude. They turned toward us gently, and they haven't accelerated in any meaningful way. They are coming at us out of curiosity, not hostile intent."

"That's not your call to make," said Weiss.

Hackett turned to face him and said, "It is my call. I command here, and if you can't keep that simple thought in your head, then leave the flight deck."

Weiss dropped his eyes and fell silent. He made no additional suggestions.

"Okay," said Hackett, turning his attention back to the flat-screen. "What can you tell me about this ship?"

"It looks nothing like anything I have ever seen," said Bakker. "It seems to have a good acceleration capability, but it doesn't seem to be using chemical reaction to create either the acceleration or to maneuver. I don't know what sort of engines it might be using."

"Atomic?"

Douglas shook his head. "No. I detect no radiation that

would suggest that. I don't recognize the readings I'm getting here. I don't know what it is."

Bakker turned and leaned over his shoulder, looking at the various readings. She said, "I don't know what these are either. Not atomic in the way we'd think of it, but there are some high end radiation readings."

"This is getting us nowhere," said Weiss.

"Everything we learn takes us somewhere," said Bakker. "A little patience."

"They're slowing," said Douglas.

"To shoot?" asked Weiss.

Hackett said, "I would suspect that they would have the ability to shoot at their highest speed, so that's not a reason to slow. I take it as a friendly gesture."

"Friendly?" said Weiss. "Are you crazy?"

"If you can't keep your comments to yourself," snapped Hackett, "get out of here. If you have something important to contribute, then stay."

Weiss made no move to leave the flight deck.

Hackett asked, "You getting anything over the radio? Any sort of communication?"

"Nothing I recognize," said Douglas. "We are getting some narrow beam, but I can't read it. I don't know what it might be. Could be a sensor probe."

Bakker moved around so that she could look at the display. She shook her head and then sat down in a vacant chair. She pulled a keyboard close and said, "I'll take a closer look at this."

Hackett watched her for a moment and then looked back at the screen. The ship, which had a long, lean body with a gigantic head that looked as if it was made of glass, was maintaining a position about 50,000 miles away. It no longer maneuvered, which meant that it was no longer a threat.

"I'm getting nothing here, Tom," said Bakker. "There might be communications in the beam somewhere, but whatever they're doing is beyond me. We'd discussed using a narrow beam for communication, but we never did anything with it. Same with laser, which might be called a narrow beam, though it's more accurate to say focused."

"These guys human or what?" asked Hackett.

"Well, that's the question, isn't it?"

[2]

BAKKER FINALLY TURNED FROM THE FLAT-SCREEN and looked directly at Hackett. "I've done everything that I can think of, and I haven't been able to read the message, if there was a message in that beam. The technology is beyond me."

"Okay," said Hackett. "Anybody have an idea of how much time has passed?"

Weiss, who had been quiet, said, "I've been running some calculations here, and this is what I have come up with. We could be as much as eighty years, maybe a century in the future."

Hackett snorted, and Bakker laughed. "How in the hell did you come up with that?" she asked. "We've no basis to make any such calculation."

"Well, I'm basing it in part on what Colonel Hackett said and a little bit on some of Einstein's work. I could be off by as much as fifty percent."

"Just what would we expect from civilization a hundred years from now?" asked Douglas. "Think of just what the twentieth century saw. Ocean travel as the quickest means to travel among the continents to manned rockets to the moon, computers in everyone's house, and instant communications. Give those in 1950 the technology that existed in 2000, and they would have been lost. They'd never have understood it. Who knows what would be around a hundred years after we left Mars."

"Like that ship out there," said Hackett.

"Wouldn't you expect the technology to improve?" asked Douglas.

"Just what I'm trying to say, Colonel," said Weiss. "That ship out there might not be alien. It could be human, but we don't recognize it, just as Orville Wright wouldn't recognize his airplanes after a hundred years."

Hackett finally tired of the debate and waved a hand. "What can you tell me about that ship standing out there, looking as if it wants us to make a move?"

Bakker said, "I've tried all the communications gear we have, and I have not been able to get a response. If there is a message buried in the signal they have sent to us, I have been unable to find it, let alone understand it. This is like trying to decode a Morse message using a laser. It just won't work."

"What do you propose?" asked Hackett.

"What we did when the aliens entered the Solar System. Broadcast on a wide spectrum and hope these guys have the ability to understand us and put together a message."

"Or we could just get the hell out of Dodge," said Weiss. "Retreat from the system."

Hackett shook his head. "They'll follow us."

"But would they be able to keep up?" asked Weiss.

Hackett realized that it was quite likely that a ship designed for interplanetary flight would not be able to keep up with one designed for interstellar. It would be like a Cessna trying to keep up with an airliner. Different missions, different capabilities, and certainly different speeds.

Bakker said, "We could retreat to the Kuiper Belt or the Oort Cloud and study the situation carefully. Give us a chance to think of something."

"Not an option," said Hackett.

"Well," said Bakker. "We don't know that these are humans. Could be aliens. We seem to have gotten away from that attitude here."

Now Hackett rubbed a hand over his face. He looked down at the deck, at the light gray carpet that had the little loops of velcro so that his slippers would stick. Surely, if they were living in the future, someone had come up with a better solution to the problem of zero 9.

"I need some information," he said.

Bakker said, "Why don't we fire up the regular engines and move slowly toward that other ship?"

"Or," suggested Weiss, "move toward Mars. That's where we launched from."

"I don't like either of those ideas," said Hackett.

"Well, you better do something," said Douglas, "because another ship is coming our way."

[3]

"THAT'S A MAN-OF-WAR," SAID HACKETT. "THAT is a hostile gesture, if I ever saw one."

"They don't know who we are," said Bakker. "How would we have reacted if an aircraft that vanished a hundred years earlier suddenly reappeared. We wouldn't even recognize it."

"This is gone on long enough," said Hackett. "Begin to broadcast every way that you can. Let them know that we are on a mission dispatched by the Galaxy Exploration Team and we are returning after a trip to Alpha Centauri."

Bakker didn't move for a moment, and then she began to type. She activated the radios, the television, and the lasers. She looked up at a camera that had swiveled around so that the lens was pointing down at her. She smiled up at it.

She said, in carefully enunciated English, "We are a returning exploration team and would like to make planetfall at our original base on Mars. We are carrying no weapons and will not resist any attempt to board."

She repeated the message twice and then cut off the

camera and the radio. As soon as she had, Hackett demanded, "Who in the hell gave you the authority to tell them that we would not resist an attempt to be boarded?"

She looked at him sweetly and asked, "And just what would you do if they began to board us?"

He stared at her hard but finally nodded. "Okay. There wouldn't be much we could do, but you didn't have to put the idea into their heads."

"Listen, Colonel," said Weiss, "they have to be human. They'll see we're human. We all speak English, though ours might sound funny or accented to them, but they're going to know who we are. Let's just end this nonsense."

Hackett dropped into one of the chairs bolted to the deck. He studied the flat-screens, looking at the two ships that were now near him. One seemed to be a transport of some kind. Maybe it had been engaged in mining operations in the asteroids, or on one of the moons of Jupiter. The other looked as if it was a military vessel, though he could see no weapons on it. The only good news was that no one had fired a shot.

Bakker suddenly laughed. The sound was out of place and grated on his nerves. He spun toward her.

Bakker held up a hand and said, "I just had a thought. We've done this before, but on the other side. We went out to meet the alien ship, discussed what we would do and could do, and then watched as that ship departed the Solar System. Now we're the alien ship entering the Solar System. Fortunately, history is on our side here."

"Meaning?"

"We took a don't-shoot-first attitude. They seem to have adopted a similar attitude."

"They're maneuvering closer," said Douglas. "What do I do?"

"They get too close," said Hackett, "and they cut off our escape route. We fire up the generators and anything near us is dragged away with us."

"That's not necessarily a bad thing," said Bakker.

"What if they have weapons? They're moving at the same speed as we are. They shoot at us because they think we've captured them, what does that do to us? We have no real capability to defend ourselves."

"Then we either have to jump before they get too close, or we figure to stay put," said Bakker.

"They're sweeping us again. Sensors maybe. Communications, maybe."

"In response to us?" asked Hackett.

"I don't think so," said Bakker. "They're still using something that I don't understand. We broadcast using a fairly primitive method . . ."

"Primitive," said Douglas.

Bakker looked at him. "If we are more than a hundred years from our launch time, then it would seem primitive to them. They might not have the equipment to respond."

"I don't want to get into another discussion about our traveling into the future," said Hackett.

"Not traveled in a science fiction sense," said Bakker. "We just managed to accelerate ourselves into the future."

"Sarah, this is not the time or the place for that discussion," said Hackett, "Especially with a man-of-war floating out there."

"So what do we do?" asked Douglas.

"We remain nonthreatening," said Hackett. "We watch them carefully, and at the first sign of hostility, or that they're not human, we go. Rapidly. I would suggest that you plot a course that will avoid asteroids and planets and moons. One that will take us back outside the orbit of Pluto where we can make a few more observations."

Bakker laughed again and said, "We'd just seem to vanish. One instant we're here and the next, we're gone. That might frighten them a little."

"Unless they understand faster-than-light drive," said Hackett. "Then they would know that we have it."

"Which they probably know already."

Hackett took a deep breath and wondered what the

commander on the other ship was thinking. Probably looking for weapons but was finding nothing. He might be scanning old records, looking for anything that matched the ship he was now facing. Looking at the records of craft that vanished. Maybe looking at the records for the generation ships and wondering if one might have turned around to return to the Solar System.

"All we can do," said Bakker, "is continue to broadcast our message and hope they eventually figure out how to receive it. That would sure uncomplicate things."

"Colonel," said Douglas, "they've launched a small object. It's coming straight at us."

"Weapon?"

"I don't know, but it's not moving very fast."

"Sarah, what can you tell me about it?"

"It's traveling fast enough to reach us in a couple of hours, but not so fast that we couldn't maneuver to avoid it. Maybe that is the welcome home committee."

"Or the boarding party."

[4]

HACKETT LEFT THE FLIGHT DECK, WALKED slowly along one of the darkened corridors, and stopped near a computer terminal. He thought about sitting down and asking a few questions, but there wasn't much that he needed to know that the computer could tell him. All the information in it was the information they'd left Mars with less than a year earlier, yet it now seemed to have been a century earlier. Time dilation had confused the issue, and no one had really thought about it back then.

When world exploration really began, at the beginning of the sixteenth century, some of the voyages lasted years. Travel around the world was a very dangerous proposition. By the twenty-first century, it was so simple that some people did it by accident. A trip to Europe fol-

THE EXPLORATION CHRONICLES: F.T.L.

lowed by one to India with an excursion to Australia and the quickest way home was suddenly flying east to California.

But when Magellan and his crew sailed from Spain, someone had to be waiting for their return. So that when the surviving ship appeared on the horizon, people knew what it was. They didn't sail out to meet him with force, and had they done so, they would have recognized the ship for what it was.

Someone, somewhere, in some data bank or information retrieval system had to have a record of Hackett's launch. Someone would be aware that they were still out, traveling around a small section of the galaxy and would someday return. Maybe that was why it had taken them so long to make a decision. They had to identify the ship and then realize that communication would be impossible because the radios or communications gear would no longer be compatible.

So Hackett sat there, staring at the blank screen, wondering what question he could ask that would clarify the situation. But there was no question, and all he could do was wait for the enemy, no, not enemy, but *other*, ship to arrive. Then, he would have to be prepared to resist if it turned out to be a threat, but what, really, could he do. They had no real weapons. Just a couple of personal pistols and rifles taken in case they made planetfall and found dangerous beasts.

Once or twice he put his hands on the keyboard, but he couldn't think of anything to ask. He couldn't think of what he needed to know. The computer wouldn't be able to recognize the ship coming at them, because there had been nothing like it when they left.

He knew he was just killing time until the ship got close enough for them to make some kind of decision about it. He had two choices. Stay where they were or flee. He didn't like either of them. He wanted a third option. But there just wasn't one.

There was a quiet, metallic click, and then the intercom said, "Colonel Hackett to the flight deck."

It meant that it was time to decide.

[5]

AS SOON AS HACKETT STEPPED ONTO THE flight deck, Douglas pointed at the screen and said, "He's about to the point where, if we engage the faster-than-light drive, he'd be sucked along with us."

"And if he launched a weapon," said Weiss, "we would no longer have the time to react to it."

Hackett dropped into one of the seats and said, "We could pull back a hundred thousand miles . . ."

"And accomplish what by doing that?" asked Bakker. "More delay is all."

"Granted," said Hackett. "We need to end this now, one way or the other."

"Colonel?" asked Douglas, his voice now high and tight. "We've got to do something."

"Hold for a moment," said Hackett, while his mind raced. He could see clearly, the consequences of both actions. Run now, and they would be pursued. Hold, and they would be boarded. Neither was a good answer."

"Colonel?"

"Tom?"

Hackett held up a hand for silence, knowing that the decision was about to be taken from him by actions outside his ship. If that vessel came too much closer, he'd be forced to stay.

And then he realized the chance those on the other vessel were taking. They had put their lives in his hands, knowing that almost any action he took would result in the destruction of their vessel in some fashion. They were trusting him.

"We hold where we are," he said quietly. And then, with more force. "We hold right here."

"Colonel," said Weiss, "I'm not sure that this is a very good idea. I think we should . . ."

"The decision has been made. Anything else we do would only prolong the agony. This way we get our answers quickly. We find out what we must know."

"They've slowed," said Douglas.

Hackett turned and looked, but the ship, whatever it was, had not stopped. It was still coming at them, aimed at them, and would contact them somewhere near what Hackett considered the bow.

"If it is a weapon," he said, "it's a very cleverly designed one. Military thinking suggests that weapons be small, hard to hit, and fast. This one is anything but."

"I have signs of life-forms on board," said Douglas.

"Meaning?"

"It is warm in there. They seem to have an atmosphere on the inside, and one of the engines is not functioning properly."

Hackett laughed, almost with relief. "Well, I'm sure they're not that clever. They wouldn't launch a weapon at us that had a misfiring engine."

"Decoy," said Douglas.

"No, I don't think so."

"They're now maneuvering to bring themselves in line with one of the hatches. I think they want to enter," said Douglas.

"Which hatch?"

"B-4. At the rear of the station."

Hackett stood up and said, "Sarah, you, Weiss, and Wilson come with me. Douglas, you stay here. If anything goes wrong, we jump to light speed and get out. If not, I'll let you know."

"Might be too late once they've docked with us," said Douglas. "We really don't know anything about who's on that ship."

"Just be ready to jump if I give the word. You watch everything that goes on."

Without thinking about it, Douglas said, "Yes, sir."

As they reached the rear hatch, Douglas announced, "I think they'll be here in ten minutes."

"Don't we need to do something to get ready?" asked Wilson.

"What would that be?"

"I don't know. Something. Clean uniforms?"

"Maybe a band?" said Weiss, sarcastically.

"Maybe."

Hackett said, "We don't know what we're going to face here. We are not in a foreign system. We've come home after a long journey. If anyone should expect a reception, it's us."

"They're along side," said Douglas. "Hey, I thought they would use a tube to connect us, but four people have just stepped into space."

There was a flat-screen near the hatch. Hackett looked up and saw that Douglas had already keyed in a view for them. He could watch these . . . people . . . as they stepped out of their craft. All he could really tell was that they were human, or rather humanoid. They had two arms, two legs, a single head. The hands seemed to end in fingers.

The suits were smaller, meaning less bulky, than those that Hackett remembered. Improvements in material probably could account for that.

All four of the people seemed to swim toward the station and then the hatch. There was no visible means of propulsion, which, of course, didn't mean there wasn't any. It only meant that he couldn't see it easily.

Douglas said, "They've reached the hatch, and I have initiated the cycle. They should be inside in about a minute or so."

The lights near the interior hatch glowed red, then amber, and finally green, meaning that it was now safe to open the interior door.

Hackett was suddenly frightened. He didn't know what to expect and wasn't sure that he wanted to open the door. But he reached up and touched the button. There was the grinding of a servo, the snapping of bolts being drawn back, and then a hiss as the door swung open.

The first person out was a young man with light hair, a stocky build, and a rosy complexion. He held his helmet under his left arm and his right hand out to be shaken.

In a strangely accented voice, something that sounded vaguely Australian, he said, "Colonel Hackett, I presume. Welcome home."

EPILOGUE

[1]

Mars had radically changed in the time they had been gone. It was no longer a red planet covered with vast deserts and craters from meteoric impact. Now it was a miniature Earth, terriformed so that there was a vast ocean covering nearly half the planet, ice caps that were miles deep with ice made of water, and a system of roads and magnetic railroads that linked the cities together. There were no more domes, because the air was sweet and mixed perfectly for human respiration and the outside air temperature was kept to an artificially pleasant seventy-two degrees.

From orbit they didn't know about the temperature, or the fresh air, but they could see the changes made since they had left. Hackett and Bakker had figured their journey at something just over eight months, but on Mars more than a century and a half had passed. Technology had taken over and turned Mars into a human paradise. Earth had taken a different path, and though they hadn't seen it, they had been told that rather than a bright blue planet filled with the hope of humanity, it was now a dirty yellow ball that had been left to those who just didn't care enough to get out into space.

Hackett and Bakker, sitting side by side, watched as their view changed from one that gave them a picture of the whole planet to one that showed them only the city where they would soon land. It was a sprawling complex that had a central core of high-rise buildings, their height regulated by the amount of oxygen in the air. Once they had climbed only a couple hundred feet, the air thinned to the point of danger. Of course there were taller buildings, but each had its own oxygen supply and fewer and fewer windows. Explosive decompression was a real danger on the upper floors.

They landed at a terminal, were checked quickly, and then guided to one of the high-speed magnetic trains for the run into the city. They moved too quickly for Hackett to see much of the countryside. Though he psychologically believed that he had been gone less than a year, in reality, it had been much longer. The countryside was radically different.

Bakker sat close to him, surreptitiously holding his hand and just a little frightened. She was more than a century and a half into a future that she didn't know. Everything she knew about physics and astronomy was now as outdated as that learned by Kuiper or Copernicus. To get to where she had been would take three or four years, if she could even understand it.

"This is not going to be easy," she whispered to him.

"No, I expect not. But look at the bright side," he said. "We're together."

"Yes, there is that."

The train slowed smoothly, not with the jerking motion that had marked the trains on old Earth. They just gently slid into the terminal, and the doors opened quietly. The air was fresh, clean, and just a little cool.

They didn't exit into a climate-controlled building that

was sealed to prevent loss of oxygen, but out, onto a platform that was exposed to the weather. The sky was nearly cloudless, and Hackett wondered if it was always that way. The evaporation of water had to be tremendous, given the size of Mars and the lack of water vapor in the atmosphere, unless there had been compensation for that.

Coming through the doors in front of them was a small man with a large head. He had wide-set eyes, a pointed nose in the exact center of his face, and a mouth that seemed to be a bit too low. It was as if his face had been assembled from the parts left over from others.

He held out a massive hand, and grinning broadly, he said, "Welcome. Welcome. I'm Juan Gonzales. We didn't know when to expect you. Your expedition was launched so long ago."

Hackett took the man's hand and shook it. "You've been waiting for us?"

"Well, there was never any indication that you had been lost, and we did detect periodic signals suggesting you were still out there somewhere."

Bakker pushed forward and asked, "Why didn't you come to look for us then?"

The smile briefly left the man's face, but returned quickly. "Why, we couldn't do that. We don't have the ships to do that."

"You mean we're still confined to the Solar System?" asked Hackett.

"Please, let's get you processed through here, and then I can answer all your questions. Once you have those answers, everything will make sense to you."

"There sure has been progress here," said Bakker.

"Yes. Once we were able to artificially increase the gravity on a planetary scale at least quite near the surface, some of the problems we'd faced were diminished. We don't have to worry about the atmosphere slipping into space now, but we still haven't gotten all the problems worked out."

Gonzales led them through a door into a room that was reminiscent of an Earth-based train station of the early twentieth century. Tile floors, wooden benches for the passengers, though the wood was synthetic, and a small restaurant for those waiting to board a train.

Gonzales waved a hand and beamed, as if he had created the station himself. "We're quite proud of this," he said. "We wanted a retro look, and I think we've done just that."

They walked through and out into a parking area that had been surrounded by green plantings and colorful flowers. The only clue that they weren't on Earth was the sun, which was smaller than it should have been.

Gonzales pointed to a vehicle that looked like a late-twentieth-century minivan. Still grinning, he said, "We're quite into the retro look these days. This runs on electricity, so that we don't pollute at all."

Once they had climbed in, were strapped in, but before they began to move, Gonzales turned and looked at them. "We'll get you debriefed later . . ."

"I still don't understand why no one came to look for us," said Hackett.

"All your questions will be answered in time."

For a moment, Hackett could only think of the old science fiction stories in which the returning astronauts were lured into a false sense of security by crafty alien creatures. He didn't understand the feeling, but he knew that if it were true, then he had no way to escape.

[2]

THE HIGH-RISE WHERE THEY HAD LIVED, INSIDE the dome, was no longer there. It had been replaced with a newer, modern building that was just as tall, but that had been constructed with techniques that had been developed in the last fifty years.

There was a huge lobby of glass and steel and open doors. On Mars there were no pesky flying insects, though some bugs had been introduced during the terriform process. No mosquitoes or bloodsucking flies, and very few spiders. The lessons learned as the brown rat was transferred from Europe to the New World, and as rabbits began to overrun Australia, had been remembered. The introduction of species had been carefully regulated to prevent the sudden explosion of one of those populations. Given that, people could leave their doors open without fear of invading bugs or animals.

Gonzales said, "Apartments have been arranged. You have become quite wealthy in your absence, so don't worry about expenses now. All has been taken care of. I will call on you in the morning for a debriefing." He turned to go.

"Wait," said Hackett. "You can't just abandon us here."

"Why not?"

"We don't know the system. We don't understand how things work. We've been out of touch for a long time."

"Not to worry," said Gonzales. "You have apartments in the building, and we have arranged for them to operate just the way those you had when you left operated. There are clear instructions. I'll return in the morning."

Hackett wanted to protest again, but Gonzales had turned and was hurrying toward the door. He stepped out into the sunlight, held up a hand in a motion that looked as if it belonged on Earth, in Manhattan, hundreds of years earlier, and waited. A vehicle slid close, the rear door opened, and Gonzales got in.

Bakker looked at Hackett and asked, "Do we each have an apartment?"

"I don't know."

They stepped up to a central pillar that had screens on each of the four sides. He reached out to touch the center of the screen, just as he would have done had they been in his own building on Mars, now so long in the past.

"Good evening, Colonel Hackett," said a surprisingly pleasant, feminine voice. "Is Doctor Bakker with you?"

Without thinking, Hackett said, "Yes."

"Do you need a single accommodation for this evening, or will you require two?"

Hackett glanced at Bakker who couldn't conceal her smile. "I guess they know. One will be fine."

"Please follow the green lights. They will lead you to your apartment. It will open as you approach. Please have a good day."

Hackett saw a light on at the far side of the lobby. He said, "That's it, I guess."

They followed it down a short corridor, into what looked like an elevator, and were taken up several floors. Once out of the elevator tube, they saw a door halfway down a brightly lighted corridor swing open.

"That's got to be it," said Bakker, pointing.

"Got to be."

The interior didn't look much different than those of their old apartments. There was no flat-screen on the wall, but there was an area that looked as if it was a screen. As Hackett looked at it, the area brightened into a welcome display.

Ignoring that, they checked out the rest of the apartment. In the bathroom was a tub and shower combination, and the kitchen was tiny, little more than a device that looked like a microwave oven, but no refrigerator and no cupboards other than a single one mounted above a tiny sink.

Bakker said, "Looks like cooking at home is a thing of the past."

Satisfied that they understood the apartment, they sat down on the couch that was across from the screen. As they got comfortable facing it, the display brightened, and a voice asked, "Do you have any suggestions?"

Hackett glanced at Bakker and said, "History of Mars for the last one hundred years."

"No, history of space travel for the last one hundred years," said Bakker, "beginning with experimentation into faster-than-light drive."

"Yes," said Hackett. "Good."

For the next hour they sat quietly while the history of interstellar travel was revealed to them. They learned that the generation ships, launched so long ago, were still traveling toward the stars, but communication with them was limited. Scientists had even visited one or two of the ships and offered the opportunity for them to speed their journeys, but all had elected to continue at their slow and prodding pace.

Finally Hackett and Bakker understood the history of space travel and knew why there were no faster-than-light ships anymore. They understood the problem, because they were living it. Faster-than-light took too long.

[3]

THE CONFERENCE ROOM WAS NOT WHAT THEY had expected. Rather than a table with chairs surrounding it, they were all sitting in chairs that reminded Hackett of one of the better theaters. They were arranged in three lines, one behind the other, with each line elevated above the one in front of it. They all faced a blank wall that, when activated, revealed people in other conference rooms seated in a similar fashion.

The screen was split, showing conference rooms in two other locations. They were warned that one was on Earth so that there would be a delay in transmission, and they were advised that some of the questions asked might be irrelevant by the time the signal was relayed back and forth.

Hackett, Bakker, and the others, were seated in the front row, so that everyone could get a good look at them. They faced what had been a blank wall that now displayed those other conference rooms. It looked as if they were sitting in another room twenty feet away.

For an hour they explained what they had seen, the effects of the faster-than-light drive, and what they had observed around them. Questions were asked, though the people on Earth seemed not to participate for the first minutes and then were suddenly engaged in the briefing. They asked no questions.

Finally the questions for Hackett and his team ended and someone asked if he had any questions. Hackett sat for a moment, looking down at the floor, amazed that it was, in fact a floor rather than a deck, and then looked up.

"Yeah. Tell me again why you scrapped faster-than-light drive."

On the Martian screen, a woman stood up and said, "If I might? Faster-than-light drive sets up a paradox that we've been unable to solve. Yes, we can reach the stars in weeks. We can cross the galaxy in weeks. But time dilation expands with the increase in speed, so that those who launched a hundred years ago, two hundred, are just beginning to return. They have survived the journey, but their civilizations have not."

"You're still here," said Hackett.

"The society you left is not," she said. "There are still teams out there who launched in the decade after you left and who will probably not return for a thousand years. They will fit in no better than Merlin the magician would fit in here."

"That's no reason to take the stars away from the human race," said Hackett. "Exploration and expansion, science and humanity, have advanced, often at great cost to society and the humans who forced the issue."

The woman stared at the camera as if she was staring into Hackett's eyes. "You don't understand. We have the stars. We own our part of the galaxy. We do this without the sacrifice of the brave souls who would make the same choice no matter what the circumstances."

"I don't understand," said Bakker.

"We travel to the stars. We have a system that allows us to move from one planet to the next by folding space and stepping through a portal. We have the stars, and it was your journeys that made it possible."

Hackett sat for a moment and then understood. They had found a new method of defeating the distances of interstellar space. The wormholes of old had been found. Humanity had the stars.

Kevin D. Randle is a captain in the U.S. Army, an authority on alien abduction, and the author of numerous works of fiction and nonfiction. He has appeared as a guest on many television programs focusing on extraterrestrial activity, including *Unsolved Mysteries, Larry King Live, Good Morning America, Alien Autopsy,* and *Maury Povich.* He also coauthored the bestselling *UFO: Crash at Roswell,* which later became a popular Showtime movie, and *The Abduction Enigma.*

The Exploration Chronicles
by **Kevin D. Randle**

Book One: SIGNALS
0-441-01039-3

In New Mexico, devices monitoring the desert skies
pick up faint but unmistakable sounds: signals
coming from a mere fifty light years away and
headed toward Earth. But will the approaching
beings be friendly? As Earth struggles towards a
unified response, one thing becomes clear—
We are about to meet our neighbors.

Book Two: STARSHIP
0-441-01128-4

Starship Alpha is a "generation ship" on an
interstellar journey to locate the souce of the
extraterrestrial signals first heard on Earth over two
hundred years ago. Now, as new generations born
aboard the ship threaten to abandon the mission,
humanity's destiny lies in the hands of one boy.

Available wherever books are sold or at
www.penguin.com

A006